HAIL CAESAR

GO THERE.
OTHER TITLES AVAILABLE FROM **PUSH**

HAIL CAESAR

THU-HUONG HA

SCHOLASTIC INC.

NEW YORK TORONTO LONDON AUCKLAND SYDNEY
MEXICO CITY NEW DELHI HONG KONG BUENOS AIRES

ISBN-13: 978-0-439-89026-7
ISBN-10: 0-439-89026-8

12 11 10 9 8 7 6 5 4 3 2 1   7 8 9 10 11 12/0

Printed in the U.S.A.   40
First printing, February 2007

For my family

ACKNOWLEDGMENTS

Thanks must go first to the Ha/Tesler clan; cám ơn Bố, Mẹ, Rich, Chị Hai, Chị Ba, Siêu, and Liêm for your incessant nosiness. Special thanks to Chị Hai and Rich for harboring me (and many others) in all times of need. Without you, there would never be any PFB moments and I would have no idea how to play pool.

Thanks to one superhuman man, David Levithan, whose books have been such an inspiration and whose words have been such an encouragement. Thank you for your patience, friendship, hospitality, wit, and overall ability to make mixes like no other being on Earth.

Thanks to the entire PUSH family: Anica, Josh, Ranya, and those two lovable interns. Chris and Jeff: Thank you for the infinite wisdom you gave so willingly (in both literature and life) to the small Asian girl who showed up one day in the office.

Thanks to all the friends and teachers whom I have met on this long and crazy journey and who have believed in me so unquestioningly. Special thanks to Lyndall Soden, Jo Archer, and Jamie DelPiano for your unwavering support and to Ilona Bito, Sami Dercher, and Sam Wuu for helping me grow as a writer. (Lony, thank you for your constant need to leave behind a mess wherever you go, because without it, I never would have found those rhinestones.) Thanks to my best friends in the entire world, who for the past few years have endured my nervous breakdowns with unbound patience. You know who you are. I love you so much. Also, thanks to anybody who has ever heard me reference this book with only the words "Oh GOD."

Thanks to every asshole I've ever known or loved.

Finally, thanks go to William Shakespeare. You genius, you.

CHAPTER I

Darkness. Silence. It's a peaceful slumber. Closed eyes and nothing but breathing. Just breathing. Inhale. The sound of silence. Exhale. And then, without warning:

Loud. LOUD. LOUD! SHUT UP!

The alarm clock buzzes, *GETUPGETUPGETUPGETUP!* My arm comes crashing down on the snooze button, and all is quiet again.

But it's too late. In the next room, my sister has heard The Call. It's days like this that I wish she was a heavier sleeper. I hear her thump out of bed and angrily swing open the door. She stomps into my room and jumps onto me with morning breath and disheveled hair. Kelly is not a morning person.

It runs in the family.

She shakes me with as much vigor as her puny thirteen-year-old body will allow.

"GET. UP. YOU. STUPID. LAZY. MORON. I. HATE. YOUR. STUPID. LOUD. ALARM. CLOCK!" Kelly grunts between words, pushing and pulling at my immovable body.

"GET UP!" she screams right in my ear.

I'm up.

I roll onto my feet and grab her by both flimsy shoulders, my eyes half-shut.

"Get off, you —" she starts.

I shove her back onto my bed and walk out of the room.

"Morning," I mumble through a yawn.

The steaming-hot jet streams wage war on my tired body. I close my eyes and let the water run down six feet of thick basketball skin. I scrub some hydrating herbal goop through my dark, getting-too-long hair. It figures Kelly uses this crap.

Five minutes later, I stand clean in front of the steamy bathroom mirror. I wipe away part of the blurry image to reveal myself standing in a towel and still wet.

For better or for worse, I smell pretty fucking good.

I push a comb through my hair, attempting something presentable. A useless and tiring struggle. With one hand, I push it all back and open the bathroom door.

Peggy, my five-year-old sister, dawdles in the hallway, munching on the remnants of a piece of toast. I scoop her up under my arm in the direction of her bedroom. She squeals with early morning giddiness. I fake a pass and then dunk her right onto her unicorn-themed bed.

"Got clothes?" I ask her.

"Nope," she says.

I open her closet. "Pick," I say.

"Nope," she repeats.

"Pick."

"Nope."

"*Pick.*"

"Poop."

She scrambles off the bed and thumps toward the closet to a red T-shirt and the matching red pants.

Game point. I always win.

Slam the car door. I stride into the parking lot and toward the brick school: Laurence High School, Home of the Lions. Roar. Life in suburbia's public high schools doesn't get much more complicated than dicks, chicks, and a lot of kicks. I may be living the great American teenage cliché, but I've got no complaints.

Enter Sophie. She's got that slinky come-hither look that's worked so well on me in the past, but now all I see when I look at her face is the orange tint of her fake tan.

"Hey, baby," she croons. "Where were you this weekend?"

She touches my arm.

"Around," I say, my stride not slowing.

She pouts and trots along to catch up with me in her too-high high heels that make me think of the nails I want to drill in her fake blond head.

"Let's cut today and go to the beach," she suggests.

"Maybe later," I say.

She smiles a fake smile and wraps an arm around my neck, pulling my face to hers. She whispers something to me — soft words against my ear, silky syllables I don't hear. I press my lips to hers just to get rid of her, and she's gone as soon as she gets what she wants.

And then there is nothing.

3

*   *   *

I shove my backpack into my locker and shuffle through papers to find my bio book. I slam the tarnished blue locker shut and spin the dial.

Jake is at my locker. When did he get here? He's talking.

"Yo, Caesar? YO?"

Oh, he's talking to *me*.

"Huh," I grunt.

"Did you see Jenna? She's looking for you."

"Great."

"Did you?"

"Did I what?"

"See her?"

"No. And if you see her again, tell her I'm home."

"What's wrong with Jenna?" he asks.

This is a routine of ours.

I shrug.

"Nothing specific. Just . . . y'know. The usual."

I shrug again.

"How can you not be satisfied with *anyone*?"

I don't know.

"I don't know."

"They all *want* you, man."

He points a finger at my chest. I smack it away.

"Don't touch me," I say without thinking.

"Why do they all want you?"

He gives me the why-can't-we-switch-places look that I know so well. I wish I could just punch him and put him out of his misery, but he's my best friend. I guess there's something to be said for that.

I play along.

"I don't know. But I think it has something to do with the sex."

"You bastard."

I resist a grin.

"Hey, it's not my fault."

"Be that as it may, you're still a bastard. The girls of Laurence — and the surrounding towns, for that matter — have been at your fingertips for years, and you have yet to show an interest in *anyone* that's lasted for more than three weeks! Forgive me for my frustration!"

"Jake, Jake, Jake," I say with mock pity, patting him lightly on the back. I pause and give him a harsh look. "Shut the fuck up before I punch you."

And that's that. I start to walk away from him, which means he'll either follow me and the conversation will be over, or he'll walk the other way and the conversation will be over.

He follows.

I haven't been able to stay awake in homeroom since I was a freshman. You'd think my homeroom teacher would be used to this by now, but for some reason she has this ridiculous idea that I need to be awake in order to be present. Today is no exception. As soon as I sit down, I lean forward, and soon I'm falling . . .

"Miller."

My eyes are closed and it's dark.

"Miller?"

I'm warm and it's nothing but breathing.

"*Miller.*"

Rude voices fight their way into my rhythm.

"He's here."

5

Don't let them wake you up. Block out. Black out.

"I know that. But he needs to wake up!"

Not here not here not here.

"JOHN MILLER!"

Loud voices. Getting louder . . . no, they don't exist.

"Yo, Caesar." Someone taps me on the head.

I whip out of my seat and knock my victim back.

"Don't. *Touch me*," I growl.

I right my chair and sit back down in it while TJ Minchin backs away from my desk with a frightened look. Probably shouldn't have done that.

"Nice of you to join us, Mr. Miller," comes the voice of my homeroom teacher.

I lay one on her, all twenty-eight of my teeth in perfect rows, and the trademark wink. "Anything for you, Mrs. Clancy."

She can't resist the Caesar charm. She blushes in spite of herself and moves quickly on to Brittany Modina.

World: 0. Caesar: 2.

I sleep again.

Mondays are always uneventful. English, gym, history, the day drags on. After lunch, I leave the cafeteria with the smell of French fry oil and hamburger juice stuck in my hair. I nod as Jake complains about his older brother coming home from college for Thanksgiving break. Sometimes I think I'd do anything for a brother. Just so I wouldn't have to leave the house every day smelling like the Victoria's Secret Endless Love body wash that Kelly uses. I like my sisters and everything, but, God, it's hard raising girls. What the hell do two grown men know about bra sizes and tampons?

Jake interrupts my thoughts: "Do y'ever wish you were an only child, man? Life would be so good."

"Sometimes," I answer as we walk slowly to pre-calc, taking our sweet time.

"It could be just you and your dad."

I shrug, say, "I doubt I'd like that."

"Why not?"

"I get tired of him."

"How? You guys could do whatever you want and drink and watch sports all the time and not have to worry about Peggy getting hurt or whatever."

"Yeah, but me and my dad don't know what the hell we're doing. At least with the girls around we try to cook and clean and shit."

"So?"

"It would be gross."

"I guess."

"Besides, without Kelly and Peggy, my dad and I would never talk. We need them to have something in common."

"I guess."

We enter A121 and slide into two desks in the back.

"Yo, man?" Jake says after a moment.

"Yeah?"

"Do you ever miss your mom?"

"Yeah."

And it hurts.

I manage six periods of Avoid the Girl (i.e., Jenna). But of course, at the end of the day, just as I am congratulating myself on a game well played, guess who rounds the corner? I pretend not to see her, but those calculating eyes catch the look on my face too fast. She may be shallow, but she's easily the quickest member of the Caesar Fan Club.

"Caesar!" she exclaims. "Where the hell have you been? I've been looking for you all freakin' day!"

I lean against my locker to look her up and down.

"Around. Class."

She rolls her eyes and puts her hands on her nonexistent waist, pulled tight by those jeans that make your legs look like they're suffocating.

"Don't roll your eyes at me."

She fakes a smile that reminds me of Sophie. In truth, I find Jenna more entertaining, but it's not a huge difference. She puts her arm around my waist and leans her body against mine, holding my hands in hers.

"Jenna . . ." I say.

"Let's go eat," she says.

"I have practice," I answer. I almost feel bad for her. "Maybe later."

Her face is right under mine, and I can smell her hair. Smells like my sister's shampoo. I imagine I'm at a game while Jenna keeps talking about God knows what. Dribble. Dribble. Sneakers squeak against the gym floor. The crowd is loud, but I can't hear them. All I hear is my breathing — shallow, ragged, as the sweat drips from my head, and I blaze down the court. As I'm about to make the winning shot, Jenna appears next to me and gives me a giant bear hug. All the other guys stop and look at me with incredulous eyes.

"CAESAR! WHAT THE HELL ARE YOU DOING?" they yell. "FOCUS!"

I look down, and Jenna is still wrapped around my torso. In real life.

"Thanks, baby. 'Bye!"

She gives me a quick kiss and her heels *clickety-clack* on the linoleum floor as she disappears down the hall. Uhh . . . no problem. I wonder what I said to her.

Basketball practice. Dribble, dribble, bend knees, shoot. Swish. Dribble, dribble, bend . . .

"Caesar!" Coach calls me over.

"Keep going, guys," I shout over the noise of sneakers and bouncing rubber.

"What's up, Coach?" I say.

"Don't forget we're going to Chelsea next week to check out the competition, yeah?"

"I won't forget."

"Good kid."

For once.

I run back over to the foul line and dribble, dribble, bend, shoot.

We run laps, do lay-up drills. Brian Marsh slacks on his defense, and the rest of us score up the points. Coach yells. Brian repents. I sweat.

Hit the showers.

Clean and smelling like Irish soap, I sling my duffel bag over one shoulder and my backpack over the other. I head to my car, my beautiful open-topped black convertible. Gift for my seventeenth birthday. So we've got some money.

I dump everything into the backseat and open the front door when I hear an all-too-familiar voice behind me. Michelle.

"Hi, Caesar," she says.

I can hear a smile in her voice. I don't turn.

"Hey."

I get in the car. I really don't feel like talking. Maybe if I don't look at her, she'll go away.

"You going home?"

No such luck. Michelle leans against the car.

"Maybe."

The truth is, on paper, Michelle's not so bad compared to some of the others. I mean, the girl's got brains. But as far as I'm concerned, she doesn't have much else going for her; she's annoying as hell and tries way too fuckin' hard.

"How was practice?"

"Good," I say.

I rev up the car, hoping to give her a hint.

"Good," she says.

She's not getting the hint. I smile and lay the Caesar charm on thick to weaken her spirit. Or her knees.

"You . . . wanna go get something to eat?" she asks.

"Maybe later." I smile wider.

"Okay . . . 'bye," she manages.

I smile my widest and my tires squeal against the pavement as I rip out of the student parking lot, toward the lake.

I flip radio channels in search of something to distract my ears from the tired afternoon silence.

Flip. Flip. Flip.

Stations *bzzt* in and out, fuzzy and clear, soft and Spanish. I leave the dial on the loudest station I can find and cruise down the road.

Wind. Air. Hair. Breathe.

My baby races on. Trees pass, nothing more than waving green arms. All I can feel is the wind hard against my skin.

Numb.

I pull up onto the pine-covered grounds by the lakeside. There's a real parking lot on the opposite side of the lake, but I like this spot better since most kids never come near it.

Laurence Lake is just an excuse for girls to drag their boyfriends around and for families to have picnics or some crap with their dogs. But I've never seen anyone come near this area, so close to the deepest parts of the lake. I don't think people even know it's here. The spot is partially covered by trees, but once you pass a couple of those, there's a whole clearing with an old gazebo and everything. There isn't even really a place to park; I've just parked here for so long that the earth has sunken in to create a place for my car. I sling my backpack over my shoulder and duck through a few pine trees before I get to the grassy hill overlooking the lake. It's almost romantic. Which means I wouldn't screw a girl here.

I skip up the brown wooden steps to the old hidden gazebo and drop my backpack on the floor. I stretch out on one of the side benches and soon I'm falling fast . . .

Asleep.

Hours later, I wake up to a light layer of darkness creeping up around me; already I can see the lights across the lake reflect in little orbs on the water. I check my cell phone. Eight o'clock. Should have been home an hour ago, but over the past few years, my dad has learned not to worry. I don't blame him for not caring; usually I don't bother to check in, either. But I do today.

The house phone rings. *Click.*

"Hello?"

"Kelly."

"John." There is muffled speaking and I hear my dad's voice in the background.

"Did you guys eat dinner yet?"

"We were waiting for you." She sounds annoyed.

"Really? Why?"

"Remember? You promised Dad you'd be home tonight for dinner so we could eat together?"

Ah, crap.

Deny, deny, deny.

"I have no idea what you're talking about."

She sighs irritatedly into the phone. "Whatever. The pasta's getting cold. I hope you're already in the car. Dad says — no, Dad —"

There is arguing and shuffling for the phone, and I hear Peggy in the background.

"John! Jooooohhhhnnn!" her little voice screams.

Kelly wins and Dad's voice can be heard in the background once more.

"John?" she says, a little out of breath.

"Yeah," I say, holding the phone away from my ear.

"Go!" she yells, and hangs up.

I stare at my phone for a little while, with its blinking ellipses at the end of END CALL, and finally pick up my backpack and head to my car.

CHAPTER 2

The front door clicks shut behind me and I enter muddy-footed into the white-tiled foyer.

Kelly appears from the kitchen.

"You're late." She crosses her arms.

I say nothing and we both enter the dining room.

"John," Dad says.

"Dad," I say.

"How was your day?"

"Fine," I answer.

Harmless enough. I take off my shoes so I don't track any more mud around the house, and we all sit down at the dining room table.

I watch the Millers in all their dysfunction, my father and two sisters, trying their best to do the family thing.

My father is a business guy, the CEO of some huge software company. He's starting to gray, no thanks to the three of us. Peggy sits in her red outfit from this morning, staring intently at her plate. Kelly is more than a head shorter than me and sports

13

the popular dyed-blond hair and too much makeup of a thirteen-year-old. Some of the girls in her grade are bigger skanks than seniors I know.

We eat and nobody speaks.

Half an hour later, I heap the last of the cold rotini onto my fork and shove it in my mouth, not bothering to be polite.

Dad does the same.

Peggy is quieter than usual. A lot of times I wonder if she's more mature than she should be. I mean, I know she's young, but she's had to grow up knowing Mom died giving birth to her. These things don't just happen without leaving some scars.

Dad tries to make conversation.

"Kelly, did you get your math test back yet?"

Kelly stops mid-chew and swallows hesitantly.

"No, Dad." She smiles sweetly, her braces catching the light from the chandelier overhead.

Liar. I taught her how to do that.

"John?" Dad starts. "How 'bout you? You haven't told us about school for a while."

There's a reason for that.

"Eh."

"How are your college applications going? Finished any?"

I grunt again.

Poor Dad. The communication thing really doesn't work for him. He stares at his three kids expectantly, and we all avoid his gaze, gulping the last of our drinks or scarfing down pasta.

He gives up and continues staring at his own food. Just as he looks like he's thought of something else to say, Kelly jumps up.

"Done!" she says quickly, and runs upstairs.

14

Poor, poor Dad.

Kelly's voice floats down the stairs, already engaged in a phone conversation about (gasp!) what she (get out!) said to him (no way!) and why they (oh my God!) broke up. Dad looks to me to say something and save him, but he's on his own. I take my dishes over to the sink and leave Dad to stare despairingly at Peggy, the only one left in our verbally challenged family.

9:30. I lie in my bed, watching the ceiling. It doesn't move. Hmm. Maybe if I stare long enough, it'll disappear . . .

Nothing. Maybe not.

I stare at the red digits on my alarm clock . . .

Why do I think staring at things will make them do something?

I don't want to get up.

I stare at the ceiling. God's only response is Kelly's muffled voice on the other side of the wall.

I get out of bed and take a seat at my desk and take my pre-calc book out of my backpack. Cosine crap. I scribble illegible numbers and hope she doesn't collect the homework.

I turn on my computer and wait while it boots up. Whirring, illumination. My face glows bright from the reflection of the screen. For lack of anything better to do, I log onto AOL Instant Messenger. Three messages pop up.

Thug4Lyfe (11:33:01 PM): yo
Italianhottie85 (11:33:05 PM): yo
ShOppAHollCBayBie21 (11:33:12 PM): yo
HotCaesar1 (to all three): yo

I open Internet Explorer and check my e-mail. Junk mail, the worst. I surf for a while, checking sports updates and that kind of thing.

> **Thug4Lyfe (11:34:38 PM):** sup
> **HotCaesar1 (11:37:15 PM):** nmu
> **Thug4Lyfe (11:37:56 PM):** jc
> **Thug4Lyfe (11:38:01 PM):** im hungry
> **Thug4Lyfe (11:38:18 PM):** u wanna get sum food
> **HotCaesar1 (11:41:20 PM):** come over here
> **HotCaesar1 (11:41:23 PM):** we got shit
> **Thug4Lyfe (11:42:18 PM):** aight
> **Thug4Lyfe signed off at 11:46:02 PM.**

Ten minutes later, the doorbell rings. I open the front door.

> **Thug4Lyfe (11:54:28 PM):** yo
> **Me (11:54:29 PM):** yo
> **Thug4Lyfe (11:54:30 PM):** sup

We walk into the kitchen and he sits down at the table. I walk into the pantry and stare at the contents of chips.

> **Me (11:56:27 PM):** sour cream and onion, salt and vinegar, cheddar, or regular?
> **Thug4Lyfe (11:56:29 PM):** bring 'em all

I grab all four bags of barely eaten chips and close the pantry door. I put them on the table.

Thug4Lyfe chows down on one bag at 11:57:04 PM. I open the sour-cream-and-onion bag and grab a handful, inhaling the smell of processed potatoes.

Thug4Lyfe finishes the salt-and-vinegar bag and reaches for the regular chips at 12:08:57 AM. He is a monster. We crunch and munch and lick and chew and swallow in complete silence. I feel strange all of a sudden. And I can't think of anything to say. Neither of us says anything for five minutes. Me and Thug4Life finish off the salt-and-vinegar bag at 12:20:48 AM. I smell like processed chips and grease.

Thug4Lyfe (12:23:36 AM): jake lent me the championship game tape yesterday. have you seen it?

Finally.

Me (12:23:40 AM): yeah

Me (12:23:46 AM): awesome game

Thug4Lyfe (12:24:09 AM): yea, triple overtime. it was sweet!

Me (12:24:13 AM): yeah

Thug4Lyfe (12:26:17 AM): did you see that shot —

Me (12:26:18 AM): yeah!!

Me (12:26:20 AM): steven was unbefuckinglievable

Me (12:26:21 AM): two seconds left!!

Me (12:26:22 AM): (speechless)

Thug4Lyfe (12:26:29 AM): oh man i know!

Thug4Lyfe (12:26:34 AM): i was like no fucking way you just did that!

Me (12:26:35 AM): from halfway down the court!

Thug4Lyfe (12:26:40 AM): come over tomorrow, we'll try it out

Me (12:26:42 AM): hell yeah

Thug4Lyfe (12:26:45 AM): oh man, steven was increeedible!

We grin, unspeakably worked up and in a state of amazement. We breathe basketball.

Me (12:46:02 AM): later, dan.

Thug4Lyfe (12:46:03 AM): later.

Thug4Lyfe leaves at 12:46:10 AM.

I lie in bed, worn but still awake. I stare at the still-red digits on my alarm clock: 1:57. The house has been asleep for hours.

I roll off my bed in the dark and stand facing my reflection in the full-length mirror on my wall. Wavy brown hair and dull brown eyes, like Mom. I guess I think I'm good-looking. But it might just be because everyone else seems to think so.

I flop back onto my bed and soon I'm fast
asleep.

Friday night: out with the Boys. We cruise in the nicest cars in town, among them, my jet-black Mercedes SL550 roadster. My baby. Marsh and a few other kids drive somewhere behind Jake and me. We drive with no destinations, our usual Friday night agenda before we decide where to go.

The night is warm, summer air still lingering for a few more weeks before the end of September. With the top down, Jake and I don't talk much as we whip down the road with nothing more than fields in sight. The wind is like waves against our hair and eyes, but our smiles are the widest thing under the velvet night sky.

My cell phone rings. Keeping an eye on the mostly empty

road and a hand on the wheel, I fish the phone out of my pocket. Marsh's cell.

"Who is it?" Jake asks from the passenger seat.

"Marsh," I say.

I flip the phone open.

"Marsh," I greet.

"Yo, Caesar. What are we doing?" comes the voice on the other end. "Who's on your list tonight?"

I grin into the phone.

"I don't think that's yo business, man."

He laughs. "Sure, sure," he says. "But I gotta know if we're gonna decide where we're goin'."

"I'm thinkin' Stacy's party," I say slyly.

"In *Magville*? Dang, boy! You got another thing coming, Caesar. You must be crazy to do it with a Magville girlfriend on enemy territory!"

From the passenger seat, Jake gives me a look. "Magville?" he says. "Do you have a death wish, man? If you show up in Magville you are a dead dictator. No way, Caesar. No way! I am *not* going over there, and I bet Marsh agrees."

I grin again.

"Hear that, Marsh?" I say into the phone. "We're makin' it a night in Magville."

Jake shakes his head, but there is a glint in his eye, and he can't help but laugh.

On the other end of the phone, Brian and the boys whoop in the wild night as we speed out of town.

Half an hour later, we near Stacy Kinder's house. She lives in a freaking mansion, but then again everyone in Magville is pretty well off. The house is raging, and we hear the noise of the party before we even get onto her street. Jake looks at me expectantly.

"Who's on the list, Caesar?"

I laugh loudly and it mingles with the roar of the party. He knows he won't get an answer, but he always asks.

"We'll see," I say, wiggling my eyebrows.

He laughs back his approval, and we swerve up against the curb. Cars already litter every available spot, some even parked on Stacy's lawn. Over the din of screaming and splashing of pool water, I recognize the blaring radio of Marsh's car just making the turn onto Stacy's street.

In addition to cars, kids are *everywhere*: drinking on the roof, hanging out of windows, dancing in the driveway. I slip my keys into my pocket and take in the smell of nighttime air and booze — my two favorite smells in the world. Especially together.

Jake and I cross the lawn to the back of the house, hoping to go unnoticed before slipping in. I could take most of the guys here, but I'd rather wait for Marsh and the boys in case anyone wants to start anything. I kick a Sam Adams and it rolls away from our path. Within a few minutes, Marsh, Dan, Jared, and Matt have joined us. As Dan lights a joint, all six of us round the house to the back where the noise is louder and the smell is stronger.

Stacy is in a red bikini, dancing atop the diving board with some Magville scum I recognize from over the summer. I was thinking of nailing Lindsey Jacobs tonight, but I really hate the shit-for-brains guy Stacy's dancing with.

So tonight, Stacy *is* the list.

Dan follows my gaze to Stacy's bare legs and glances anxiously at the other guys.

"Stacy Kinder, man?" Jake says. "She's off-limits, even for you. She's *Mike Jennings's* chick. There's no way."

"She doesn't look like she's with him right now," I say. "Besides, no one is off-limits for me."

I do not think. I do not breathe. I am in party mode. I am the Dictator.

The boys feel the change in the air, and they know: No one will stop Caesar. They all grab beers and disperse, leaving me to it. Jake looks like he wants to say something, but Jenna appears and wraps a skinny arm around him, pulling him off somewhere. For once, she's done something smart.

I take off my shirt and toss it onto a lawn chair. *Deal the cards.* Stacy looks up from the guy she's with, and, as we lock eyes, a slow grin crosses her face. *Fake him out.* She whispers something into the guy's ear and kisses him as he walks toward the house, a triumphant look on his face. No, loser. Nothing for you tonight.

It's all me.

Stacy steps off the diving board and comes to my side. I feel nothing but the thrill of the hunt. I take a slow sip of Corona with a cool face. She takes the bottle from my hand and swigs, throwing her long blond hair back. She points a ruby-frosted nail at my bare chest accusingly.

"You're not supposed to be here," she teases.

I look down at her.

"What are you going to do about it?" I say. *Play the game.*

"The question is," she says slyly, placing my arms around

her waist and down the back of her bikini bottoms, "what are *you* going to do about it?"

I win.

Saturday morning. Have I been sleeping since Monday? No, wait . . . I remember a party. I remember . . . a girl. I remember a bed. I remember being drunk and eventually passing out and getting dragged into someone's car and tripping up the stairs to . . . here. Well, that would make sense. This explains the pounding in my head. Agh. Moan. I bury deeper beneath flannel covers to escape the steady *badum. badum. badum* of my screaming temples.

Kelly swings through my door, right on time.

"Get up."

"Euhh."

"Get. Up."

"Ehhhhuhh . . ."

"JOHN!"

Why does she do this to me every morning? She pretends to be annoyed, but I think Kelly takes some twisted pleasure in dragging me out of bed. I do not answer her.

A mistake.

She pounces on me.

"Aaargghhhhhhuhh!!"

The bed shakes and wriggles, springs squeak and a pillow thumps onto the floor. Legs kick and limbs flail in every direction. This is starting to become routine. Oh, why fight it?

I get out of bed, leaving Kelly punching my covers. She recovers quickly and follows me out the door. We enter the kitchen together. The clock on the wall says 1:14.

"It's still early!" I protest.

My father pokes his head out from behind an erected newspaper at the kitchen table and glares with a raised eyebrow.

"Eat," he commands.

I hate it when he's authoritative. It means he's in full CEO mode. Which means he has a meeting. Which means he's very edgy. Which makes him authoritative. And snappy.

I pour myself orange juice and sit down next to Dad. I pick up the sports section of the newspaper and drink.

"*Eat,* I said," comes the voice behind the front page.

No point in arguing with this family. They already suckered me into getting up. Might as well humor Dad. I crack an egg over the stove and pop some toast into the toaster oven. Yellow and white crackle and fizz on the oven top and I wait patiently while the egg fries. When my dad isn't looking, I clutch my head desperately to get rid of the wonderful pounding sensation. I grab two Tylenols and chug them down with orange juice, looking up to see Kelly staring at me from across the kitchen.

She says nothing, only raises her eyebrow. She looks just like Dad when she does that. Except she reads the comics. I give her my usual don't-tell-Dad shrug and she rolls her eyes.

Peggy is not at the table, but from the thumps upstairs, I get the feeling dancing to Barney is on today's agenda.

Little sisters are the best.

CHAPTER 3

September 13. Fall's just waiting for its chance to bite, but we do our best to cling to those oh-so-precious days of sandal-wearing weather.

I cruise down the empty road, hardly able to keep my eyes open on the way to school. With the top down, the wind breathes life into my dark hair and the pale sun is only a distant thought in the early morning sky. I hear nothing but birds and the hum of moving tires against pavement.

I park my car and sling my backpack over my shoulder, before crossing to the other side of the student parking lot.

Next thing I know, there's a car on top of me and I'm almost eating blacktop for breakfast. The dark blue sedan screeches to a halt and the horn blasts impatiently. I slide out of the way right before the front bumper can total my legs, and I stare wide-eyed at the driver. From behind the windshield, she looks like she might be Asian, but her dark sunglasses make it hard to tell. She must be a senior, but I don't recognize her. I do not move.

"Hello?" the girl yells out her window. "Do you mind?"

I glare into the window and flip her off.

What the fuck?

I stare at my reflection in the mirror in my locker. Nothing I haven't seen before. I grab my bio books and shove a pen into my pocket before I slam the locker door shut.

Jake appears.

"Yo" is the usual greeting.

"Hey," I reply.

He grins.

I ignore it and walk past. Jake follows, grinning wider than ever. He doesn't say anything.

"*What?*"

"Stacy?"

"Yeah, so?" I shrug.

"*So?*" Jake repeats, the smirk now stretching the length of the hallway.

I relent and smirk with him, letting him think I am as low as he is.

"So *what*," I say with a hint of conceit in my voice.

"Ha-haaaa! I *knew* it, man! *You* are a *god*," he exclaims, gesturing wildly.

I grin. "Julius Caesar was a dictator, though many may have considered him a god . . ."

Jake slaps me five, and for a second, I feel good. And I have to add another little bit just to set him off again:

"She wasn't *that* good." I shake my head with mild distaste.

Jake goes crazy and repeats himself, "*You* are a *god*!"

I know.

*   *   *

25

When Jake and I enter the gym, our friends have congregated near the bleachers. Today's topic of conversation is the Magville party Friday night. As we near the circle, Jared shouts out:

"Here's the man of the weekend! The conquest of the inconceivable: Stacy Kinder!"

I shrug with a who-gives-a-shit air, but I know what I did was risky. Of course, I never think of these things until after I do them. Shrug. Breathe. It's a routine.

The guys whistle and applaud, but the girls look rigid. Jake slings an arm around Jess.

"Jealous, baby?" he teases.

She shakes him off disgustedly. "Jake," she whines and pouts. "Of course not."

I stretch out on a bleacher and lean back on the one behind me where Sophie sits, her legs on either side of my head. I stare at her from upside down. I generally can't stand Sophie, but flirting with her seems unavoidable. She wants me — that much is obvious — and sometimes it's fun to play with her.

She wraps her arms around my neck.

"Tell me the truth," she whispers in my ear. "Who was better, me or Stacy?"

In my opinion, neither was anything special, but say that to a girl, and she gets really offended.

"You, of course," I say, lifting her chin. "Stacy's such a whore."

She winks and looks proud of herself. And you're not? She holds my face closer to hers and engulfs my mouth. Lips, hard, kiss, tongue, wet, breath. I feel nothing, only lips. Sophie pulls away and brushes her long fingernails through my messy brown hair, but I barely pay attention. She is nothing.

26

Dan turns to me and raises his arm to punch me in the shoulder when he looks at my face and reads it as a warning. His arm hesitates and his smile falters, and he slaps me a safe high five. He quickly turns away.

As the discussion continues, I survey the rest of the gym and the other students gathered here. The seniors are the most relaxed class in the school. We don't do our work, cut our classes, skip our tests. Despite pre-college anxieties, we're all just bumming around long enough to graduate.

I watch a guy from the team freestyle with his friends in the doorway of the gym. When he finishes his turn, something catches his attention and he loses focus for a moment. I follow his gaze to a dark-haired girl crossing the middle of the gym. She looks vaguely familiar, but I can't put a name to the face. She turns toward me, and then I remember the face from this morning and the annoyed glare from behind the blue sedan's wheel. It's the bitch who almost ran me over.

Jared notices me watching her.

"Fresh meat?" he says, nudging me. His voice is suggestive and I shoot him the Look of Death.

"No way in hell, Fisher. Who is she?"

Jared shrugs. "She just moved here, I think."

The rest of the crew turns to join our conversation. From behind me, Danielle pipes up.

"She's in my homeroom," she says. "Her name's Eva or Ava or something."

"She's kind of hot" is Jake's only contribution.

"She's half" is Danielle's reply.

"Whatever," I say.

And that's that.

27

Jared, Matt, and Dan continue their conversation about the Jets game yesterday, and I zone out, almost falling asleep.

Minutes later, I open my eyes, and there is Nicole Slater standing in front of us with this Eva person. Nicole is the president of our class and one of those ambitious types who we all tolerate because she's so overwhelmingly nice to us. Her main goal in life is to plan the best senior prom in the history of Laurence High School. She's irritating but mostly harmless.

"Hey, you guys!" Nicole says with a smile that seems ever-plastered onto her bright, cheerful face.

Everyone greets Nicole with smiles and hellos. Being rude to a person like that is like torturing a fluffy white bunny rabbit.

"I want you all to meet Eva. She just moved here, and so today I'm taking her to meet everybody!"

The girl smiles politely. "It's *Ay-va*, actually. It's just spelled like Eva."

Nicole bursts out laughing, presumably at her own stupidity.

Everyone exchanges confused glances before repeating the same smiles and hellos to Eva. Jake is notably friendlier than everyone else.

Up close, Eva's unusual features that I mistook to be Asian are even more unusual. The color in her hair and eyes is just a little bit off, but I guess that's because she's half. A lot of her looks are just a little bit off, but I have to agree with Jake when I say some things about her are just completely . . . *on.*

She is pretty.

"And this is John," Nicole says, finally reaching me, "but —"

"They call me Caesar."

Eva laughs. "*Caesar?*"

28

"You heard me." I am unusually defensive.

"Are you some kind of salad?"

Excuse me? Are you laughing at me? The muscles in my arms tighten.

The kids around me, including Nicole, exchange nervous glances. Control, Caesar, control. I know she knows what she's doing. This is her subtle dig at me for giving her the finger earlier this morning. Her wide eyes say she doesn't sense the tension, but it's Eva's quiet smirk that betrays her.

"Where'd you get that macho nickname? Thousand Island's already taken?"

Jake can't resist and chuckles at her joke.

At his expense.

I grab him by the neck of his shirt and glare right into his now-wide blue eyes.

"S-sorry, Caesar, buddy. I . . . uh . . . y'know. Sorry," he manages.

Eva says nothing but her smirk irks me. She knows she got me. I glare at her, too, but I don't dignify her with a response. Nicole smiles a falsely cheerful smile while Dani tries to make amends.

"When we were kids, the boys went through this weird phase with ancient Rome. John always got to be Caesar, and "

"Don't bother," I say coldly.

I stand up and walk away from this stupid mess of pestering losers. I knew I should have stayed home today.

The morning is slow. I slouch in my seat during English and listen to Mrs. Donahue drone on about *Hamlet*. That woman really doesn't shut up. It's all right, though, I don't mind; her

29

monotone voice makes sleeping easier. Except I can't close my eyes, because whenever I do, Eva runs madly through my head.

You can't show me up like that. *You can't.*

I look around the room. Other kids raise their hands, scribble notes, highlight lines in the play. The pen on my desk lies untouched next to my closed notebook. Mrs. Donahue stares at me.

What?

"Caesar, pay attention," she says. "What year was *Hamlet* first performed?"

Uhhh . . .

Maybe it's time to open my notebook.

The bell rings.

Saved.

As I grab my duffel bag from my locker at the end of the day to get to practice, I spot Eva coming down the other end of the hall headed toward the exit. She has haunted me all day, and now she's come to finish the job. As she nears me, I brace myself for a snide remark or at least a sassy word or two. I get all my comebacks ready, get my cool stare down.

And then she walks right by me, not even glancing my way.

What a bitch.

Night. I lay in bed in the quiet darkness. A steady breeze brushes through the open windows and across my face. Breathe. I let the night bathe me in cool air as I try unsuccessfully to fall asleep. The digital alarm clock on the nightstand next to my bed says it's 2:41. So tired.

I blink and my room comes into dark focus. When you first turn off the lights at night, you can't see a thing. But the longer you stay in the dark, the more you see. Usually after I lie in bed for an hour, I can see my entire room in shadowy detail.

As I drift into quiet slumber, the last thing I see is Eva's face.

CHAPTER 4

Saturday afternoon, I lie in my bed, zoning out and surrendering to iO's two hundred eighty-seven channels. Flip, flip, flip. The Argentina game, Beyoncé's new video, starving children in Somalia. Flip, flip, flip. I close my eyes and stare at the black behind my eyelids.

I sleep.

I dream I'm in Stacy Kinder's room again. I lay stretched out in her bed without my shirt on, my back to the bedpost, the TV on, and the remote in my hand. Stacy has one knee on either side of my legs and she tries to get my attention, but my head ducks around her to watch the game on TV. She starts to kiss me, and my tongue responds automatically, but my eyes do not leave the screen.

Stacy rips the remote out of my hand and flings it across the room, the channel stuck on ESPN.

She is aggressive.

I grin.

She probes my tongue with hunger, and I slide our bodies farther down the bed. She's still wearing her bikini, but this is easily remedied. She lies on top of me completely naked, her jaw still detached, her lips swallowing my face, and her body moving against mine . . .

A little *too* aggressive.

She grabs the back of my head and a good portion of my dark hair. My hands move up and down her body, and she reaches down to my jeans. Before they're flung across the room in the pile with her bikini, I hastily retrieve a condom from my pocket. The next thing I know, we are melting together, and Stacy is gasping for air. It's then that I realize the face of the girl I'm having sex with is not Stacy Kinder's.

It's Eva's.

I awake with a start, my heart racing and my hair sweaty. Oh God. Oh God, no. What the fuck. What. The. Fuck.

My hand gropes for a grubby white undershirt off the floor, and I slip it over my head. I slam the windows open as wide as the hinges will allow and unlatch the screen of the window above my bed. I lay the screen on the floor and crawl through the window out into the cool night. The breeze washes over my lean body and I stand quietly on my roof in dark midnight bliss.

I rake a hand through my hair and rub my eyes. Contemplate. Freak out. Okay, let's think about this sensibly. I had a dream — normal. I had a sex dream — normal. I had a sex dream about some sex I had last week — normal. I had a sex dream about a girl I never had sex with who almost ran me over and showed me up in front of my friends. And who I despise.

NOT NORMAL.

33

I lie down on the level part of the roof and stare up at the velvety sky. The sky is smooth, speckled, black. I am smooth, muscled, white.

Eva smiles, Eva smirks, Eva points, Eva laughs, Eva breathes, Eva . . .

haunts.

SHE IS TOTALLY MESSING WITH ME.

I am delirious.

Leave her be, Caesar. So what, she's new — she doesn't know what she's saying or who she's dealing with. She can't hurt your pride. You're Caesar! The king! The man!

And a total idiot.

I close my eyes and let basketball slowly into my mind, hoping to find a distraction by soaring effortlessly through the air toward the net. I sleep.

The air is cool. I jerk awake, lying on the roof. I haven't moved far since I fell asleep, but it has been several hours judging from the light of sky and the moon already far from where it was hanging above me. I step back toward my open window and crawl back inside. My room is drafty, both windows wide open, and filled with shadows. I can see everything clearly now, and though it is dark, nothing lies hidden. My alarm clock says 4:54 as I crawl under the covers and sleep again.

Sunday morning is pretty droopy. I wake up around 4:00, and probably would have slept longer if Kelly hadn't woken me up with our daily ritual of thrashing and yelling. I laze around the house, shoot some hoops, watch some TV.

I finally have to wear a jacket. It's not very heavy, but it still

34

pisses me off. The air is getting too cold too fast. I jump into my car and start the ignition. I turn off the blaring radio and spin left out onto the road and toward the lake.

On the way there, Eva's face flashes into my mind, so I turn the radio back on to drown her out. I pull up into the slump I use as a parking spot and walk through the bushes to the gazebo.

I stroll out to the short dock jutting out into the water and take my shoes off. I sit on the edge and let the clear lake water drift up to my knees. I watch the people on the other side, with their little kids and their kites and their picnic baskets and their smiling faces and I wonder what they do for a living. What kind of cars they drive. What they were like in high school. If they hate their lives.

I sit a while longer, let my legs float gray and distorted in the lake water. My cell phone beeps, and I reach for it instinctively, but my hands drop away. Let Jake wait. I pull myself out of the water and slip back into my sandals, stroll back to the gazebo. The sun is starting to set, the sky lemonade pink and the night breeze creeping into the air.

I avoid Eva's face, dart around, try to find a distraction in something else. Past girls run through my head: perfumed hair, pouty lips, perfect breasts. Stephanies, Saras, Stacys. No thinking or feeling or wishing or waiting, just the simplicity of sex.

I can't think of anything else to do, so I leave the clearing and head back to my car. As I turn onto the road, I check my messages. Jake's voice comes in short bursts.

"Caesar. We're at the diner. Come meet us."

I glance into my rearview mirror. At the sight of an empty road, I swerve into a U-turn and drive back the way I came in the direction of the Laurence Diner. When I get to the parking lot, I pull up into a spot next to Jake's bright red car. I get out of the car and walk up the steps and into the dimly lit diner.

Jake, Jenna, Marsh, Dan, and Chris all sit at a booth in the back. They wave me over, and I slip into a place next to Jenna. She kisses me on the cheek in greeting. Everyone greets me, and Jake hands me a menu.

"Where were you?" Marsh asks. "We didn't think you were coming."

I shrug. "I was around . . . sleeping."

Jake grins. "But not sleeping around?"

Jenna shoves him. "Don't be a pig," she teases.

He grins again and grabs a fry off her plate while I call the waitress over. A tall brunette with dark, full lips comes to our table.

Chris stares deliberately at her breast pocket. "Hi . . . Molly," he says, pretending to squint at her name tag. She looks down at him in disgust and starts to walk away. I touch her arm gently and pull her back.

"Wait," I say, flashing her a smile and laying on the Caesar charm. "You didn't let me order."

She looks at me, unsure, her eyes deciding, making her judgment. She cocks one eyebrow.

"Yeah?"

The table watches me expectantly, and I don't take my arm off her.

"Would it be cool with you if I had a classic burger and a strawberry milkshake?" I look her right in the eyes and give her an innocent stare.

Her eyebrow rises higher and she stands next to the booth, my arm resting on hers, trying to decide whether or not I am serious. I keep a straight face, and everyone else immediately tries to look occupied with each other or their own food. I wait for her to say something.

She comes to her decision and smiles suddenly.

"Yeah, I think that would be all right."

"Can I ask you for one more thing?"

"Sure, anything you want."

"Well . . . I dunno." I wear my mask, flirt with her, pull her slowly into my trap. "I don't know if I should . . . I don't want to trouble you."

She leans over me, her low-cut uniform dangerously close to my head. "Try me."

I pretend to shift uncomfortably. She eats it all up. I beckon her closer, and she leans her ear close to my mouth.

"I don't like pickles," I whisper. "Do you think you could help me out?"

She straightens up and winks. "I'll see what I can do."

"Thanks," I say, faking a sigh of relief.

"Anything else?"

"Nope, that's it."

As she walks away, I call her back.

"Wait, Molly, come back, there's something else."

"Yes?"

"Well . . ."

She laughs. "Yes?"

"I don't know . . ."

"You can trust me; I'm a very competent waitress."

"You think you can do me one more favor?"

"Anything you want."

"So I'll see you Friday night?"

She leans away from me and pouts a little.

"You're a sneaky one, aren't you?"

I shrug and smile. "You said anything."

She twists her lips to one side. "I'll see what I can do," she tells me again, and walks away, her hips moving side to side slightly more noticeably than before.

After she has left, the guys slap me fives while Jenna giggles. I know I've gotten her, but now she just has to go to the bathroom and fix her hair and makeup. When she returns with my food, I notice she looks smoother than before, and the top of her uniform has been unbuttoned more. She slides the plate onto the table and winks at me again.

Another one bites the dust.

An hour later, she comes back with the check. Jenna glances at it and smirks. She hands it over to me, and I see a handwritten number sprawled next to my order on the bill. I punch the digits into my phone and smile. Eva has completely left my mind and new prey has replaced her.

I am so good.

After dinner, we loiter at Jake's place with nothing to do.

"What time is it?" Dan asks.

Marsh glances at his watch.

"Almost nine."

"Mm . . . where are we going?" Always the same questions.

No answer. Chris and Dan both pull out paper and start to roll and light joints. They make their rounds, the group smoking in silence. Jake disappears into the house and returns after a few minutes with a six-pack of Corona and a plate of freshly cut limes. We settle on the roofs and trunks of each other's cars and make small talk. Jenna sits with me to share my beer, and Chris leans against the car facing us.

"Yo, where were you all weekend?" Chris asks Jenna.

She grins slyly. "My parents dragged me up to the city to visit their friends, so while they were out I gave their son a little . . . eye opener."

She winks and adjusts her shirt to reveal what Jenna Farrell is all about.

"The Jacobs?" Chris asks.

"No," Jenna says, grinning. "The Neilsons."

Chris almost drops his joint.

"The Neilsons? Isn't their kid twelve?!"

An innocent smile plays on Jenna's lips. "Never too young to learn," she says.

I smirk, imagining Jenna in the lap of some poor zit-faced junior high kid. He probably never saw 'em coming.

"That is *so* nasty . . ." Chris chuckles stupidly out of the corner of his mouth, the joint quickly taking effect. "Don't you think so . . . Thousand Island?" Chris's laughs are short, but he can't stop. He gives me a playful shove.

WHAT? As his hand makes contact with my chest, I grab it and squeeze it in my fist. I grab him by the collar and pull him to his feet.

"What did you say," I say in a low, deadly voice.

Jenna, not fully sober, just laughs along, a half hiccup, and pushes Chris into me. Chris laughs nervously and tries to push my arm away . . . unsuccessfully.

"C'monnn, dude, take a joke," he says, laughing the whole time.

The adrenaline pumps fresh and hot through my body,

the levels erratic and uneven. I clench my fist at my side harder, trying to keep steady control of a force I know can never be tamed. Chris takes my hesitation as a sign of forgiveness and tries to shove my arm off casually: *mistake*. He fights to gain control of his slowing mind, intoxicated by the pot, but loses miserably and says something he knows he will regret for the next two weeks.

"Do you want croutons with that? I think Eva did . . ." Chris drawls jokingly.

Eva. The name whispers across my mind, a quiet but clear taunt.

Swift and soundless, my right fist makes hard contact with Chris's jaw. The light is extinguished from his eyes and he stumbles away from me, the blow unexpected. The amusement has left Jenna's eyes as well, and she backs away from us. The others have taken notice, and Jake tries to step in between us.

"Caesar!" Jake shouts. "C'mon, man! Marsh, c'mon."

Brian tries to pull me off Chris, but my arm cannot stop. Chris is now fighting back, and he is no small force to be reckoned with, either. He is strong, but I am faster by nature, and the pot and beer have made us both dumber.

He swings, I swing: stomach, up, jaw, fist, knee, round, hair, blood, swing, swing, swing.

We are on the ground. He is under me. Jenna is shrieking and Jake and Marsh are a blur of bodies trying to rip us apart. All the while my eyes are locked with Eva's dark brown orbs staring right back at me. I elbow Jake off me and nail Chris in the eye. That will teach her to mess with me. But is she the one? Or is it Chris?

Or is it me? Faster, faster. I round Chris and he slows, lagging.

Ready to give up, kid? *C'mon, let's dance,* my mind taunts between shallow, ragged breaths. I taste blood on my lips, but it is quickly spat out and the breathing resumes. Finally Marsh and Jake both get us at the same time and Jake pins me hard against his car. He is strong from wrestling and I can't move.

I give Jake a strong shove and he stumbles away from me. I jump in my car and pull out my keys in one motion, then squeal away from the curb, barely missing Chris, and down the road away from Jake's house.

CHAPTER 5

Halfway down the road and halfway through a mental chew-out of Chris, I realize drinking, driving, and reeking of pot won't look good if I get pulled over. I swerve onto a smaller road and park the car. From what they can see at Jake's, they think I'm furiously tearing down the back road, looking hot and pissed off at the world. Nobody has to know that I'm thinking clearly. Or as clearly as possible, given the circumstances. If I'm going to be a pussy, I might as well do it in secret. I lean back in the black leather and quietly run my fingers over my closed eyes. I finger my bloody bottom lip and the scratches on my arms.

Another fight. I never really stop to think about why or what or why or who or why I'm fighting until it's over. Instinct just kicks in. I like the way it sounds. So I just do it, swift and hard. Just fight, because it's easy. I'd rather fight someone with my fist than fight myself with my mind. Control someone else because I can't control myself. It's just easier.

I can't stay here, but I can't go anywhere else. I sit quietly in the driver's seat, wondering what to do and where to go and why when Eva brushes through my mind and Chris whispers in my ear.

No, Caesar. Control. They are nothing.

I push them out, grapple with Eva's haunting smirk and Chris's stoned laughter, and fall asleep on the side of the road.

When I wake, the moon has risen and the cool almost-autumn air has settled. I check the clock on the dashboard. The green lights blink 11:23. I've been asleep for more than an hour.

I turn the key in the ignition and back out of the quiet road onto the street dotted with straggling cars. Head home.

The house is quiet when I arrive, so I settle silently on my rooftop with a cold beer.

I set the bottle next to me and stare out into the distant night and wonder where it might take me. Will I go far? Or are the burbs it for me?

I think about those overambitious seniors who are getting ready to apply to Princeton and Yale and Harvard and all that, and it makes me wonder what the point is. Is that what they did all through high school, just studied their asses off to make the grade and a 4.0 GPA and get into an Ivy League? It hardly seems worth it.

And then there's me.

When I was in junior high, I was pretty popular. Jake was my best friend then, too, and we started hanging out with a lot of

43

high school kids. I started messing around with my dad's old punching bag in our basement, and after a while at the gym and playing basketball, I became a pretty strong guy. I got into a couple of fights, and anyone who wanted to face me would get his ass whupped — and not even because I was the strongest guy out there, but because I was the best fighter.

When Jake and I got to high school, it seemed like everything was within our grasp. Girls wanted me, and all of a sudden I was a big-shot freshman, which is unheard of. Everyone treated me with this kind of respect, the guys because they knew what I could do in a fight, and the girls because they knew what I could do in a bed. All the clichés came true; anything I said was instantly cool, and I just got used to it — being Caesar.

No one can blame me; it's good to be the king. No one questions me or messes with me.

Or did, I guess.

And then there's Eva.

The next week is slow and passes drudgingly, and while for the most part I desperately hope for the weekend to come, there is the occasional fleeting thought of Eva or Chris, though I see neither of them all week. Which is fortunate. For them, that is.

Still, I know she's around.

On Thursday, Jake announces:

"I'm asking Eva out."

"*What?*"

"I'm asking Eva out."

You idiot. I heard you. I'm just pretending you said, "The gas thing gave out." In my mind, I slam my hand against

44

the locker door and dent the blue metal. In my mind, I throttle Jake and pin him to the wall and shake him fuckin' hard, shout at his wincing expression, ask him what the hell he is thinking. In my mind, I ask a million questions and buzz with a million answers, none right. Et tu, Jake? How can he . . . why is he . . . what about me?

What *about* me? What's the big deal anyway? In my mind, I'm torn. In my mind, I stand helplessly in front of a silent Jake.

In real life, I shrug.

"So?"

"Nothing." Jake shrugs back. "I just wanted to tell you."

"Why should I care?"

"Then you don't?"

"I don't give a shit."

For a fleeting moment, Jake eyes me like he might know, like we might be having one of those rare moments when we can read each other exactly, but it passes and he says nothing. He believes me.

Fool.

As soon as the last bell rings that day, I am out of Spanish and in the parking lot. Jess is right on my heels, trying to catch my attention.

"Caesar," she calls, struggling to match my strides.

I ignore her as the black of my car comes slowly into view and kids filter quickly into the parking lot. Five paces ahead of her, six paces, just a little farther . . .

"Caesar!"

Finally I am next to my car. But I'm too slow, because now Jess is next to me. She is dark and pretty, a full head shorter than me, with a mouth to make up for it. It's too late to pretend I don't notice her.

"What the hell is your problem?" she asks when I turn to face her.

"What?"

"I don't know why I even talk to you."

"Me, neither." I move to open the door of the driver's seat and she steps in front of it before I can.

"Caesar . . . ?"

"Yes?"

"Don't you get it?"

"Get what?"

"It! Everything! All the things I'm trying to tell you."

"No . . . I have no idea what you're talking about."

Jess fidgets and looks at the ground.

"You're so oblivious," she says quietly.

"Thank you," I say with an edge in my voice. I hate when girls play stupid games and think we know exactly what they're talking about.

She bursts into tears and I feel a little bad.

"What's wrong?" I ask her, trying to feign concern.

"Caesar, why can't I get away from you?"

I wrap an arm around her and she presses her face into my chest. I roll my eyes heavenward and she sobs brokenly against me.

"No one can," I joke.

She chokes out a laugh and wraps her arms around my neck, pulling me closer. I feel her tears stain my thin gray shirt and her small hands rub the skin on the back of my neck. What the hell is going on? Jess is the PMS queen, I knew that, but this is just too much.

"That's why I love being with you," she says, finally pulling away. "You make me feel good, but at the same time . . . I can't stand you."

Then why do you?

She takes a step away from me. "I'm tired of this, Caesar."

I don't give a fuck, but I guess I can't say that. "Tired of what?"

"Wondering if you even like me. Wondering if we're even friends!"

"What do you mean? I see you every day. We always talk."

"*We* always talk or *I* always talk? God, I'm so tired of trying to make you understand."

Understand *what*? is what I wonder, but I am scared to ask any more questions. Jess is clearly unstable. If she hates me so much, why the hell does she still follow me around everywhere?

"You don't appreciate me at all. After everything I've done for you, you still treat me like crap. I'm so stupid."

But I'm tired of pretending to care. I know what she wants. I know she wants me to tell her no she isn't — she's not stupid, she's great, I love being friends with her. I know it. But the truth is, she is, she isn't, and I don't. She is filled to the top with self-pity, and I hate that. I hate girls who cling to you and try to make you feel bad if you don't like them. If you're an ass, they should figure that out and get on with it.

"Who cares if you think I appreciate you or not?"

"You're supposed to say you do. You're supposed to say I'm not stupid. Don't you get it? You don't understand anything!"

47

"I'm not going to be your fucking ego boost. I don't need this! If you don't like me because I treat you like shit, STOP HANGING AROUND ME!"

It feels bad, but goddammit, I don't care anymore. I hate girls who manipulate you and have to be complicated about it and need you to tell them how much you care about them, how much you need them and appreciate them and all that shit. Goddamn.

"Caesar!"

I throw my backpack onto the passenger side and get in the car.

"You asshole!" is the last thing I hear as I tear out of the parking lot.

Instead of driving straight home, I drop by the gym for an hour. As I walk out of the thick, sweaty air and into cool, crisp autumn, I spot Jake pulling up into the parking spot next to my car. He steps out and slaps me five.

"Hey."

"You done?"

"Yeah, I'm gonna head home."

"A'ight, man, I'll catch you later."

I burn to ask him about Eva, but I nod swiftly and get into my car.

"Yo, Caesar, hold up," Jake says, turning around again. "I gotta tell you what happened with Eva."

"Oh," I say with mild indifference, as if I had forgotten about the entire incident. "What'd she say?"

"Yo, it was the craziest shit, man."

"She said yes?"

"She said no!"

I let out the breath I didn't know I was holding and say, "That sucks, man. Did she say why?"

He shrugs. "Eh, what the hell, she was just like, 'you're not my type.' I should have known better than to try and get with a *brain*. You know how they are. Fuckin' snobs."

She said he isn't her type? "Yeah, forget that bitch. I don't know why you wanted to go out with her in the first place. I can think of a million better girls on the spot."

"Not like her, man. Not like her."

"What do you mean?" What does he know that I don't?

"It's just like, the way she moves, y'know?"

"Jake, all chicks move the same. Well . . . all the good ones."

"Naw, Caesar, not this one. She's got . . . class."

I snort. "Class? In Laurence?"

"She's from New York."

"You talked to her?"

"Yeah, a couple times. She's so hot, man."

"Forget her, Jake! Let it go. She thinks she's too goddamn good for you, whatever. It's her loss."

He shrugs and the left corner of his mouth tips into a smile. "Whatever. I'll catch you later, Caesar." He turns and walks toward the glass doors of the gym.

"Peace."

I climb into the car and grip the steering wheel, then breathe easy.

Relieved, Caesar? Why the hell should you be relieved? Why the hell are you happy? Your best friend just got rejected

49

by some girl who just moved here and already thinks she rules the fuckin' place. I mean, really. Who the hell does she think she is?

When I get home, Kelly and one of her friends are in front of the TV with glazed looks in their eyes, not moving, barely blinking.

"Don't you have homework to do?" I say, standing deliberately in front of the TV.

"We have a big screen, dumb-ass. We can still see what's happening."

"Touché."

Kelly's friend stares at me with the same glazed expression. I settle in the love seat closer to the TV and channel surf.

"We were watching that!" Kelly says.

"What?"

"*Seventh Heaven!*"

"C'mon. That episode is on so often, even I've seen it."

"It doesn't matter; we were here first! Go watch TV in your own room!"

"It's not a big screen," I respond distractedly, engrossed in the Jets game.

"It's okay," Kelly's friend says. "I like football."

"See, you can learn from your friend," I say as a commercial comes on.

"I'm Jenna Tyler," the girl says, flashing me a toothy grin. "You're Caesar."

"Yeah, how'd you know," I answer.

Kelly rolls her eyes. "I *hate* football," she whines. "And his name is John."

"Hey, I know a girl named Jenna," I say just to piss Kelly off.

"I know," Jenna says, wide-eyed. "I heard the two of you had sex when you were in seventh grade."

I chuckle, not denying it. "Where did you hear that?"

"Everyone knows it."

"Who's everyone?"

Kelly interrupts on this one. "The entire Laurence Middle School," she says to me. "Could we *not* spend your afternoon here talking to my brother about his sex life?"

Kids say the darnedest things. "Yeah, you girls should be off playing Barbie or something. Isn't that what you middle school kids are doing these days?"

Kelly glares at me as she drags Jenna out of the room. I grin mockingly at her.

It's good to be me.

CHAPTER 6

Late Friday night I open my eyes and find myself in an alien bed sleeping next to the waitress from the diner. Her long dark hair spills over the pillow, and her slender hand rests on my bare chest. She's asleep. Groggily I recall the whole night, the dinner and the drive and the fooling around. And the sex.

Finally, it's the weekend. Relief has settled in and things are back to normal.

I said I'd stay the night, but this sleeping together without sleeping together thing is just a little too cozy for comfort. I slip out from under her hand and pull my jeans and shirt on in a flash. A note is probably in order, but who's got time for such formalities?

I'm gone.

Saturday morning I get up early to go to the gym, but I realize sitting at the kitchen table that I don't feel like going as much as I did last night. After two bowls of cereal, I pull on a sweatshirt and call my dad's cell. I leave a message reminding him that it's Kelly's week for her dance carpool and to pick her up at 4:30. Dad always works weekends.

"Kelly, I'm leaving!" I yell before slamming the door shut behind me and heading out to my car.

Outside is dank and gray, a rainy September day. The sky is a sheet of cloud and the pavement underneath my feet is slick. Raindrops skim my skin and graze my head. As I pull out of the driveway, I flip the switch to pull the top back up over the car.

I take the main road out to the lake and soon arrive and park my car behind the bushes. I head out into the clearing where the old gazebo waits patiently. I sit inside the brown shelter and stare out at the water, the massive body that divides and connects us all. The rain has let up and now a slight drizzle mixed with fog hovers on the gray and faceless lake.

I feel like going for a swim. So who cares if it's cold and raining?

I toss my sweatshirt and T-shirt on the bench and shuffle my shoes off. I walk out of the gazebo and start running toward the water as soon as my foot hits the ground. I run straight at the edge of the dock and jump far, far, far out where they can't get me, and I fall with a deafening splash.

When I resurface, my hair is slicked back and there is a huge grin on my face. That felt amazing. It's raining on me and I'm freezing and I have goose bumps all over and my shorts are weighing me down, but *damn* it was worth it. I smile like an idiot.

I hear a voice behind me. Laughter.

Feminine laughter.

I turn around in the water and —

There. She. Is.

Her.

She says nothing, only smiles at me looking at her. She stands off to the side where I couldn't have seen her from the gazebo. She is alone and has a bag at her feet and a camera in her hand.

Maybe I can get her. Maybe. The best way to act around her is treat her like all the other girls. Maybe I'll even score.

Play with her, Caesar. Make her beg. Make her kiss your feet for what she said about you.

I flash her a grin. "Hey!" I call out.

"Hi," she answers, putting down her camera and walking to the end of the dock as I swim toward it.

She is taller than I remember. Her long legs are covered in jeans and her top is all black. She slips her shoes off and swings her legs over the edge of the dock while I tread at her feet.

"You're Monica, right?" I say, flashing her the pearly whites again.

She smirks at me. "Yeah, how did you know? Have we met?"

Uh-oh. She plays my game. I am at a loss for a moment, but I compose myself. *You're the master, the king at this game. Don't let this chick think she can win.*

Keep talking.

"I'm Caesar." I hesitate when I remember her reaction the last time she heard this. *Keep talking.* "I'm sure I've met you somewhere."

"Caesar . . . oh yeah, I remember now. Thousand Island." The left side of her mouth tugs upward, but she continues. "Your name is John."

I smile and duck under the water to slick my hair back more. When I come up, I spray her with a handful of water, half flirtation, half challenge. She stares at me a moment and does not move.

"I'm already wet." She points heavenward, telling me my efforts are useless.

Damn.

I shrug; *duh*, a careless gesture.

"What are you doing out here?" I ask her. "It's cold and raining and no one likes to come to the lake when the weather is crap."

"Except for you?"

I hold out a hand to the drops.

"Yeah, I don't mind the rain. And I like it when no one's here."

"Why?"

Why? Isn't it obvious? Because I'm a secret loner and it intrigues you! At least . . . that's what I'm going for.

I shrug, try to look sad and misunderstood, look down at the water. This is taking longer than I thought it would. "I like being alone out here with none of my friends to bother me. Gives me time to think." That's right, sell it, sell it, you're an angst artist who loves introspection in nature's company.

"Seems a bit cliché, don't you think?"

She doesn't look impressed. Or intrigued.

At all.

This is going to take quite a performance to pull off. I *have* to get this girl. No one matters but this one.

"Cliché is okay. As long as I get the job done."

"Typical male answer." She laughs. "Who cares how you get her in bed, as long as it ends with a dirty condom."

Ouch.

55

"Well, what difference does it make if I like to be alone in a novel way or a cliché way or whatever? Is one search for peace of mind better than another?"

DAMN, I'm good. That one even surprised me.

She tilts her head at me and finally looks like she sees me. "All right, John, you win."

She called me John. Why did she call me John?

Don't make an issue of it, Caesar. Keep talking.

"I usually do."

I smile without showing my teeth, a more genuine approach. I grab on to one of the spikes jutting out of the dock and pull myself up so I'm sitting next to her. Instinctively she leans away from my dripping body, and I smile with fake innocence.

"Don't worry about it; you're already wet," I say.

She stares blankly at me, though I know she's computing an answer. She's starting to crack.

Finally she says, "As much as I would like to exchange playful banter with you all day long, 'Caesar,' I'm here for a reason, and you're getting in my way." She gets up from her sitting position and stands over me.

"To get away from everything?" I stand up, too, revealing my lean, muscular body in all its glory.

She rolls her eyes. "Oh, please." She gestures to the bag lying in the grass on the bank. "I'm taking some pictures."

"You know, Eva, you're kind of a snob."

A smile draws slowly across her pretty face and her dark brown eyes lighten just a shade.

"Monica."

I freeze. I've been busted. Totally busted.

HOW COULD I LET HER WIN?

I am startled into shock. How could this happen? I've never slipped up before.

WHAT'S WRONG WITH ME?

"I . . . uh . . . right. Eva," I stumble.

I shake my head, at a loss for any other comeback. I give up. How . . . did I let this . . . what's going on?

With nothing left to say, I mumble "sorry" as I brush past her.

"C'mon, Caesar." She laughs again. "Stay and play a while."

She waves mockingly as I walk away from the water and to the gazebo to retrieve my clothes.

Don't look back.

But as I enter the bushes to get to my car, I turn to see her still standing at the edge of the dock watching my retreating body.

"Nice shorts!" she shouts and turns toward the water.

Dang. She's good.

In the car, the dashboard clock says 11:21. Backing out of the parking spot slump, a thought hits me. *What if I do stay? What if I go back to her? What if I really talk to her for once?*

No. I can't do that. I can't go back.

Luckily, before I make up my mind, Marsh calls and asks me to check out TVs with him. When I get to his house, he's standing in the driveway with a BestBuy catalogue in his hand.

"Yo," he says, sliding into the passenger side and clicking the seat belt over his lap. He opens the catalogue.

"Find anything good?" I say, nodding at the open page in his lap.

I pull out onto Dober.

"I don't want anything too big," he answers. "All this stuff is so high-tech and shit. I just want something that can support good porno whenever I need it."

I laugh. "*That's* what you want to pay three hundred bucks for? An outlet for your porn collection?"

Marsh has a notoriously extensive porn collection that he mooched off his uncle in the "movie" business.

"Well, what else?" He shrugs. "I don't want anything too fancy. Do you think they make stain-resistant screens?"

"Aw, man, that's nasty." I laugh. "I don't want to think about you doing any of that."

He laughs, too. "Why? It's nothing you don't do yourself."

"Yeah, but . . . *dude*. What you and your hand do for fun on the weekends is your own goddamn business."

"Oh, fuck it," he says, tossing the catalogue out the window. "Let's just go."

"That's what we're doing!"

At BestBuy, we get out of the car and walk through the automatic sliding doors, and a wave of computer room ACed air washes over our faces. After half an hour, Marsh decides on a $200 Panasonic that will fit in the most ideal place — right next to his bed.

"This is sweet," he says, grinning as we load the box into my trunk. "College is going to kick ass. Nonstop partying, all the hunnies we want, and none of our parents' shit. I'm gonna have girls in my room all the time. My roommate isn't going to have any space for his crap."

"You think you'll get into Rhode Island?" I ask, getting into the driver's seat.

"Hopefully. Only for basketball, though. Otherwise I've got no chance."

"It's tough."

"I know. If not, I can still go to Rutgers. My grades aren't terrible."

"They're not amazing, either."

"You don't need to be a flaming genius to get into Rutgers."

"True."

"So where are you planning . . . ?"

"Don't know."

"Dude! You better get on it. It's almost October."

"I know. I guess, Rutgers. Or Ravens."

"Don't go to Ravens — fucking community college's got no dorms!"

I laugh, but it is not a warm laugh. "I don't know if I can get in anywhere else."

"Yeah, you can. You did decent on the SATs, right?"

"Yeah."

"And you're captain of the team, Caesar. We've been playing awesome lately; once the season starts, we're gonna go really far. I can feel it. I think you can definitely get a scholarship somewhere."

"Probably."

"So why don't you?"

"Eh. Who cares." I shrug. I don't feel like discussing it anymore. College is such a burden.

Marsh shrugs, too. "Whatever."

Dribble. Dribble. Left. Right.

Move.

Get out of the way.

Left.

Bend.

Shoot.

Swoosh.

I spin, I turn, I fake left, fake right, dribble, dribble, bend, shoot, lay-up.

Make it in.

I always make it in.

I push my hair back and wipe the sweat off my forehead with my sleeve. I stand back from the net and hold the ball poised, ready. I stare down my opponent, stare down the lean black pole and the grimy imitation-nylon basketball net.

I wait. I breathe. I count.

I shoot.

I make it in.

It's like poetry.

After an hour of playing in my driveway, I return to my house, drenched in sweat and feeling mighty good.

It is now almost 5:00. I jump in the shower and hot, clean jet pressure meets natural, sticky cool sweat. They blend together with the soap and the three of them enjoy a ménage à trois on the surface of my skin. I lather my way-too-long hair and the smell of sweat washes away and makes a sucking noise as it swirls down the drain.

I open the glass door and the steam is released into the rest of the bathroom, fogging up the mirror. I stand with a towel wrapped around my waist and my bare chest rising and falling in the heat of the room. The air is thick and I can't see my reflection in the mirror.

Where's Caesar?

CHAPTER 7

The rain does not let up for the entire weekend. Sunday afternoon, I drive to Jake's house. Marsh's and Sam's cars are parked out front when I pull up to the curb.

I ring the doorbell and Dan answers the door.

"Yo."

I follow Dan into Jake's basement where Sam, Marsh, Jake, Jenna, and Ashley are already hanging out around the pool table, drinking and making merry. Jay-Z blares from Jake's surround-sound speakers. Jake hands me a beer and Ashley hands me her cue.

"Here," she says. "I don't feel like playing anymore."

"Thanks," I say.

"Caesar, you're on my team," Marsh says. "Solids."

Sam grins. "Good thing, too, Marsh. You need the help."

Ashley settles on the couch and leans against Jenna as they watch the game. Dan sits in the love seat and chills quietly with his beer held close.

"Your shot," Jake says to Sam.

She moves around to the left side of the table and chews her hair softly, cocking her head to the side. She makes a decision and leans against the wooden edge, aiming her cue at the cue ball. It spins at a forty-five-degree angle and hits the felt wall, then makes its way toward the corner pocket. Sam sinks the nine without batting an eyelash.

"Sweeeet," Jake says, and he hugs her around the waist.

I forgot how amazing at pool Sam is. She smiles modestly and swigs from a half-empty beer bottle sitting on the coffee table. Marsh grins and shakes his head.

"Damn! I've never met a chick who can sink 'em like Chansett. I hope you can bring us back on this one, Caesar."

I laugh. "I can try."

Sam winks. "Yeah, you can."

I decide on the three and hit it right in.

Clunk.

One clean, satisfying clunking sound.

Cake.

"SHWAY!" Marsh exclaims, clapping me — lightly — on the back.

Sam grins. "Hot, Caesar." She offers me a sip from her Corona as props to my shot.

"Thanks, babe."

"All right, let's do this," Jake says importantly, rolling up his sleeves and setting up his next shot.

I wink at Sam and she smiles like we share a secret. When did she get to be so sexy? Her dark hair falls quietly to her shoulders and her eyes have a hidden sparkle. Sam doesn't talk much, but she loves to have a good time and isn't obnoxious or loud about it. We go way back to the third grade, when she first moved to Laurence. She was such a cute little eight-year-old.

Now as I watch her in her worn jeans and simple green shirt, I can't imagine why we never hooked up. She was with that James guy for a while. But since they've broken up, she hasn't been involved with anyone else. As my eyes travel up her slim body over jeans and cotton, all I can think about is ripping them off her. Sam catches my eye and winks back at me.

My smile grows wider and my eyes gleam.

This day is looking up.

After ten minutes, me and Marsh are tied against Jake and Sam, each with one ball left. The shots are impossible, and a ball isn't sunk for another ten minutes. Jake and Marsh look at each other and silently agree to give up. It's down to me and Sam.

When she misses her first shot, I know I can beat her. I've got this one. Let's show her how it's done. A look of concentration is sprawled across her face. I want to draw her attention away from the game and onto something infinitely more important:

Me.

Of course.

I lean so that I'm in full view of Sam's pretty hazel gaze and tap the cue ball gently, sending it ricocheting off the green felt wall and into the five ball, which spins gracefully into the left side pocket.

Cha-*ching*.

"Right side pocket."

I move around the side of the table and send the cue ball straight at the eight ball. It goes right in. I am fully ready to gloat, waiting on my prize for winning, which, if I calculated right, should lead to some interesting backseat activity after I leave Jake's. It's Sam's turn to make a move.

But no such luck.

She gives me a limp smile and leans under the table to retrieve the balls from the ball drop. She places them back on the table and racks them up to use again. She doesn't so much as look at me.

Can't say the same for Marsh.

"FUCK YEAH!" he cries and claps me — harder — on the back.

Watch it. My eyes tell him this, and he backs away.

"Nice," he says, coolly this time.

"Dammit," Jake says.

I wait for a reaction from Sam.

Nothing.

"Good game," I say in a feeble attempt to get her to say or do something . . . *anything*. A wink, a laugh, a scowl.

She hangs up her cue and turns back to me. She smiles her limp half smile again and then shrugs apologetically to Jake. She sips more beer and doesn't finish the whole bottle. She hands it to Jake as if in consolation.

I wait.

Nothing.

Ugh. No interest? So fuck her!

Except I really do want to.

Fuck her.

Sam joins Jake and Marsh on the couch in front of the game. Still not a word. I sit next to Ashley and Jenna and listen to their idle chatter in the background of the game.

"He's just so *gross*. I mean, I can understand her situation and all that, but, God, hooking up with him just screams DESPERATE! It's disgusting."

"I know. And she told me . . ." Ashley leans into Jenna and cups her hand over her ear. She whispers something — some deep, dark, horrible, juicy secret, I'm sure — and Jenna pulls away with an oh. my. God. look on her face, her jaw slightly dropped.

"You're shitting me. YOU'RE *SHITTING* ME! With HIM?" She turns away in disgust. "Ew. EW. EWWWWW."

Ashley nods her head knowingly. "Uh-huuuuuhhh."

I watch Sam like a hawk waiting to attack its prey and I just don't understand how she has no reaction to it. I didn't impress her? I didn't get her attention? She wasn't the least bit interested?

WHAT DOES THIS MEAN?

It has to be a mistake.

Suddenly, she speaks.

"Jake, do you have the new Game CD I asked you for?"

Not quite the first words I would have picked to come out of her mouth.

"Uhhh, yeah, it's in my room . . ." he answers distractedly, eyes glued to the screen. "You want it?"

"Yeah, can I get a copy of it?"

"Yeah, it's in my room . . ." he says again. His focus does not leave the TV.

"Where?" Sam looks at him expectantly.

"Huh?" Jake says, finally tearing his eyes away from the game. "Where is it?"

"It's under my — OH MY GOD, HOW IS THIS

POSSIBLE?!" Jake jumps up and starts to dance around the basement, doing his ridiculous victory dance.

Sam grins patiently as he kisses her on the cheek and dances her around. He plops back down on the couch.

"Jake," Sam says with a twinge of annoyance as her smile fades away. "Are you going to give it to me or not?"

"Do you need it now? I need to see this plaaaaay!"

Sam looks at her watch. "I need to go to work soon. And I won't have time after that, so can I copy it or what?"

Jake does not answer. At the moment, he doesn't know anything but left pass. Marsh and Dan contribute nothing, both equally engrossed in the game. Jenna and Ashley are busy going on about God knows what, and Jake shows no signs of moving for the next hour.

This leaves me.

"It's under his bed," I break in, a knowledgeable source of Jake's living habits. "I'll get it for you. Come upstairs."

She smiles. "Thanks." She throws Jake a mockingly dirty look. He does not notice.

The plan is back in action.

Two flights up, the rain pelts Jake's windows and the sunless sky casts gray shadows into his room. Sam sits on the floor next to me as I sprawl out on my stomach with my head hidden beneath Jake's bed. After rummaging around for a moment, I pull out a handful of CDs and hand them to her.

"All the crappy hip-hop you could ever want and more."

"Thanks."

She lies down on her back to flip through the CDs and I can't help but think about how tempting she looks when she's lying down.

Dammit.

I lie down next to her and somewhere in my hormones, a desire for her to kiss me starts to grow. This gets the better of me and I gently pull the CDs out of her hand.

She laughs and props herself up on one elbow to face me.

"What are you doing?"

I gently nudge her onto her back again and lean over her, placing a hand on her waist.

I hope she's as horny as I am right now. I look in her eyes for a few moments, hoping to build up a romantic atmosphere before I go in for the kill. She stares back, and I see a longing in her open hazel eyes. I touch her arm and pull her slightly to me and lean in to her . . .

"I know you want this . . ." I whisper, hardly inches from her face.

"Caesar!"

She pulls away abruptly and sits up.

Or not.

"What?"

"What are you doing?!"

I don't answer for a moment.

I'm doing the hokey-pokey.

WHAT THE FUCK DO YOU *THINK* I'M DOING?

"C'mon, Sam," I say with a cocky grin. I can't help it. "C'monnnn, Jake won't know."

"That's not what I meant! What makes you think I want to do this?"

"I'm . . . Caesar?" I say confusedly.

"You're such an asshole!"

Okay, different tactic.

67

"I'm sorry, that was a joke. I didn't mean it."

She furrows her eyebrows and turns away from me. "Stop."

I sit up and place my hand gently on her waist, pulling her to me again.

"I'm sorry. Will you listen to me now?"

She stares at me and makes eye contact again.

God, she's hot.

"I didn't mean that," I say. "I don't want you to think I'm insensitive. I just really like you."

And right now this bed is really tempting.

"Bullshit. You just want to get laid."

Hmmm.

"Are you saying that you don't want to be with me?"

"Yes!"

You're not allowed to do that!

"Now you're the one bullshitting," I say.

"Is it really so unbelievable that I'm not interested in you, Caesar?"

Uh . . . yeah, it kinda is.

I stare at her. "It's all right, Sam. I know James treated you like shit, but I won't hurt you."

She gives me a withering look. "Well, I'm not a virgin, so that shouldn't be a problem, now should it?" she says sarcastically.

"Why do you think I only want to get you in bed?"

"Because you do!"

"That's not true!" I exclaim, hearing the lie crack in my own voice.

Actually, I just really want to see you naked.

"Really," she says, not believing. "Is that so?"

"Really! I think you're great, and I wanna be more than what we are right now."

Because right now, we're wearing clothes.

"Which is?"

"Friends."

If being friends means I want to see you naked.

"We're not friends, Caesar. You don't know anything about me, only the shallow details, like who I'm with, who I was with, who I'm going to be with . . . which, I can tell you right now, does NOT include you!"

"Then give me a chance!"

. . . to see you naked.

Why is she putting up a fight?

"Caesar . . ." she trails off.

Forget it, talking is getting me nowhere.

I pull her gently to me and kiss her moist lips. I feel her respond with pressure against my own mouth, but in a fraction of a second, she pushes me away.

"No," she says.

"What?"

"No. I said no. Now leave me alone."

"But you kissed me back."

"I can't help but be physically attracted to you, Caesar. But I can't be with you."

I'm not asking for you to *be* with me, I'm asking for you to BE with me. Like in a bed. Like in *this* bed.

"Why not?"

"I told you! I can't be . . . I'm not . . . I'm not interested."

"Yes you are. Listen to yourself! Who are you trying to convince, me or you?"

"God, you're so fucking cocky!" she says defensively. "I hate that about you! You waltz around like you own the goddamn place!"

You mean I don't?

"You look at every girl like she's some kind of fucking object that you can just use and then toss her away with a dirty condom."

"It wouldn't have to be that way! You last longer than condoms."

"Wow, that's real romantic. I hope you don't plan to propose like that."

"Sam, please —"

"I don't think —"

"Don't think. Just kiss me."

Her eyebrows knit together and all the light I thought I saw in her hazel orbs is now gone.

"Fuck you," she says, low and cold.

What did I say NOW?

She stands up and walks out of Jake's room.

"Don't you want The Game?" I call after her as she starts down the stairs.

My balls tell me to chase after her, but my brain tells me there will be others. Better ones.

"Forget it," she calls back.

This is followed by the sound of the front door slamming.

I rake my hands through my hair and fall back onto Jake's bed. I stare at the stark white ceiling and close my eyes and stare at the dots behind my eyelids until I get dizzy. I stare until all I can see is black and then I know what just happened. Then I know I was just rejected.

For maybe the first time in my life. By Sam. Sam. Who the hell is that girl anyway? I try to remember memories with her, try to recall her face and the smell of her hair, and suddenly I can't. Who is she? Why did I care? What just happened?

But I know, I know. I know what just happened.

CHAPTER 8

Not long after Sam leaves Jake's, I leave, too. I don't say anything to Jake; I just get in my car and leave. Leave because I don't know what to do, sitting alone in his room and having to face what just happened. Leave because maybe if I leave, it will mean what just happened didn't just happen. And then maybe it'll be okay.

Maybe.

The rain pelts the windshield and the wipers slide them away, a steady thumping rhythm.

Thump.

Slide.

Scrape.

Thump.

Slide.

Scrape.

Thump.

The rain flows away in steady streams down the side of the windshield and I drive down 38 with blurred vision. The drops come down harder, and though I know I should slow down, it only makes me want to speed up.

When I stop the car, I'm at the lake. The slam of the car door, a few quick steps, and I'm in the gazebo. I'm in the gazebo and it's raining on me. If I were slightly more distraught, I would jump in the lake and go swimming.

But I'm not distraught; why should I be? It's just Sam. Just a girl, just some girl . . . but it's more than that, and I know it. It's my reputation, my pride . . .

I sit down on the bench that runs along the inside of the old brown gazebo, trying to imagine what Jake will say, what Marsh will think, what the girls will wonder. What whispers will grow between mouths and ears in the girls' locker room. What will the next girl I meet already know about me?

The back of my neck is soaked, my hair clings to my forehead, and I rise from the bench.

Fuck this. Fuck this and fuck her.

I leave the steps of the old brown gazebo behind me and get back on the road in the heavy rain. The cold from outside seeps past the walls of my car and chills me. I turn on the heat and turn up the radio. I drive down, down, down the slick black pavement and trace the familiar roads I take every week. I can't control my hands, they have some life of their own. The roads become more and more familiar as I drive on, and finally I come to a stop in front of the last place I'd expect to turn to:

Home.

I park my car in the garage and pocket my keys, but I do not start toward the garage door. I grab the worn basketball from the shelf and dribble out into the steady sound of rainfall, like a shower of beads against a wooden floor. After five minutes, my shirt is soaked and I have to slick my hair all the way back to see. I hear the rain, a contact sport between water and pavement, an ugly duel between nature and man. I hear my feet, squeaks and pivots on the smooth black of my driveway. I hear the *thump, thump, thump* of the tough leather and my arms pumping in steady motion. I feel like I'm in a movie, moving in slo-mo, fighting to keep my neck above water as my feet leave the ground and I extend my arm and flick my wrist and suddenly —

Swish.

The movie music plays and my feet take an eternity to come back down again, and then I am grounded. My soaked shirt clings to my frame and my fingers make a squeaky grip on the air-tight basketball. I will not give in to this. I fight the cold, sweat it out, until I feel nothing left of it in my bones. Half an hour passes. My feet squish in my sneakers. My jeans, dark from the rain, weigh me down, and a steady stream of wet runs down the length of my body. Another half hour.

And still I don't stop.

Dribble. Bend. Leap. Dribble. *One. Two. Three.*

Jump.

Breathe.

I fight my imaginary opponent, grapple with him, fight to keep the ball in my possession. It's mine, it's my ball, my win. My life. I turn, fake him out, pivot. Left, right, left, right. Which way am I going to go? He tries to smack the brown victory from my hands, but he can't. I'm too quick for him. I suddenly lunge to my left, dribble *one, two,* and leap for a lay-up.

And it's in.

I win.

And another half hour. My body feels so heavy. One last

shot. It bounces off the rim and out toward the end of the driveway. A swift arc.

The sound of rubber against tar. *Bounce. Bounce. Bounce.*

It rolls away, down the driveway. Into the street. I chase after it and scoop it up, dribble it up the driveway, and dump it back on the shelf in the garage.

I strip out of my wet clothes. They're heavy and dragging, and stick to my skin as I try to peel them off. Even my boxers are soaked, and I get rid of those, too. I change into new ones and put on shorts and crawl underneath my covers where it's just black. When I close my eyes the scene doesn't change.

I fall asleep.

When I regain consciousness, it is only because there is a little person on me, shaking me awake.

"John! John! Johnjohnjohnjohnjohnjohnjohn!"

It's Peggy.

"Wakeupwakeupwakeupwakeupwakeupwakeupwakeup!"

Her little fists pound into my back, and I feel it in my lungs.

"Uuunnnnnnnhhhh" is the sound that comes from my mouth.

She must be taking lessons from Kelly.

"Hurryhurryhurryhurryhurry!"

Sam's face flashes through my head and I hear the slamming of Jake's front door.

"UUUUNNNNNNNNNNNNHHHHHHHH."

I feel Peggy's breath on my face and I open one eye. Her eyes are wide and she is right in my face, blowing up her cheeks and making faces at me.

"Grroff," I grunt into my pillow.

Peggy squeals and pummels my back more.

Get up, my mind whispers.

I sit up, grab Peggy, and jump out of bed, dragging her out of my room.

"John! Guess what we're having for dindindindinnnnnerrrr?"

"What."

"PAAAASSGHETTIOSSS!"

"Congratulations."

She giggles the entire way downstairs and I carry her into the kitchen by her feet.

Sitting at the table, we are the picture of domesticity. White family with a father and three kids. Forget that there's no mother. They miss her and love her, but they continue to live their lives, loving each other and helping each other to cope.

Yeah fuckin' right.

I can't remember the last time I even spoke to my dad. I mean, it's not like we don't talk, we just don't . . . talk. He's not a brooding old man who never got over his wife's death, either. He's just . . . he's there.

"John."

"Dad."

"Hi."

"Hey."

"How was your day?"

Played some pool, got rejected for the first time in my life. . . . Great day, Dad. How about you?

I shrug. "Fine. Yours?"

"Fine. Kelly?"

She stares at no one and mumbles through her drink. "Fine."

Peggy hops up and down in her seat and no one needs more than that. She never runs out of energy, goddamn. We eat in silence, except for Peggy, who makes noise even when she fucking walks. She squeals and bounces and is forever asking questions.

And then she starts to fucking sing. Oh God, no, not the singing.

"Who lives in a pineapple under the sea?" she croons.

My beautiful, tiny, curly-haired, dear baby sister. Please. PLEASE. PLEEEEEASE STOP SINGING.

Kelly and I stare at each other from across the table with pained expressions while Dad forks broccoli quietly into his mouth.

"SPONGEBOB SQUAREPANTS!"

It becomes a race of who can get away from the table the fastest: who can shovel food the fastest, who can chug water the fastest, who can mumble "mayibeexcused" the fastest. Kelly and I are old competitors, since the days when food shoveling was a contest of pleasure, up until it became a mechanism for survival. I am on my last meatball when Kelly stands up triumphantly.

Not fair. She had a smaller serving than me.

"Sit down."

Dad's voice is firm.

I smirk at her.

"But I have —"

"*Sit.*"

"But Dad —"

He glares at her.

He's usually pretty passive, but he can be scary when he wants to be.

Kelly sits back down grumpily.

I say nothing.

"C'mon, someone must have *something* to say."

Fuck. I didn't think he was going to try the let's-be-a-family approach. It's worse than I thought. He must be feeling bad about something. Something must have happened.

"Dad, did you have to do layoffs today?"

"What?"

"Did you?"

"No, what the hell are you talking about, John?"

"Nothing."

"Have you been reading parenting books from the library?" Kelly asks.

Another glare.

It's not that we're dysfunctional. It's just that we don't really have much to say to each other.

"No one is moving until we talk about something."

"Sports?"

"Politics?"

"SpongeBob?"

We stare at each other.

"About *us*."

"What about us?"

"Exactly."

"Exactly *what*?"

"There's nothing to say about us."

"So?"

"That's a problem."

"Since when?"

"Since now."

"Dad . . ." Kelly says.

"Kelly, how is Anna?"

Her eyebrows tilt up questioningly. "Um, we're not friends anymore, Dad."

"What? Why? I thought she was your best friend."

"Yeah, last year. We don't talk anymore."

"Did you get in a fight?"

She shrugs.

"What about?"

"What difference does it make?"

Dad sighs. Poor guy.

"Boooyyyssss," Peggy squeals.

"Boys?" Dad repeats.

"Peggy!" Kelly says.

"Booooooooyyysssssss." Peggy laughs. "She's always talking about boys."

"Ugh!" Kelly shakes her head frustratedly. "Everyone in this house is crazy."

"What *about* boys?" Dad asks Kelly.

I chuckle.

"Dad!"

"What *about* boys?" Dad asks Peggy.

Sam's face flashes into my face and I stop mid-laughter.

Sam.

I'd hoped to have slept that off, but I guess that doesn't always work. There goes my coping mechanism for every situation I've ever been in.

Well, there's always Corona.

Dad gives up on Kelly and turns to me.

No, no, no, no, no, no, no, nooooo.

All the sleep and beer in the world couldn't save me now.

"John, say something."

"What?"

"Say something."

"About what?"

"I dunno, anything. You don't ever say anything. You dating anyone these days?"

Kelly snorts.

"No," I say truthfully.

"Really? You? Why not?"

"I just . . . y'know. I'm not. I'm . . . busy. And all that."

"Busy with schoolwork? Because that seems a little improbable."

"No . . ."

"Did you get a job?"

"No . . ."

"Then what are you busy with?"

I shrug. "Things."

"Things." He stares at me, half wanting to get angry and half wanting to give up on his verbally challenged family.

"What is wrong with us?" he asks nobody.

"Nothing," I answer.

"Everything," Kelly says.

"Can I have more pasghettios?"

By 8:00, the torture is over. I sit in my room staring at the TV, waiting for something to distract me from the events of the day.

My phone hasn't stopped ringing all afternoon since I left Jake's. Sam must have told somebody and that somebody probably has a big mouth. It's not like this recent news can be ignored.

Caesar? Rejected? *The* Caesar? Surely, you jest.

I flip through all the ESPN channels digital cable has to offer and fall against my pillows, tossing my phone and all its unanswered calls into a pile of dirty clothes on the floor. Sleep? No, that doesn't seem to really work these days. What else is there to do? Going to the gym could result in meeting Marsh or Jake or one of them. I sure as hell can't call up any of my friends; they all will have heard by now. How will the girls react? Will they consider me somehow less valuable than before? Dude, fuck that if it happens.

Ah, crap.

What else is there to do? I'm afraid to go out in public. I'm *really* afraid to go to school tomorrow. It's not so much that I'm embarrassed or any of that pussy shit, but I just don't want to have to fucking *deal* with this. I have to talk to people, face Jake and his questions, face the girls and their judgment, face Sam and her rejection.

Ouch.

I need to get out of here.

Gazebo time.

Again.

CHAPTER 9

When I get to the lake, it's dark out and still raining, harder now. I climb up into the gazebo and watch the lake being pummeled with sheets of rain, waves of drops never-ending. It's not gray and dreary but dark and frightening. Just enough light for me to see as far out to the lake and that's all. A few drops manage to spray me from under the rooftop and my hair starts to stick to my face sadly, almost depressingly.

But maybe it's me that's depressed.

I've never been depressed before. I've only been angry or annoyed or a combination of the two. What's happening to me? I do feel annoyed, but at the same time, I feel almost . . . dejected. Like I don't want to see anybody, like thinking about the incident makes me disgusted, like I never want to go home. If it wasn't so cold outside in the rain, I'd probably sleep here tonight. My thin undershirt flaps about in the wind, and I lean against the side and watch the night. I fold my arms against my chest and feel the rain pelt against my face and soak into my shirt.

The longer you stare at the dark, the more you see. The more the shadows become clear, the more the subtle light from an unknown source becomes obvious, the more the night reveals itself to you. I watch until everything is clear to me, until I see every leaf, every wave, every drop suspended in the air. Where does the rain go when it falls? It seeps into the ground and washes the dirt away.

The cold whips against me and the rain lashes my arms and face. I step down onto the grass and toward the dock. The waves call to me. The turbulence of the water, the feel of the wash over my face, they beckon. I want to peel off my shirt and jump right in, but the water is probably freezing. Which is actually a good incentive.

I walk back to the gazebo, toss my shirt and sandals inside, and get a running start toward the dock before I plunge feet-first into the lake of icy daggers, rain pelting and waves rolling. A rush runs quickly from my feet to my face, and I feel like I'm naked and drowning in snow. The chill runs through my body, and all at once I feel clean. I feel clean and cold and free and fresh and everything good and wonderful.

I surface, and the warm air and cold rain collide with my face from all sides. It's dark all around and I can hardly see in front of me. I feel so cold, so blind, so alone in this place. Yet free.

I lay out on my back and float in the darkness, staring up at the sky, completely clouded over. When you float on your back, the world becomes something serene and beautiful and effortless. You can't hear any of the world's troubles, can't feel anything but numb. Underwater, the world is slow and muffled and peaceful. There's no such thing as Eva or Sam or fathers or college or phone calls or world hunger. When you're floating in the water, there's nothing at all; there's just you and the cold and the rain and the night.

And that's enough.

The rain continues to hail war on my face, and I lay there, not moving, not listening, cold and alone. And then without warning, there is warmth. A warm hand on my shoulder sends me to my feet in a second. I whip quickly around and come face-to-face with none other than the ghost of a girl, Eva.

"Hi."

"Hi." I can't hide the surprise in my voice.

"Fancy meeting you here. Again."

"Wh . . . what are you doing here? Where did you come from?"

She points to the other side of the lake.

"I was swimming. I saw you, and . . . sorry, should I leave you alone?"

"No, that's fine. Stay. I'm just surprised to see you here. Again."

I kind of smile, but I have no idea what to say or do. Everything I've been feeling the past few weeks floods into me in one shot. All the things I imagined I'd say to her, all the rational thoughts I had about her . . . in a few seconds, everything is gone, and I have no idea what to do. Should I leave? Should I talk about what happened last time I met her here? Should I keep smiling? Should I try to kick her out? Something about this appeals to me, making her be the one to leave this time . . . but now that I see her, the last thing I want is for her to leave.

"Do you come here a lot?" she asks.

"Uh, yeah, actually." Why did I just tell her that? "Do you?" Stupid question. She just moved here. I'm an idiot.

"Since I found it a month ago or so, I've come pretty often. It's a really nice place. Even when it's pouring."

We stand crouched in the water, trying to keep warm, only our heads bobbing above the black water. She looks as if she's been here a while, swimming and floating, too, no doubt.

"What are you doing here so late?" she asks.

I shrug. "Swimming?"

"Right. Me, too." She laughs, both of us trying to swim around the awkwardness.

"We must be crazy," I say, to try and ease it.

"Yeah. Or maybe it's everyone else."

I smile, sure this time. Because I know it's true.

We tread in silence, both fully aware of the cold and the rain and the wind and all the other things that make us crazy. Both not caring.

"How long have you been here?" I ask.

"A while," she says. "Maybe like half an hour. I don't know what possessed me to fucking swim in this weather, but I thought it would feel good. I think you gave me the idea the last time I saw you here. The water's fucking nuts."

I nod. "I just got here. I'm freezing my balls off."

"Yeah, I saw you when you walked into the gazebo. I didn't want you to see me."

"Why?"

She doesn't answer but hugs her arms to her chest, and for the first time, I realize she must not be wearing very much to be able to swim around freely.

"When I saw you jump in, I changed my mind."

She looks around us into the darkness and above us into the sky and closes her eyes to all of it.

"It's amazing here," she says, eyes closed.

"I know." I practically have to shout over the din of the rain hitting the surface of the lake. A million drops and a million sounds make it hard for just one guy to say what he wants.

"Do other people ever come here? Your friends or anybody?"

"I don't usually see other people here. They don't really know about it. The gazebo is hidden from the other side of the lake, and the dock is old. Mostly people go to the picnic area on the other side so they can play with their fucking Frisbees."

"You have some kind of grudge against Frisbees?"

I laugh. "No, that's not what I meant. They just don't come here."

She nods. "I see. So you have this place all to yourself?"

"Yeah, I guess."

"Until now."

"Right.

"I'm sorry."

I shrug. "I don't care."

"Are you sure? If I had a spot like this all to myself, I wouldn't want anyone else coming here, either."

You're different, I want to say. Instead I shrug again.

"Doesn't matter to me. It's not like I own it."

"We can't keep coming here at the same time like this."

"Why not?" Shouldn't have said that.

"Well, I don't know about you, but I come here looking to be alone. Look how alone we are now."

It's not such a bad thing.

"Yeah," I say.

"It defeats the purpose of coming here at all."

"So find somewhere else to go." Shouldn't have said that.

"Well, that's what I was saying."

"Oh."

I had thought she offered to stop coming for my sake, because I wanted to be alone. But I guess she really just doesn't want to be here with me.

"But maybe . . ." she says, hesitating.

"Maybe what?"

"Maybe . . . we can share it," she says finally, shrugging.

"Okay."

We float around each other awkwardly. My gut says to stay, but the awkwardness is getting louder.

Before I make a decision, she turns away from me and stands up in the water. Her clothes cling to her body, letting me get to know her better than either of us probably intended. She pulls herself out of the water without so much as looking back at me. Soaking wet, she walks up onto the bank and lies down in the grass, eyes closed and face upturned to the rain. She spreads her arms out and then doesn't move.

She looks right out of a movie.

I am left messing around in the lake, standing awkward and alone. I want to follow her, but I don't know if I can allow myself to chase another girl after what happened with Sam. I turn away from the bank and face the rest of the water. Everything is dark, and the shadows spill from the trees and picnic tables, and the rain just keeps on falling, cleansing everything in Laurence. Finally I turn around and pull myself up onto the bank next to Eva.

Neither of us knows what to say; after all, we've barely ever spoken.

Still shirtless and completely soaked, I sit down a couple feet away from her and wrap my arms around my knees, watching the rain callously take over the world.

"If you don't mind me asking," she says suddenly. Her eyes are still closed and only her lips move. I prepare to defend myself against the worst. Her lids open. "Why are you here?"

"Huh?"

"You didn't deny that you're here to be alone. So what happened?"

I shrug. "Shit. Shit happened."

"Me, too." She nods. "It's worse when there's no way to describe it except that way. When you don't even know what it is, you just know it's shit."

"Yeah," I say, but it's a lie, because I do know what it is.

Her name is Sam Chansett.

A shiver runs up my bare spine and I suddenly long for the inside of my car with the heat turned up all the way. I step over Eva's still body and into the pass that leads up the hill to the gazebo. I pull my shirt on over my head and sit down inside. Eva follows, clutching her arms and holding a bundle of clothing, obviously freezing.

"This is what I get for following my impulses," she says with a laugh, still shivering. She sits across from me in the gazebo and wraps her legs in her arms, trying to keep warm.

"You don't have anything dry?" I ask.

She shakes her head and holds up the ball of clothing she carried.

"I left it out on the grass and it got soaked."

I laugh, not meaning to sound cruel. "I'm sorry," I say to suppress it. "Just seems like you'd have more sense than that."

She laughs, too. "Yeah, I normally would. I'm fucking

freezing. Can't believe I was that dumb. And my car is all the way around the other side. I walked here from the picnic area."

"So I guess we *are* crazy."

"Yeah, something like that."

We sit in silence, not uncomfortable, but not completely relaxed. We stare at the ceiling, out at the lake, at the floor, toward the trees, anywhere but at each other. I feel the wind in every bone of my body, and my shirt sticks soaked to my body. After a few minutes, I can't take it anymore and I stand up.

"Fuck it," I say. "I really, reeeaaallly didn't want to go to my car because the inside's leather, but I'm fucking freezing my ass off. Come on, it's parked right here."

I pull on my shoes and we hurry out of the gazebo and into the bushes, where my car has sunken into its usual spot in the dirt. I open the passenger door quickly, and then slide into the driver's side. We huddle in the car, our wet asses squeaking against the black leather seats. I turn up the hot air all the way and we cup our hands over the vents.

"I'm sorry about your seats," Eva says into the silence.

"Me, too. It's a very heavy loss. But my dick breaking off would be a far heavier loss."

"I agree. The female population of our school would be losing a valuable asset."

I laugh. That's totally something I would have thought of myself.

"What's *up* with that?"

"With what?"

"You and girls."

"What about us?"

"I dunno. I've heard some stuff since I moved here."

"Really? It's only been, like, three weeks."

"Yeah, well. I get around." After a moment, she adds, "Not like you, though, apparently."

I grin. "I'm one of a kind."

She snorts.

"What? I am."

"I've met a million guys like you."

"Like me? What's 'like me'?"

"Assholes."

I nod. "Mm, yes, you're right, that is my only quality worth mentioning," I say drily. "Some would say it's the only one I have."

"And are they right?"

"You tell me."

"I don't know you yet, John. But don't make the mistake of thinking that I'm willing to let that slide."

"That's a weird threat to make."

"You might change your mind after you know me better."

I laugh, though I am admittedly a little frightened. She intimidates me.

The car is warmer by now, though we are not much drier. Eva's hair is pulled back, but the water from my hair still drips down the sides of my face. I pull my shirt off and try to use it to towel off my hair and the rest of my body. Not very successful, seeing as the shirt is pretty wet itself. I hold it unfolded in front of the air vent, trying vainly to dry it. Eva looks over toward me, eyeing me quietly without my shirt on. (Or is that just my imagination?) We sit in silence, both trying to beat the quiet with useless tasks.

90

The awkwardness kills me. I want to kiss her or kick her out of my car or jump back in the lake or fucking tell a joke or *something*, anything to break this tension and make me feel like less of an idiot for letting a stranger ruin my leather.

"Thanks a lot," Eva finally says after an eternity of silence.

No, thank you for finally fucking saying something so I didn't have to kiss you. Or tell a joke. Or both.

"For what?"

"For letting me come in your car. It's fucking ridiculous out there."

"Yeah, well, if you're as crazy as me, you deserve a little hospitality."

She smiles, and before the silence comes back, I blurt something out.

"It's a good thing I came, then."

"Yeah, or I would have died from hypothermia."

"We both need to share this place."

She says nothing, so I go on, "Otherwise, what if I die or drown and no one realizes because no one knows where to find me?"

She laughs. "Yes, that's a great reason for me to keep coming back here. In case you die, someone needs to call the cops and alert them that the number one asshole in town is dead. Suddenly my life has meaning."

"Glad I could help."

"And what if I died?"

"I'd definitely save you."

"How could you save me? I'd be dead."

"It's the thought that counts."

"It's the thought that counts when I'm dead?"

"Well . . . I'd save your body."

91

"My corpse thanks you."

"You're welcome?"

"Anyway."

"Anyway."

Neither of us says anything and I feel the overwhelming urge to tell a joke again. God, please, please, please don't let me tell a joke.

"So a rabbi and a minister are sitting —" I start.

She turns her head to me, her eyes amused. ". . . Uh . . . how 'bout them Yankees?" I try again.

We stare at each other and chuckle nervously.

"I hate the Yankees," she says.

"Me, too."

Silence again but more smiling this time.

"Is your shirt remotely better?" she asks.

I stare at the crumpled mess of white fabric in my hand.

"No. Yours?"

"Nope."

"We're useless."

"Yep."

"What now?" she says.

I shrug. "You . . . wanna go somewhere?" I ask tentatively.

She looks at the dashboard. "Ah, no, actually I've got some stuff to do tonight. I shouldn't be out too late."

9:52. Her excuse is believable, but I can't help but wonder if this is my second rejection in one day.

Second rejection in one lifetime.

"Are you any warmer now?" I ask her.

"Yeah, I'm really good, actually. Thanks."

"No prob."

She opens the door and sticks her hand outside. "I think it's died down enough for me to walk back to my car."

"You want me to drive you to the picnic side?"

What? What? What? WHAT?

"That'd be awesome. Are you sure that's okay?"

No? No? No? No! Yes!

"Yeah, it's fine." My voice carries itself out of my mouth.

"Thanks so much, John. I really appreciate it. First you save me — and my body — from certain death, then you even ensure my safe return to my own leather-imitation vehicle. What a guy. What they say about you is wrong, dear Thousand Island."

"What can I say?" I say, shrugging.

No! No! No!

I pull out from behind the bushes and onto the main road, then turn into the actual entrance of the public lake property. At the parking lot, I pull up next to her blue sedan and she throws back another "thanks" as she gets out.

. . .

No! No! No!

As I look ahead of me to drive away, she opens the passenger door again and ducks her head into my car.

"Hey."

"Hey?"

"Thanks a lot."

"Uh, you're welcome?"

"I do hope I see you here again."

She slams the door shut and walks away toward her own car.

I pull out and find myself back on the road with the rain falling steadily against my windshield. I turn on my windshield wipers and follow the pavement back home.

Thump.
Slide.
Scrape.
Thump.
Slide.
Scrape.
Thump.

CHAPTER 10

The next morning the rain has not let up. In my half-conscious state, I hear the sounds of a gray world crying and it makes me want to never leave my bed. But I know Kelly has other plans. She'll be in here any minute now, throwing herself onto my unmoving body and trying to shake me into existence.

Until that moment, I concentrate all my energy on lying as still as possible, on being at peace with myself, and at completely ignoring the upcoming events of the day as well as I can.

Sometimes when I lie in bed, I play this game with myself and I imagine what everyone would say if I died that very moment. It sounds morbid, but it's really not. My friends always say something different, depending on whatever happened that day or the day before. Jake says, "But we were just at the gym together. . . . Now he's gone." I never really get past my family and two or three of my friends before I either run out of answers or fall asleep. It's not a very fun game; it's just a habit I have. Today Jake says, "I can't believe he got rejected for the first time in his life just before he died. . . . Now he's gone."

95

Uggggh. So much for inner peace.

My alarm clock buzzes to life, sounding its sleep-shattering calls. Loud and unrelenting, it whines in a steady rhythm. I wait to hear Kelly thump out of bed and appear in my doorway. The alarm wails with familiarity and habit, *GET UP! GET UP! GET UP! GET UP!* And my head answers, "SHUUUT UP! SHUUUT UP! SHUUUT UP! SHUUUT UP!" I extend my arm to shut it off, my face buried in my pillow and my eyes not ready to come out into the world. I drag back into darkness again, the steady sound of rain against pane singing me to sleep.

When I loll back into consciousness, my alarm clock reads 8:42. It's been an hour since it went off, and I am still lying facedown in my bed, barely awake.

It's 8:42. It's 8:42. It's 8:42. It's 8:42. My mind gropes to understand what my eyes see, to urge my body out of its comfortable recession and into my fucking car.

It's 8:42. It's 8:42. It's —

SHIT!

I leap from my bed and into the shower in less than fifteen seconds. The water has no time to heat up and I have no time to wait. Cold, cold, cold, FREEZING, no time, no time, no time. I grab blindly at the closest shampoo and claw at my hair, sickeningly sweet scents of flowers and foliage trickling down my forehead in trails. *Fuck, fuck, fuck, late, late, late, cooooooooooold.*

In record time, I leap out of the shower, push my hair back, and jump into the nearest clean clothes from my closet. It isn't until I race out of my driveway and skid away from my house that it dawns on me the reason I am running an hour late: Where the FUCK was Kelly? She always wakes me up; it's practically a guarantee that I'll never be late. The only upside to the situation is that I won't see Jake until third period and I won't see Sam all day.

I speed to school as fast as humanly and legally possible, but I still end up five minutes late to homeroom.

"Miller. You're late."

"I'm here."

"You're late."

"Okay."

She marks me late, and before I can even sit down, the bell rings for first period. I notice Marsh motion to me from the other side of the room as people pile into the hallway, but I pretend not to see him and let myself get shoved out of the classroom. I avoid usual routes and usual people and take the long way to my locker. I dump my books inside and reach for my bio book when I feel someone come up behind me.

Fuck.

Expecting Jake, I slam my locker shut and turn around, only to come face-to-face with Sam.

Double fuck.

"Hey," she says, sounding resigned.

"Hi." I can't help sounding surprised.

"Sorry I didn't call you last night."

"Umm . . . it's okay."

"I kept wanting to, kept wondering if I should stop by, but . . . I dunno."

We stand facing each other in the crowded hallway, tension in our body language.

"I didn't mean to hurt you," she says.

I snort instinctively.

"You didn't hurt me."

"I didn't mean to be mean about it, either."

"It's fine. I've already forgotten about it."

Bold-faced lie.

"Can I explain?" she asks.

"No, I gotta go to bio."

She sighs. "That's part of it, you know."

"What's part of what?"

"The fact that you are never willing to give any of your time to anyone else. The fact that you make people feel like they don't matter. That's part of why I said no."

"I gotta go."

It doesn't sink in that Sam has just tried to explain herself. I shut her words out, close my eyes to her face, and walk on to bio. I don't want to hear what she has to say; I don't want to deal with her at all. I just want to make it through the day without emotional scarring or another fistfight. It doesn't matter to me why Sam seemingly rejected me, only that she did. And now I have to deal with it.

And that's really all that registers as I walk through the rest of my Monday at school.

During electronics and lunch, Jake tries to talk to me about it, knowing full well there's nothing he could say or do to change things. I ignore him and tell him I don't really care, which is only half a lie. I know I shouldn't care, which isn't really the same as not actually caring . . . but it's close.

I leave my last class early so as to avoid any other unwanted confrontations. I grab my things from my locker and head down to the gym while the halls are still empty. I hide out in the locker room until the last bell rings, and then I head out into the gym. Practice lets me forget things for a moment, lets me drown in another kind of world, where all the other faces are a blur and I am the only person on the court. That is, until Marsh comes up to me in the locker room.

"Hey," he says casually.

"Yo."

"What up?"

"Nothing."

I grab a towel from the bench and turn toward the showers.

"Wait," Marsh says.

"What?" I say, turning.

He lowers his voice. "What happened with you and . . . ?"

I shrug. "Nothing."

"What's everybody been talking about?"

"I don't know what the fuck people talk about. People need to mind their own fucking business."

He shrugs. "Okay. Whatever. Don't tell me if you don't want to."

"There's nothing to tell."

"Fine."

"Fine."

I walk to the showers.

I think I handled that well.

At home, Kelly sits in the family room watching TV.

"What the hell?" I say as soon as I see her.

"What?"

"Why didn't you wake me up this morning?"

"I didn't hear your alarm clock," she says.

"How could you not hear it? You're such a light sleeper."

"How could *you* not hear it? You sleep right next to it!"

"Yeah, but I thought you were gonna wake me up so I didn't bother to get up."

"Great logic."

"Why didn't you hear it?"

"How the hell should I know? I must have slept through it."

"You never sleep through anything."

"Well, I was tired."

"Why?"

"What do you mean, why?"

"I mean why? Were you up late last night?"

"I don't know."

"What do you mean, you don't know?"

"Look, it's not my fault you were late! Why are you being so immature? It's not my responsibility to take care of you!"

"Why didn't you wake me up when you woke up?"

She starts to raise her voice. "Doesn't it seem a little screwed up that I have to wake you up every morning? Since I'm thirteen and you're almost eighteen and you're going to have to take care of yourself soon?"

"Well, could you have let me in on this revelation *before* you decided to let me take care of myself?"

"Yes, next time I'm ready to let you act your age, I'll be sure to let you know!"

"What's your problem?"

"Nothing, okay? Will you fucking leave me alone?"

"Fine. Jesus."

The girl has become impossible. She shuts herself in her room and talks for hours on the phone and her attitude problem has gotten worse. She's so fucking moody and gets upset so easily. Sometimes she has outbursts at me and my father that can't be explained at all.

It's not healthy.

In my room, SportsCenter helps me pass time and ignore phone calls. I get the feeling Jake has called at least two or three times inviting me out somewhere, but I haven't had the energy to get up. I know that not answering my phone is obvious and shitty, but answering and actually having to talk to one of those morons is potentially a lot worse. I watch TV until well after it gets dark and try to ignore all outside factors (time, homework, phone calls) until finally I submit to hunger. Downstairs, I rummage around in the fridge and pantry, but there is nothing except our ridiculously large supply of Lay's potato chips, a couple protein bars, and some yogurt. Bah.

I consider asking Kelly if she wants anything, but she's being a whiny brat and doesn't deserve that kind of attention. She can find her own dinner.

I drive to the Papa John's five minutes from our house and give into my conscience while I'm there, ordering a large cheese pizza for me and Kelly. I sit down to wait for the pizza, and Eva walks through the door holding a stack of pizza boxes. As she walks past, she smiles casually at me and I find myself smiling and nodding back.

She's fucking everywhere, haunting my every step. I wouldn't be surprised if she started babysitting Peggy or teaching Kelly's dance class. Ten minutes later, as I am getting into my car with the pizza, Eva walks out and opens the door to the car next to mine and puts a stack of five pizzas in the passenger seat.

"Hey, Eva," I say over the roof of her car.

"Hey. What's up?"

"I didn't know you work here."

"Yeah, I deliver."

"How does it pay?"

"Pretty damn well, actually."

"Really?"

"Yeah, and I don't have to sit around in the actual restaurant all day; I just drive around in my car."

"Nice."

"Where do you work?"

"Uh, I don't actually," I say. "Although maybe I should. Prom and all that is gonna be really expensive."

"They're looking for some people here to deliver. I could talk to someone for you, if you're interested."

"Yeah, that'd be cool, thanks."

"I gotta go," she says. "I gotta get all these done in, like, twenty minutes."

"Later," I say, getting back in my car.

I pick Peggy up from her babysitter's and head home, where an all-too-familiar blue sedan is parked in the driveway, blocking my way to the garage.

What the fuck?

I park in the street and help Peggy out of the backseat, then realize Eva is waiting on our front doorstep holding a pizza. The front door swings open to reveal Kelly holding a wad of cash.

"John," she says with surprise, seeing me come up the front lawn.

Eva turns around. "John," she says with even more surprise.

"Kelly. Eva."

"I thought you were going to get Peggy," Kelly says.

"He did!" Peggy says.

"No, like, I didn't know he was getting food, too."

"Hi, Eva."

"Hey, you live here?"

"Sadly, yes."

"Your house is huge."

"Mm. Yeah. How much do I owe you?"

"Wait, we don't need the extra pizza now," Kelly says.

"We can't give it back."

"Yeah, we can. There's a policy that if you don't want it, you don't have to take it once it gets there."

"She already lost time delivering it," I say.

"But we're not going to eat both," Kelly says.

"It's fine, John," Eva says.

Kelly raises an eyebrow. *John*.

"It happens all the time," she adds.

"Yeah, but those customers are obnoxious. Forget it, it's fine. Leave it. I'll pay for it. Take this," I say, handing her the money, "and go before you're late for your next delivery."

Kelly looks taken aback.

Eva smiles. "I'm definitely talking to the manager about you."

I laugh. "Thanks. Go."

"We're not going to finish this," Kelly says as Eva's car pulls away and we walk into the kitchen.

"Yeah, we will."

"No, we won't," she says. And then, "Did you fuck her?"

"What! Do you mind?" I say quietly, gesturing to Peggy in the family room.

"Did you?"

"No. Jesus. Why do you think that?"

"Because you were really nice to her."

"So?" Being nice to a girl is definitely not a sign that I fucked her.

"So, seems natural you'd be nice to someone you screwed."

"Who told you *that*?"

She shrugs. "Seems that way to me."

"Well, anyway, no. She and I are not sexually involved."

"Okay." And then, "Why not?"

"None of your business." I grab the smaller pie and retreat upstairs, calling back, "Get some for Peggy, okay?"

When I get to my room, I realize I have forgotten the most important element of all to a domestic hideout: Corona. I get back downstairs again and open the fridge to find the box of Coronas empty.

What the fuck?

Last time I had checked, there had been two left. Dad probably had one of them when he got home from work last night, but he wouldn't have drunk both of them. I walk into the family room and find Kelly and Peggy sitting together on the couch watching *South Park*. In Kelly's hand, the last Corona.

I stand in front of the TV.

"Hey!" Peggy exclaims.

"Kelly."

"What?" she says, craning her neck to see around me.

"What do you think you're doing?"

"Trying to watch TV. What are *you* doing?"

"Give me that."

I step toward her and reach for the bottle.

"Hey!"

"What are you doing drinking my beer?" She doesn't answer right away, and I add, "What are you doing *drinking*?"

"What? So?"

"You're not allowed to be drinking."

"Says who?"

"Says me. Now give it to me."

"You just want it because it's the last one."

"Even if it was the first one out of the box, I still wouldn't let you drink any."

"'Let' me? I don't need your permission." She tips her head back and downs half the bottle.

"Joo-oooohn!" Peggy wails, still trying to watch TV.

"Kelly! Give me the goddamn bottle!"

"Do you mind?" Kelly mimics me from before, gesturing to Peggy.

"Give it to me!" I roar.

Peggy goes silent but Kelly is undeterred. I lunge at her and she leaps off the couch and into the living room.

I follow her, wanting to grab her, but knowing I can't.

"Why the hell are you drinking? You think that makes you cool? Who the hell do you think you are?"

"Who the hell do you think *you* are? *Caesar*? Wow, you're so fucking cool! Everybody wants to be just like you! All the girls want you! My big brother is the coolest guy in high school! He drinks all the time and sleeps around; I want to grow up to

105

be just like him! God," she spits, guzzling the rest of the bottle, "you're so pathetic."

I narrow my eyes and grab the bottle from her and seize her by the arm.

She laughs crookedly. "You're abusive, too? What a guy." She starts to laugh uncontrollably.

Apparently my sister has not been drinking long enough to have a very high tolerance for it.

"Kelly, what the hell is wrong with you? Get it together! You're freaking thirteen. You should be freaking playing spin the bottle at parties, not drinking."

"Yeah, sorry we can't all be as cool as you, *Caesar*."

"Peggy, go upstairs."

Frightened, Peggy climbs down from the couch and scampers upstairs.

"You only had this one, right," I say, sniffing her breath.

"Yeah." Kelly giggles.

"You're not cool, Kelly. It took one fucking beer to get you like this," I say darkly.

"If only I could be like you, big bro."

"Go upstairs. Don't tell Peggy what happened."

She starts to laugh, but I seize her by the arm, more roughly this time.

"Go," I bark.

"Ow," she complains, but starts walking toward the stairs.

As I walk into the family room to turn off the TV and clean up the mess of pizza on the coffee table, I hear her small voice from the staircase.

"John? You're not going to tell Dad, are you?"

Her voice is slightly subdued, almost frightened. Guess she

didn't have that much after all, if she still has the sense to be afraid of Dad.

I don't answer.

"John?" her feeble voice floats down through the house.

I walk outside and onto the deck at the back of the house. I stare at the bottle in my hand and hear Kelly's suddenly scared voice from the top of the stairs and throw the bottle as far as it will go — down, down, down into the darkness of the woods behind our house.

CHAPTER 11

She doesn't wake me up on Tuesday, either, though I don't really expect her to. I drag myself out of bed, then drag myself into the shower and later drag myself to school.

School itself drags on, classes seemingly less and less important. I mostly do nothing, only maintain the minimum GPA requirements for staying on the team. College seems so far away, though everyone has tried to convince me otherwise. My guidance counselor has been all up in my ass for the past couple weeks, and we've had enough assemblies about "the future" to last us until well after our futures have arrived.

Classes pass. Lunch passes. Practice passes. Faces, voices, the sounds of high school . . . they all pass. I pass school. Pass life.

Days pass, and it's Friday. Several more attempts have been made on the part of Jake and Sam to resolve recent issues, but I tell them it's fine and I don't care. And now it's true. After practice, Jake calls me to find out what we're doing.

"I'm still at school," I say.

"Pick me up. Let's go driving."

"Okay," I answer, but I can't figure out why. I don't want to be around Jake and I don't want to go driving.

"A'ight, 'bye."

"No. Wait."

"What?"

"I don't want to go driving."

"What do you want to do then?"

"I dunno."

"Just come pick me up."

"Fine."

I slow down in front of the entrance to the lobby and she walks out, looking into her bag for something. Eva looks up and sees me in my car and stops.

I roll down the window.

"Hey."

"Hey."

"Goin' home?"

"Yeah."

I nod, and don't know what else to say. Small talk is useless, but for some reason, I just want to sit here and small talk with her for the rest of the day.

"What're you after school for?"

"Tutoring."

"What're you getting tutored in?"

"No, I'm tutoring other kids."

"Oh."

"You?"

"Basketball."

And that's the difference between us. We feel it hanging in

the air, what makes us know we're not the same, don't belong talking. It makes us want to belong.

I can't pull myself to drive away from the curb. I want to put my pedal on the gas and squeal away, maybe even leave her in the dust, but my foot does not budge.

The small talk continues.

"How's the pizza shit going?"

"It's going okay. I talked to Dave for you."

"That your manager?"

"Yeah. I talked to him, but I didn't see you during the week so I couldn't tell you."

"Thanks. You didn't have to."

"I said I would."

"What did he say?"

"That if you're pretty comfortable with driving around and know most of the main roads, that he'd be glad to have you."

"Awesome. Wait, how did you get the job? You just moved here. How do you know the roads?"

"Uh, yeah, I don't." She laughs. "I kind of just make it up as I go along."

"I have a lot of faith in Papa John's now. When should I come by?"

"Whenever's good for you."

"Cool. Thanks."

"No prob. See ya later."

"'Bye."

Finally I am able to put my foot down (literally) and pull away from school and to Jake's.

Halfway there, Jake calls me.

"Yo, are you near my house?"

"I'm on Thirty-eight. Why?"

"Just go to Dan's then. He's gonna drive us all to Jack's."

"Jackson's party is tonight? Okay, I'll be there in, like, five."
Moments later I park my car at Dan's and slip into the backseat
of his car.

"Hey," Ashley says from the front seat. "Welcome to the
party."

"Hey."

"This shit is supposed to be sick," Ashley says as Dan pulls
away from the house.

"Jackson's parties are always sick."

"He got strippers."

Dan and Jake look at each other.

"Siiiiiiiiiiiiiiiick."

We pull up at Jackson's house to find Sophie dancing drunk-
enly alone among the cars parked in Jackson's driveway. She
rubs up against the cars and eyes them as if their leather interior
and dual side airbags will satisfy her sexual hunger.

The four of us get out of the car and Sophie greets us
gigglingly.

"It's barely even dark out and look at her," Jake mutters.

Sophie leans against Dan and he ushers her up the driveway, with Jake, Ashley, and me in tow. Flashbacks from my last
visit to Greg Jackson's aptly nicknamed "House of Fun" return.
Visions of mud wrestling (better experienced as a spectator than
a participant), drag racing (ditto), and rounds of more than thirty
shots (definitely better as a participant) find their way fondly
back in my head.

We enter Jackson's enormous foyer, where probably a quar-
ter of the male population of the senior class (and a good

111

number of the female population) is packed, enjoying several eye-opening shows at once, put on by the fine working-class ladies of Club La-La in Kingsdale, two towns over. Before I even get past the foyer, Angel Emery comes from behind me and snakes her arms around my waist.

"Trying to get me naked before I've even had a drink?" I say.

I turn to her and she sends me a devilish grin. She's the kind of girl I'd be willing to hook up with at a party, but she's irritatingly aggressive. She grabs my ass and tries to force herself onto me and I slide my hand up the back of her shirt and shove my tongue down her throat so she can't talk. She starts to grind against me, and with my thumb and middle finger, I snap open her bra. Then before two seconds pass, I pull my hand, tongue, and body roughly away, disappearing into the crowd and leaving her confused, wet, and exposed.

I realize I have lost Dan, Sophie, Ashley, and Jake somewhere along the way, but I know it's only a matter of time before one of them turns up again. I see Jackson standing next to the bar from across the living room and he gestures a hello. He looks around and grabs the nearest Corona and a slice of lime from the bar, then makes his way over to me.

"Good memory," I say, taking the bottle from him.

"What's up?" he shouts over the music.

"Not too much. Except, y'know. Your party and all that."

"Right." He laughs heartily, the drink in his hand clearly not his first.

"How did you get La-Las to cover you for the girls?"

"Oh, I called in a favor with the manager. He and Dad go way back."

I nod, only half listening.

"You know, some of those girls are pretty friendly. If you want, I can arrange . . ."

"I can help myself, thanks."

He claps me on the back. "Of course you can." As he turns to walk away, he adds, "Rooms upstairs empty."

I nod and tip more life into my mouth. As I wander around the house, beer in hand, looking for something or someone to do, I am approached several more times by unsatisfactory proposals that I am forced to once again "talk" my way out of. After about fifteen minutes, someone interesting finally finds me.

Stacy Kinder.

"Hey." She sidles up to me and I kiss her on the cheek.

"You're not supposed to be here," I say, playing with her. "Where's Mike?"

She shrugs. "These days, I care less and less." She locks her mouth hard on mine and lets me taste the tequila deep in her.

"And less."

Nothing exciting seems to be happening here tonight, so I suppose Stacy leading me upstairs seems like the best thing to do at the moment. Which is why I don't resist. But only physically. Mentally, I am reluctant to being pulled any-where. Stacy stops in front of one of the doors at the end of the hallway and I slide my arm around her waist as she grabs my face. I feel her and my hands start to roam automatically, and she can only stop for one second to knock loudly on the door. A thump, a loud "ow," and a giggle later, Brad Alarsky opens the door shirtless, while some chick in the bed pulls on her own top.

"Caesar." Brad slaps my hand. "What's goin' on?"

"Seriously, Brad." Stacy rolls her eyes. "What do you think? Are you two done in here?"

"What, me and E? Yeah, uhh, what do you say, babe?" he calls to the girl.

She trips out of bed, flushed, tugging on clothing, and winks at Brad as she slaps him from behind and walks out the door without a word.

Brad laughs and grabs a half-filled cup on the floor before chasing after her.

"Eva, hold up!"

I stand numb in the doorway of the room. Stacy tugs my arm and starts biting my neck, but my hands don't make it any farther north or south from her waist before the idea of having sex with Stacy Kinder starts to repulse me. I fight the urge to follow Brad and Eva, and I allow Stacy to lead me into the room. It doesn't get any further than hot breath, roaming hands, and shed clothing, because at the first interruption that we encounter, I grab my shirt and ditch, making sure that Stacy can't follow me.

I'm not in the mood for another beer, so it seems not much can distract me from the distraction I have already set my sights on. The party in the foyer seems to have more or less broken up, so now a lot of the people have turned to each other for entertainment. Dancing wannabes give their own shows, and Jake somehow ends up in the middle of it all.

"Hey," he calls as I walk past. He grins at the girl he is dancing with and she whispers something in his ear. He looks back at me and mouths, "Thank you, God."

I find my way outside and scan the mass of milling bodies for someone — anyone — interesting. It isn't until my eyes pass over several of my highest prospects and closest friends that I realize I am not looking for just anyone, I'm looking for her. The only person I really want to see or talk to at the moment is Eva. When she winked at Brad and walked past me in the bedroom upstairs, a million thoughts ran through my head, but now they're jumbled into a mass of incoherent thoughts that really only formulate one clear idea: that she's here. And now, whatever it is I'm thinking about Eva, it doesn't matter. Because I can't stop. I can't stop thinking about her. And that's the one thought that resounds strongest in my mind:

I can't get this girl out of my head.

Even if I tried to shake her face from my thoughts, and even if I did find someone worth dispensing energy on, I still don't think I'd be properly focused. Maybe it's time to go home. I check my phone. It's only midnight. Dan won't be ready to leave yet. He doesn't go to these parties to fuck, but he hides himself with people in dark corners and closets and blazes into the wee hours of the morning. I shoulda known better than to come with Dan.

I walk back through the house and into the foyer to get Jake, but he is nowhere to be found. Guess he got with the aspiring La-La girl. Props. But now I have no ride.

I walk out the front door and wade out into the ocean of cars flooding the driveway and street around the Jackson property. I doubt Sophie is sober enough to drive home at this point, and she's probably having too good a time to leave the bar for two seconds. Who else will drive me home? I walk slowly down the long driveway and into the street, the cool autumn night biting my shirt where it's wet. I peer into the dark windows of the one or two cars that start up, but I don't recognize the drivers, and I walk past their cars nonchalantly, as if I had been looking behind them at someone else.

The night looks empty and I try hard to imitate it. Thoughts and images of Kelly, Sam, and Eva float through my mind, whispers of unwanted worry and distress. I'd give anything to get smashed and laid and pass out and forget about it all.

But I just can't.

I want to go home.

CHAPTER 12

I sit down on the curb and contemplate whether I should drink the beer sitting there in a cup to distract myself. It could be drugged. Or even worse, not a Corona. I consider this and decide against it, because it seems like I might be here all night, so I might as well just go back inside and get myself a good drink. I stand up and walk back into the driveway just as a dark car is pulling out. I just miss getting hit by the very familiar dark blue sedan. The driver slams on the brakes and I almost laugh out loud. Irony will kill us all. I walk to the left side of the car and Eva rolls down her window. Brad Alarsky is sitting in the passenger seat, leaning over to see who Eva has just narrowly avoided turning into road kill . . . again.

"'Ey, Caesar, keep runnin' inta ya."

I'm on fairly good terms with Alarsky, so I can't exactly be rude. "What up, Brad."

"You need a ride?" Eva asks.

If there really is a supreme being, He or She or It has a really fucked-up sense of humor.

"Be warned," Brad says. "She's a fuckin' horrible driver."

"That I've learned firsthand."

"You need a ride?" she repeats.

"Ah, no, it's all right. It's too much trouble to drive me and Brad —"

"It's not too much trouble. I'm not driving Brad home."

I raise my eyebrows. Goddamn, that kid works faster than his looks give him credit for. Ditto for her.

Eva laughs. "Get in."

I want to shake my head and back away from the car. But instead I say thanks and crawl into the back.

"Sorry if, uh, y'know, you guys were planning to get home right away . . ." I say uncomfortably.

Eva laughs again, a short *heh*. "I'm pretty sure Miyazaki can wait."

"Miyazaki? Alarsky, what kind of kinky girl did you pick up here?" I joke.

Brad lets out his own *heh*. "Eva? Kinky? Well . . ."

They turn to each other and snicker.

"Yeah, maybe," Brad continues. "But Hayao's got nothin' to do with it. We're going back to her place to watch some movies."

"Guess you're not into anime," Eva says to me as she pulls out into the street.

"What, like Pokemon porn and shit?"

Brad and Eva cringe visibly.

"That dragonmoonx website is really giving anime a bad name," Brad says.

"*Spirited Away, Evangelion, Akira?*" Eva asks.

I shrug.

"My little sister watches *Sailor Moon*," I offer.

Eva laughs. "That's where I got my start, way back when."

"Isn't your sister, like, a freshman?" Brad asks. "Isn't she a little too old to be watching *Sailor Moon*?"

"Nah, not Kelly. My other sister Peggy's only five. She watches fuckin' *Barney*."

Eva gets a kick out of this. "Aww, that's so cute — a little Caesar. With a little diaper, dancing around to *Barney*!"

"Shut up."

Eva won't stop. "That means it's true. Is she like you?"

"Peggy? Mmm . . . I dunno. Never really thought about it. I guess. I dunno. She's a five-year-old girl and I'm a seventeen-year-old guy. I can't tell if she looks like me or not."

"Yeah, but is she *like* you?"

"Dunno. Like how?"

Eva shrugs. "I dunno, either. Most people see the physical resemblance between me and my brother right away, but I don't think we're alike at all."

"Why, is he a slacker?" Brad asks.

"Hey, I can be a slacker," she protests.

"Yeah right," Brad snorts.

"Oh shit," Eva says suddenly. She swerves quickly to the right and swings us 180 into the left lane, sending the car reeling in the opposite direction of my house.

"What the fuck!" Brad exclaims.

Eva smiles with ease. "I forgot we gotta stop at Blockbuster first."

"We coulda gone on the way back! You didn't have to try and kill us first."

"Aw, but that's no fun." Eva grins.

I catch myself smiling as Brad says, "My God, girl, what are you on?"

Eva shoots him a look and lets go of the steering wheel.

"Goddammit, Eva," Brad says, trying to take hold of the wheel. "What's gotten into you?"

"PMS?" she jokes, taking the wheel again.

"Caesar, I told you she was horrible. Feel free to get out at any time. I'd rather walk an hour home than risk my life with this fucker behind the wheel."

"Is that so?" she says, unlocking the doors and slowing down into the shoulder. "You're welcome to get out here then, my love."

"Ah, no, see I'd rather walk home if Miyazaki was not awaiting to comfort me after the treacherous car ride. You mistook me."

She pulls back onto the road.

"Fucker," Brad murmurs under his breath.

Eva slams on the brakes. "I heard that."

In the backseat, I lurch forward again.

They sit in silence staring at each other for what seems like two solid minutes, each daring the other to move or speak or blink or breathe. "I Touch Myself" comes on over the radio and they can hardly suppress their laughter. Laughter shared but words not spoken, Eva pulls back onto the road again and we head toward the Blockbuster at the Ten Plaza.

The affection between Eva and Brad is clear. But it's not the same as that between Jenna and me or Sam and me or even between them and Jake or Dan or Marsh. Do Jenna and Jake act like Eva and Brad? I've never noticed before. I sit quietly enjoying my pocket of silence in the back of the car, not part of the comfortable atmosphere but not alienated, either.

When we park at Blockbuster, I don't move to get out of the car. Eva opens my door and pokes her head in.

"Coming?"

"Uhhh . . ."

Alarsky opens the other side.

"Coming."

We walk into Blockbuster and come out five minutes later empty-handed.

"Fuckin' fuck. Goddamn the Man and his stupid obsession with conformity to the mass white market!!"

To my understanding, of the limited selection of anime movies in Blockbuster, they are all edited and dubbed for the American market. Or so Eva says in her own Eva way.

"Eva, calm down," Brad says.

"Now we have to drive a fucking half hour out of our way."

"To where?" I ask.

"This anime video rental store in Tarrenboro," Brad answers. "We should probably drive Caesar home."

"That's another fucking twenty minutes in the other direction."

"Fuck," I say.

"Fuck," Brad confirms.

"You're coming with us, John Miller."

Eva and Brad get back in the car and I stand in front of the door, wondering if I should join them.

"Fuck it. I'll stay." I open the door and slide in.

"Did you call him John?" Brad is amused. "I've never heard anyone call you John before in my life."

"Well, it's his name, isn't it?"

"Well, yeah, but . . ."

I stare out the window at the black trees outside the parked car.

"Don't you think it's annoying when people call you Caesar?"

"If he did, don't you think he'd say something?"

"He's not saying anything now."

"Caesar?"

"John?"

"Huh?"

"Did you hear what I said?"

"What?"

Brad and Eva laugh.

Are they laughing at me? I'm not annoyed. I'm not angry.

"So are we going or what?" I say.

"Going," Eva says, and speeds away into the night.

We drive in silence for a bit, and even the music seems to drift into a comfortable lull without getting louder or softer or faster or slower, just coasting along at the same pace. I feel compelled to say something, anything, to break the comfort that has developed. I don't know how I feel about being comfortable with these people. Alarsky and I have never been too close, just friendly because he's on the team. And Eva, well . . . Eva. What is there to say about her? I could say so much about her and that's what irks me most about it all. Why her? Why this girl?

"So, uh, Eva, where did you move from?" I ask.

"New York," she says.

"Cool." That is the extent of my conversational skills.

"That's where I know Brad from."

"Really?"

"Yeah," Brad says. "I moved to Laurence from New York in the middle of last year. Me and Eva go way back."

"We used to live in the same building," Eva tells me, then turns to Brad. "I was so pissed when you left. I thought you were leaving me behind for something better."

He laughs. "Then you came here and realized that nothing here is fucking better than there."

"This is true."

"And especially now that we're together, it doesn't really matter, does it?"

They share a meaningful silence. I guess they must have been close. Really close. Sounds like some heavy, deep-rooted, unbelievably complicated relationship I would never (want to) understand.

My cell phone reads 12:44. I've been with these people for only half an hour and it's different than with any of my friends. I feel like I might like it, but is that okay? I say nothing.

Eva tones down the reckless driving and continues down the dark road in silence. Brad stares out the window, and nobody speaks for a long while. Black road, black trees, black night. Clouds cover the sky in a way that makes it look clear. But if you look, you can't actually see any stars.

We reach Tarrenboro, a slow suburban town, much like Laurence, except without the lake.

"They better fucking have what we want," Eva says, slamming the car door shut. I reluctantly follow the two of them into OSSAN: The One Stop Source for Anime Needs. Inside it's a lot like a comic book store, with posters and action figures and boxes of back issues piled high and disorganized in the aisles. When Eva finds what she wants, she kisses Alarsky in excitement and runs to the cashier. Still standing with me, Brad shrugs at me and shakes his head.

"She's crazy."

"Yeah. Are you guys . . . ?"

"Me and E? Uhh . . . it's complicated."

"Ah." I nod as if I know, as if I understand, but we both know I don't. What could I possibly understand about relationships?

It's past 1:30 by the time we reach Laurence again. Jake hasn't texted me back, so I figure he's still at Jackson's.

"You kids hungry?" Eva asks.

"Starving," Brad says.

"John?"

"Um, I'm all right. I guess I could go for food."

"What's open?"

"Diner," Brad and I say at the same time.

"That's the only thing to do at night in the suburbs," Brad tells her. "Diner's always open."

"Fuckin' hell," she mutters. "All right, where is it?"

Brad gives her directions as we go along and I realize I am still sitting in the car with these people an hour later than I'd planned. And now I have agreed to spend potentially another hour eating with them. Which involves conversing and, in the worst-case scenario, *bonding*. I open my mouth to say something, but still nothing comes out.

We get out of the car at the diner and I see that Eva has taken up two parking spaces. Not because her car is ridiculously large and can't *fit* in one space, but because she is the worst driver in the world and apparently just as bad at parking. We walk into the diner and find that there's a good number of kids in there already. Guess they had nothing to do tonight, either.

Brad and Eva choose a booth and I slide right in.

Almost immediately, I hear it.

"You."

I look up quickly, right into the eyes of a certain dark-haired, full-lipped waitress.

FUCK.

What is your name? What is your name? What is your name?

Shit. Shit. Shit. Shit.

" 'Caesar,' is it?"

She glares at me like the worst scum on earth wouldn't spit on my shoes.

What is your name. What is your name. What . . .

I crane my neck to try and catch a look at her left breast, but at that moment she tosses her hair onto her left shoulder and covers up the name tag.

Shit.

"Thanks for dicking me into giving you *my number*. And thanks for dicking me into *sleeping with you*. And thanks for dicking me into thinking, gee, maybe you'd CALL ME. And thanks for dicking me and NOT CALLING ME! You fucking *dick*!"

No problem, Mo . . . Po . . . Tra . . .

Arms folded and foot tapping expectantly, she flips her hair behind her shoulders, and for a second I catch a glimpse of the tag pinned on her left breast. Before I can squint enough to read it, she catches on to what I'm doing and snatches it off her shirt.

"ARE YOU FUCKING SERIOUS?" she shouts in my face.

Eva and Brad try to busy themselves with their menus and utensils and whatever else they can get their hands on. The people at the surrounding tables are not as subtle; they all stop what they're doing and try to look my way without looking my way.

The waitress gives me a cold stare and raises her eyebrows in a way that lets you know she's being sarcastic.

"Go ahead, you can apologize now. 'I'm sorry . . . damn, what was her name again?'"

Shit. Shit.

"What's my name?"

So far I haven't said a word. Admittedly, I would normally do something really dickish, like brush her off and then order a Coke, but . . . it feels different now with Eva and Brad. These people aren't Jake or Dan or Marsh or even Ashley or Jenna; right now they only know Caesar the Jerk, and I'd like to keep them from knowing Caesar the Asshole or Caesar the Jackass.

I don't know that I want them to know what I'm actually like.

"What's! My! Name!"

Finally, I give up.

"I DON'T FUCKING KNOW!" I bark at her.

Jesus Christ.

Eva and Brad say nothing, only try awkwardly not to stare at me, which must be difficult, since I am sitting across from both of them. Nobody says a word and I stare coolly off to the side, hoping she'll leave as soon as possible to alleviate the tension.

Fortunately, a loud and unexpected *CRACK* resounds in the air, relieving us of the silence. Unfortunately, this loud and unexpected *CRACK* is the sound of the waitress's hand coming in contact with my left cheek.

FUCK, that hurt.

The stinging's too hard to ignore and the humiliation's quickly fermenting itself into anger. She tosses her plastic name tag onto our table in disgust and turns quickly on her heel and stalks away, understandably fuming.

Molly.

Eva and Brad now cannot help but stare at me, and nobody knows what to say. I, especially, am at a loss for words. A million actions run through my mind — getting up, grabbing her by the arm, smacking her across her own fucking full-lipped face, running out the door, hitting something, anything, anyone at all.

I think I have aggression issues.

Luckily, I do not do any of the million actions that run through my mind. All the faces around me say different things: disgust, surprise, amusement. None good. I have no idea what's on my face, but only anger seems to register in my mind. I have to physically grip the table to resist running after her or out the door.

"So . . ." Eva's attempt to break the silence stops at a single word.

I do not move, only seethe quietly, staring off to the side, trying hard to imagine I'm not sitting across a diner table from a girl who almost ran me over twice and the guy I caught her fooling around with, and that I have not just been slapped across the face in front of a diner full of people by a girl I myself fooled around with and didn't call back. Needless to say, it's hard to think about anything else.

"Caesar, you wanna get out of here?" Alarsky asks.

Leaving would be embarrassing, but I don't know if I can suffer another second in this goddamn diner.

"Yeah."

We try to stand up as nonchalantly as possible and edge inconspicuously toward the door. Not the easiest thing to do, since we have to pass the rest of the booths before we get to the exit.

Eva, Brad, and I pull out of the diner parking lot and Alarsky coughs loudly.

"Well, this has been a successful evening," Eva says. "Culminating in us getting slapped out of the diner. And I'm still hungry."

"Why didn't you just call her, Caesar?" Brad asks. "It could have saved us a lot of trouble."

"Yeah, or you could have remembered her name!" Eva adds.

As if I could have foreseen this.

"Oh, so this is all my fault?" I ask.

Eva and Brad both turn around at once (fuckin' hell, watch the road!) and give me a look.

"Okay, fine."

"Where do you kids want to go now?" Eva asks.

"Food," Alarsky says.

"Mmm. . . . guess we could go back to my place. That okay with you, John?"

"What?"

Oh, hell no, not her *house*. I don't think I could handle that at this point.

"I feel it's my civic duty to introduce you to true art. What kind of art are you into now?"

Sorry, come again? "I'm not into art."

"Well, what kind of movies do you watch?"

"Comedies, I guess? Action . . . ? I mostly just watch sports on TV."

"Interesting," she says.

But we both know it's not.

We both know I'm not.

"It's all good; Brad here doesn't like art, either."

Good, because being Alarsky is my main goal in life and everything.

"It's not that I don't like art," I say, opening my mouth for the first time. "It's not one of my interests."

"What's the difference?"

How the fuck should I know? I'm just along for the ride.

"I dunno, it's not that I go out of my way to dislike it," I expertly bullshit. "It's not that I tried to become interested in art and decided against it. I just don't go out of my way to like it."

"Why not?"

"I dunno; it's not one of my interests."

"How could it be one of your interests unless you tried?"

"Why would I?"

"Why not?"

I shrug in the darkness.

"I just don't care."

"Okay, then what do you consider your interests?"

"Basketball. Corona. Driving. Sex?"

No bullshit there.

"Ain't nothin' wrong with that," Brad backs me up.

But of course, the truth isn't good enough for Eva. "Pretty limited, aren't we?" she comments.

"No. Those topics cover a lot of ground. I keep healthy, happy, and away from my house."

"Corona is healthy?"

"Happy." I figure if I'm going to be cross-examined, I might as well cross-examine back. "Why, what are your interests?" I ask.

"Oh God, don't get her started," Brad says drily. "Eva has 'theories.'"

"What theories?"

"I'm interested in a lot of things," Eva interrupts, pointedly ignoring Brad. "All things."

"Like what?"

"Everything. I'm interested in art, in people, in you, me, love, in where we're going and where we'll end up, tonight and tomorrow, in anime, in books, in Paris, in my brother, in . . . everything."

"I told you not to ask," Brad remarks.

"Are you interested in the Lakers versus the Pistons?" I say.

"Sure."

"What do you know about it?"

"Nothing."

"But you're interested?"

"Yes."

"Why?"

"Because it interests you. And that interests me."

But who cares? Why does she have to care about what I care about? When I'm not even sure I care about it? And does that mean I have to care about what *she* cares about? Does that mean I have to care?

"So," I say, "you're interested in everything."

"Yes."

"I don't understand."

"And that's interesting," she says with a laugh.

"Is she always like this?" I ask Brad.

He laughs and glances at her affectionately.

"Always."

"Two seconds to make up your mind," Eva says suddenly. "Miyazaki or no?"

"What?"

"Too late," she says.

As she speaks, we zoom right past the road that leads into my development.

Shit.

CHAPTER 13

"Eva, c'mon, let's drive him home," Brad says as I watch Knightly Road shrink out of view.

"No."

Why not?

"Why not?" Brad asks.

"Because. It's too late."

"You can still turn around."

"I'm too lazy."

"But —"

"What's wrong with him coming with us?"

"What's wrong with him going home?"

"John," she says to me, "Brad has some kind of beef with you coming with us."

"No, that's not —"

"You got a problem with it?" she asks me.

"Uhh . . ."

"Caesar, I don't have beef," Brad tries to assure me.

As if he isn't planning on jumping her the minute I get out of the car.

"Yeah, you do," she says.

"No —"

She looks him straight in the eye. "It's not going to be just us, Brad. Get over it."

"Fuck off," he mutters crossly.

"I really don't want to get in the way of —" I start.

"No, don't worry about it. You're not getting in the way of anything," Eva says slowly and deliberately, more to Brad than me.

Clearly I'm missing something.

The air in the car has changed, and the silence is worse than before. Sitting in the unbearably uncomfortable quiet, I almost feel bad for Alarsky. Funny that I should only relate to him now, when his horny plight means trying to get rid of me.

"You can just drop me off here," I say suddenly.

Am I doing something nice for Brad?

"Don't be stupid," Eva says, not even slowing down the car.

"If I go back to your place, you're going to have to drive me home later."

"I don't care."

"Yeah, but —"

"Eva," Brad says suddenly and irritably. "Just drop him off."

"It's not your choice," Eva answers shortly.

"Why are you doing this?" he says angrily.

They start to argue.

"C'mon, Brad, you told me you wouldn't —"

"Well, I didn't mean it!"

"Well, then, fuck you!"

"Why? Is it so wrong that I think we should be together?"

"No, but —"

"Come ON, why is it so ridiculous?"

"Because —"

"Why?"

"Fuck you and let me talk!"

"Forget it," he says moodily.

"C'mon, this was just supposed to be about fun. I thought
we agreed —"

Get.

"I lied."

Me.

"Why?"

Out.

"It was the only way to get you to —"

Of.

"Fuck YOU, Brad! How could you do this? You promised!"

Here.

"I'm fucking in love with you, Eva! God! Fuck you!"

Now!!!

She sighs. "Don't say that." And then, "All I did was invite
John to watch movies with us, and THIS is how you react? God,
grow up."

"You were doing it to throw it in my face. I didn't want him
to come and neither did he, and you still insisted."

Needtogetoutneedtogetoutneedtogetoutneedtogetoutneed
togetout.

"I can't believe we're having this discussion AGAIN."

"Well, if you'd be reasonable, then maybe —"

"I AM reasonable!"

134

"Then why can't —"

"You know why!"

"But you love —"

"Brad," she says grimly. "Don't say it."

Nownownownownownownownownownownow.

"Eva . . ." He regrets it.

"John, I'm sorry," she says to me quietly.

She U-turns in the middle of the road and drives back toward Knightly.

"Eva . . ." Brad tries again.

She doesn't answer, only stares stonily ahead at the road.

"You're getting what you want," she spits. "I'm driving him home."

We pull up onto my street.

"Caesar, dude, I'm sorry," Brad says to me as we pull up in front of my house.

I've had enough of this bullshit.

"Fuck you both," I say, without a single ounce of sensitivity.

I get out of the car and slam the door shut, leaving behind me a night filled with nothing but distress.

The next day I have to fend for myself against the blinding light of morning as it comes streaming spitefully through my open windows. Goddamn sunlight can't leave me alone for one fucking second?! I jam my head under my pillow and try to shut out the day and all the things that come with it.

Goddamn Eva.

A little after noon, I roll out of bed and drive to the gym. After I work out for two hours, I drive home to shower and leave for Papa John's. When I get there, Eva is just getting out of her car. As much as I want to, I don't say anything to her. I feel like a dick after last night, but they both deserved it in the end.

I enter the restaurant after her but don't acknowledge her.

"Don't be an idiot," she says, turning to me all of a sudden.

"What?"

"Forget about last night. It had nothing to do with you."

"Great."

"Whatever."

I find myself asking, "Everything okay?"

"No."

"What was it all about?"

She sighs and doesn't answer.

I nod and follow her into the back of the store.

A fairly young guy in jeans and a wrinkled button-down shirt looks up from pouring himself a cup of coffee. I recognize him immediately.

"Caesar? Is that you? God, look at you."

"Dave? Jesus. I didn't know you were the manager here."

"Yeah, I just started this year. Damn, how have you been?"

"Been okay. I've had better days."

"You're telling me," he says into his mug.

"You know each other?" Eva says.

"Dave is Dan's older brother," I explain. "I can't believe you're manager, man! Congratulations! That's a huge step up from . . ." I don't finish.

He laughs. "It's okay, you can say it. I've left all that shit behind. I'm clean now."

"*You?* QUIT? Seriously? That's . . . awesome, right? Kind of a shock, but, yeah, awesome."

He gives me a suspicious look all of a sudden. "Caesar, don't tell me you need this money for drugs."

"What?" I say, laughing. "Are you serious?"

"Yeah, man, I know you're loaded; what do *you* need money for?"

I shrug. "I'm not heavy into drugs, man. Calm down."

"Good." He wags a finger at me. "Don't start. You, either, Eva." He points his finger at her, too.

"Okay, thanks, Dad," she says.

"You know you gave me my first joint?" I say.

"Seriously? Shit," he says, surprised.

"Yeah, me and Dan thought we were so cool, smoking and whatever."

He shakes his head. "All that shit, it'll fuck with you."

"Yeah, that's the whole point," Eva says.

He chuckles softly. "Well, I guess this is what people call 'getting your life together.'"

"So you gonna spread the wealth and gimme a job or what?" I say with a grin.

"Oh, yeah, yeah, that'd be great, man. Do you need an application?"

"Do I?"

"It's a formality."

"All right."

"Eva, they probably need you out there," he tells her.

"'Kay. Later, John."

"'Bye."

I sit down to fill out the application as Dave finishes off his coffee.

"How's everything?" he asks casually. "Goddamn, you're graduating this year, aren't you? That's insane."

"Yeah."

"Are you psyched?"

"I guess."

"You should be. No more high school bullshit."

"Yeah."

He nods. "You're gonna like it a lot, I think."

"Yeah."

"You have anything more than 'yeah' to say about your future?"

"No."

"Kid, don't sass me."

I shrug. "It's not a big deal, I guess. I'm relieved to be leaving."

"You're not excited?"

"Should I be?"

"One would think."

"Everyone keeps talking about it, but . . . I'm not sure if I care."

"Well, what schools are you looking at?"

"I don't know. I'll probably just end up at Ravens."

"I always thought you were smarter than that."

"I'm not."

"Oh."

I hand him the application.

"Cool. I'm supposed to ask you some questions, but fuck it. You can start on Monday."

"Nice. Thanks for this."

"No prob. You know how it works?"

"Eva can explain it to me."

"Okay. She's a good kid."

"Yeah, she's cool."

"Are you guys . . . ?"

"What? No. Noooo. Noooooooo."

He laughs. "Okay, just asking, Jeez."

"'S okay," I say.

"How's Dan? I don't get to see him much."

"He's good. Hung out with him last night."

"Did you? He's all right."

I contemplate telling Dave how heavily into drugs Dan is these days, but I reconsider. It's not really my place.

"Dan's my boy. He's cool," I say.

"Good. I hope he stays out of trouble."

"As an older brother, what do you think about letting him make his own mistakes?"

"No. That's what I think."

And that's the end of that.

Dave and I shake hands, and I leave.

As I pull out of the parking lot and into the late afternoon, I think back to my first joint, and to the dopey smile on Dave's face as he handed it to me. I didn't get high, but I didn't care. All I cared about was that moment, that story I could tell all my friends the next day, about how I smoked up with Dave and all his high school buddies, how bloodshot his eyes were, how cool our laughter was. All I wanted was to be Dave, to tell his stories like they were my own. How could I have known that his story ran deeper than a simple bowl in someone's basement? How could I have known the things he'd do to take the sensations to a new extreme? And how could I know that five years later, there he'd be, totally clean and legit, hiring me for a job?

I wonder what went through his mind when he hit rock bottom. I wonder if he knew when he saw it, saw how cold and hard and endless the bottom really was. I wonder if he knows now. If he knows about Dan. If he knows Dan at all.

CHAPTER 14

The next week passes more or less without event. I see Eva every day, but as of yet, we haven't talked long enough for me to say anything real.

Then on Thursday, my shift ends early and I walk out to the parking lot to see Eva getting in her car.

"Hey," I say, walking over to her.

"Hey."

"What's goin' on? How're things?"

"Okay. How're things with you?"

"Okay. How's everything with Brad?" She doesn't answer at first, and I add hastily, "Sorry if that's not my place."

"No, it's all right. Things with Brad are . . . complicated. And gradually getting worse."

"What's going on between you two?"

She sighs.

"Sorry," I say.

"No, it's just . . ." She closes the door to her car and leans against it, facing me. "Hard to think about."

"You don't have to talk about it if you don't want."

"I want to talk about it, I just don't . . . want to. Know what I mean?"

No.

"Yeah."

She shakes her head and sighs again, then looks at me, standing in front of her in this open parking lot in the middle of the night.

"Is your love life as complicated as mine?"

My love life isn't complicated, period.

I shrug in response. "Not really."

"You have a girlfriend?"

"Nope."

"You looking for one?"

Why, are you offering?

"Nope."

"Why's that? Bad experiences with past girlfriends?"

"No experiences with any past girlfriends."

"What do you mean?"

"I mean I've never had a girlfriend to speak of."

"You've never had a girlfriend? But aren't you supposed to be like Don Juan or something?"

I laugh. I've been called a lot of things, but Don Juan is a first.

"I don't have girlfriends. They don't interest me."

"But girls do."

"Right. But not girlfriends."

I can tell that Eva's *interested* in this.

"Why is that?" she asks. "You can't commit?"

The C-word. Even when girls think they're using it casually, there's always subtext, whether they intend it or not. I *hate* the C-word.

"Commit?? Why would I? I hardly ever even sleep with the same girl more than twice."

"How many girls have you slept with?"

Besides "who's on your list?" this is probably my most frequently asked question. I've got all sorts of answers, most of them facetious comebacks to avoid answering honestly. To Eva, I only answer the very vague truth: "A lot."

"How many?"

"A lot. I lost count."

"How many?"

"You don't want to know."

"Apparently I do."

"The number is between one and a hundred."

She gives me a look. "Fine, don't tell me. I have other sources."

"There are some that nobody knows about. I doubt there's anyone you could talk to that will have the full count."

"What about Jake?"

"Even he doesn't know them all."

If he knew about all of them, he probably would have stabbed me in the back a long time ago.

"Do you write them all down?"

I snort. "What do you take me for? Despite popular belief, I'm not one of those guys that freakin' hunts girls for sport. I don't keep a little diary of all the girls I've fucked."

Lie.

"So if you don't do it for sport, what do you do it for?"

"Fun?"

143

"Isn't that the same thing?"

Why does she always have to pick me apart?

"No. Yes. Maybe."

She looks at me ruefully. "Do you lie to girls?" she says, half-serious.

I hesitate.

"Yes," I finally say.

"Like what? What do you lie about?"

Anything. Everything. To get them in bed. Or to get them to go away.

"I'm kidding. Of course I don't lie to girls. I'm not some kind of cold-hearted bastard."

Lying, lying fool.

"Yeah, right." She looks amused. "I bet you'd say anything to get a girl in bed."

"Nuh-uh."

Gooooood one, Caesar.

This just seems to amuse her more.

"What about you?" I say, curious. "How many guys have you slept with?"

You don't get to ask all the questions.

"John! That's a very personal question. You can't just ask someone you barely know about that."

Not that I thought that would really work, but it was worth a shot.

"What?! You asked me first!"

"I'm a girl; it's different."

"Why is it different?"

"It just is."

"What about treating girls the same as guys, blah blah blah?"

"That's bullshit. Do you open doors for guys?"

"No. But I don't really open doors for girls, either."

"Didn't your mama teach you better than that?"

I stare at her. "My mom's dead."

She opens her mouth to laugh, then looks at my face and closes it. "Oh God, I'm really sorry."

I shrug and look away. "It's all right."

We don't say anything for a moment. I know she wants to ask me about it, but neither of us wants to make the first move.

"Don't worry about it," I say finally.

"How did she . . . when did she . . . ?"

She smiles weakly.

"I don't mind you asking. I was twelve. She died giving birth to my sister Peggy."

"That's rough. I'm sorry."

I shrug. "Yeah."

"I feel for your sister," she says. "Imagine growing up knowing you're the reason for your mother's death. Imagine the self-blame. God, I don't know what I'd do if it were me."

"Yeah."

"And she's only . . . what, five? Six?"

"Five."

"Jeous."

"Yeah."

"Were you close with your mom?"

"Not really, I guess. I mean, not in the way that I told her everything and we spent all our time together. But to some degree, yeah, I guess we were."

"What about your dad?"

"What about him?"

"Are you close?"

"Umm . . . no, not really. We weren't really close before my mom died, either, though. I don't see him a lot."

"He a workaholic type?"

"Yeah, something like that. He works weird hours."

My father's recent attempts to unite us as a "family" flash through my mind.

"I see," she says, nodding.

"You close with your family?" I ask.

"Mmm . . . my parents? Not really. I don't like my dad that much. He's kind of a jerk."

"Do you have siblings?"

"Yeah. My brother, Adam. He's twenty-five."

"Adam and Eva?"

She laughs. "Yeah, um, my parents have a fucked-up sense of humor."

I laugh. "That's cool, that's cool. Are you close with him?"

"Adam? Nah, not really. I don't see him often. He lives in Jersey, but he doesn't come home a lot. Nobody really misses him."

"Why, is he a jerk, too?"

She laughs. "Funny you should say that, because I was just thinking about how much he reminds me of you."

"Me? Why?"

"In high school, he had a reputation a lot like yours."

"Here I was, thinking I was one in a million."

She snorts. "I think we've been over this before."

"Have we?"

We share a smile.

"Are you close with your sisters?" she asks.

"Kelly? Maybe in the way that I was close with my mom. It's not like we hang out at the movies or something, and it's not like we're friends or whatever, but we don't hate each other."

"Tell me what she's like."

What am I supposed to say? I can't get up in the morning unless she wrestles with me first? Her friends know more about my sex life than my own best friend does? Her shampoo makes me smell pretty?

"Uhh . . . she's short. She has blondish hair . . . it's not real. That's about it. She's pretty much your standard pubescent eighth grader."

Well, what the hell do you expect?

"I'm sure there's something fucked up about her, you just don't know it. Not to imply that your family's fucked up . . ." She trails off and then continues, "I just think that normal families don't really exist."

And then it comes out.

"Well, I did catch her drinking one of my beers the other day. Pissed the fuck out of me."

"Why, how old is she?"

"Thirteen."

"How old were you when you started drinking?"

It's different.

"Thirteen."

I swear.

"But that doesn't mean it's okay," I add.

"Is that what you said? When you caught her?"

"I just yelled. Told her she wasn't cool."

"Did you think you were cool when you got drunk the first time?"

147

I think of Dave.

"Yeah, of course. Thought I was cool as hell."

"So don't you understand why she'd think she's cool now?"

Of course I understand. Of course I thought I was cool, of course she thinks she's cool. *But that doesn't mean it's okay.* Why doesn't anyone get that?

"Just because she thinks so doesn't mean it's true. She's too young."

"You drink pretty often, right? So how can you tell her she can't? She's been to, what, maybe, two, three parties where there's beer?"

"She shouldn't be drinking," I say emphatically. "What if she hangs out with the wrong kids? Something could happen to her without her knowing."

She nods. "It's different when she does it; I understand. But what, you're afraid she's going to get raped or something? Are thirteen-year-old boys really that fucked up?"

"If they are, they'll fucking pay for it. I'd fucking kill any kid who touched her."

Eva laughs. "Adam would let me rot."

"Then he's nothing like me."

"It's not like he's a jerk," she says thoughtfully. "It's just that . . . I can't really imagine him being that protective of me. Our family's not really like that. He lets me make my mistakes and fend for myself, even if I can't."

"That seems a little harsh."

"Would you do anything for Kelly?"

"Not *anything.* I don't baby her. If she does something stupid, I'll probably let her learn from it. Sometimes kids have it coming to them. But I mean, if she was in, like, serious trouble, of course I'd help her. You don't think if you had a serious problem that your brother would do something about it?"

"I can't think of any serious situation where I'd need his help. I mean, I guess if something serious happened, he'd feel obligated to do something, but it's not really a brother-sisterly thing. We're not close." She shrugs. "I don't see it as good or bad. He's just a guy who used to live in my house and then he left. I don't see why we should have to be close or get along or even like each other. He doesn't really have anything to do with me. Except we have the same parents."

That's pretty fucked up. But of course, I don't say this.

"Well, that's enough, don't you think? Being family."

"Why does it have to be? It's not like I chose him as a brother. I don't need him for anything. We don't need to talk, we don't need to hang out, I don't even need to like him. Much less love him."

That's also pretty fucked up. But again, I don't say this

"You don't love your own brother?"

"I don't know him. Do you love your sisters?"

"Yeah, of course."

"Why of course?"

"Because they're my family."

"Do you love your friends?"

"My friends? I guess. Not really. I dunno. Sometimes."

"See, but don't you think that's weird?"

"What?"

"Your friends are the ones you choose to surround yourself with, and yet you only love them sometimes. Your family is just random people you were born into, and yet you are taught to love them unconditionally."

"You don't love your family?"

"Why should I?"

"But do you?"

"Sometimes."

"You love your friends unconditionally?"

"Doesn't it make more sense that way?"

"I think that's fucked up."

There. I said it.

"Why? Just because society dictates unconditional love and loyalty to your family? Why should you have to love those you are stuck with and not those you choose to be around? That just says something about your judgment."

I'm starting to think this is another one of Eva's "theories." But I do my best to keep up.

"But still . . . they're family," I counter.

"Why does it have to mean so much?"

"I don't know. It just does. I can't explain it."

"They're just random people."

"No, I don't think that's true. They're not random. You're tied to them by blood."

"So?"

"So, that *means* something."

Right?

"What? What does it mean?"

"It means you're linked. You have something in common."

I'm right. I know I'm right. You're not going to win this one.

"And therefore you should love them? What if I don't like what we have in common? Should I celebrate it with such a thing as strong as love? It doesn't make sense."

"I don't know, I can't explain it. I just know that if you're in trouble, you're supposed to turn to your family. And I think your brother would do something to help you if you were in trouble."

"Only because he felt obligated to. Truth be told, I don't need my family. Just because Adam's my brother doesn't mean I have to like him . . . or depend on him."

"If you don't depend on your family, who are you going to depend on?"

"Why do I need someone to depend on? What's wrong with being dependent on myself? I'd think you'd understand that."

"Yeah, of course I do. It's not like I talk to my dad enough to depend on him or something. It's not like I go to Kelly for advice about all my problems. It's just . . . it seems natural that people depend on their family for support."

"What's wrong with friends?"

"I guess people would say that friends don't last forever."

"Nothing does."

"Family does."

"Yeah, but it doesn't help if they're fucked up."

"Friends are fucked up," I point out.

Am I still winning?

"Well, yes, like I said, everyone is fucked up. But it just seems like families have a higher frequency of being fucked up."

"Maybe it's *because* of the fact that everyone is expected to love each other."

"And it doesn't always work out."

"No, I guess not."

We don't say anything else for a moment, just look past each other and sigh into the darkness. I feel our heavy words hanging in the air, and it makes me feel strange, like I'm heavier because of it. And now, after all that, I don't know what to say.

But Eva's going again before I even have a chance to worry about it.

"Is it true, then, do you think, that friends aren't always expected to love each other?"

"Yeah, I think a lot of people are friends with people they don't really like."

"Then why are they friends with them? Are you friends with people you don't like?"

"I want to lie and say no, but the truth? The faces of almost all the girls I've ever known just flashed through my head. And maybe half the guys. Does that make me a bad person?"

"Sadly, no. You're right — everybody has some friends they pretend to like."

But I pretend to like *all* of them.

"But with some girls, even if I don't pretend to like them — even if I'm mean as hell to them — they still consider us friends. I don't understand that. I mean, I don't fight it; it makes it easier to get ass, but still. It's twisted," I say.

"Yeah, girls do seem to dig the asshole thing."

"Do you?" I ask without thinking.

She takes me seriously. "In theory, no. Assholes have something to prove. It's an image thing. I think that's stupid."

I feel my ego deflate ever so slightly.

Then she adds, "But I think that sometimes a guy who plays hard to get is undeniably attractive."

Snaps for Caesar.

"Guys feel the same way about girls," I say. "But I don't really run across any."

"Any what? Girls who play hard to get?"

"Yeah."

"Oh yes, I forgot. Girls just throw themselves at your feet."

"You say it like it's bad."

"It's amusing."

"I'm glad I amuse you."

"Me, too. We should hang out more often; I need more amusement in my life."

We share a look and it feels light in the dark of the night. I want to slap the smile off my face, but I can't.

She has one, too. It looks like mine:

Happy.

"You know what I like about you, John?" she says after a moment.

"What?"

"I don't know!" she says, laughing. "I can't figure out why I'd want to talk to a guy like you." She laughs again. "Or why I'd say that to your face."

I smile the Caesar smile. "I'm irresistible."

"Don't get ahead of yourself."

In the comfortable silence of the night, I feel like it's my turn to say something

"Hey, thanks for getting me this job," I say finally.

"What are friends for?"

I don't know.

But I smile anyway.

I don't know who's winning now. But I'm pretty sure I don't care.

CHAPTER 15

"Hey, Caesar! Hey!"

As I pass through the first wing hall on Friday morning, I hear Jake calling my name from somewhere in the crowd behind me.

"Caesar!"

I stop at my locker and he catches up.

"I've been calling your name for, like, five minutes."

"I didn't hear you."

"You're going deaf."

"Shut up."

"Where were you last night? I called you."

"Working."

"You got a job?"

"Yeah. Papa John's. Delivery."

He nods. "Pay good?"

"Yeah, it's decent."

"Working tonight?"

"I might. Why, did you want to do something?"

He shrugs. "Yeah, I guess. I might have some people over."

Just then, I see Eva stepping down the hall in my direction. I open my mouth to say something, but she just says "hey" in passing and doesn't stop.

I open my mouth again to reply, but Jake beats me to "hey."

His eyes follow her down the hall and I don't say a thing. He shakes his head slightly, the expression on his face a twisted mixture between disgust and admiration. Then he catches me looking at her.

"What?" he says.

"What?" I say.

He shrugs.

I shrug.

I close my locker and we walk down the hall.

I spend the first three periods of the day clock-watching and the next three half-sleeping. By sixth period, I am more than ready to leave school, but I still have to make it through one more period and then practice. The rest of the day passes, and after basketball, I find my way to the lake.

As I leave my car behind and walk out into the clearing where the gazebo stands, I expect to see her sitting there inside or out on the dock or floating on the water.

But the gazebo is empty and the water ripples pathetically.

I feel disappointed, but I push it back and replace it with thoughts about plans for tonight. Then I stretch out on the bench and replace all thoughts with comforting darkness.

The next time I open my eyes, darkness is indeed what I see. I missed the sunset and night has fallen. I debate a bit between going to work for some extra hours or calling up Jake, then Jake himself calls me before I come to a decision.

"'Ey," I greet him.

"You coming over?"

"Who's there?"

"Marsh, Ashley, Dan, Jenna . . . Sam." Some muffled speaking in the background, then Jake replies, "It's Caesar . . . I dunno, that's why I called him."

For a second, I am tempted to go, but it hardly seems worth it to be in such a close environment with Sam.

"Caesar? You there?" Jake's voice comes through the little earpiece.

"Yeah. I'm not coming."

"Why not? You working?"

"No."

"Why not?"

"I don't feel like it. Later."

I hang up and lean back against the side of the gazebo. There's a restless feeling growing inside of me that I can't quite put into words, but it's nothing a little female companionship can't solve.

I flip through the numbers on my phone for someone interesting. Let's see, which of these ladies can I consider worthy and interesting? There's Lindsey Jacobs, whose company I missed out on a couple weeks ago at Stacy's . . . oh, and then of course there's Stacy . . . I scroll around some more. There's Jamie Nell; she's always reliable to deliver. I finally decide to call Lindsey.

She answers on the first ring.

"Hello?"

"Lindsey."

"Caesar? Oh my God, what's up? I haven't seen you for so long."

"Yeah," I say. "I miss you."

"You do?"

"God, of course I do. What are you doing?"

"Right now? I'm home."

"Anybody else there with you?"

"No."

I smirk.

"Do you want to . . . ?" she asks.

"Maybe."

"Then why did you —"

"I'll be right over."

Ohh yeahhh.

I pocket my phone and skip down the steps and around to the clearing. Happy little shit songs play inside my head and I am almost tempted to whistle, but I resist for the sake of my own dignity.

A night with a girl I haven't seen in a while. A night without any regrets. This is what I need.

As I walk behind the bushes, a dark blue sedan pulls up dangerously close to where my car is parked in the ditch. Suddenly all the happy tunes get louder and more high-pitched.

"Hey," Eva says brightly as she slams the door shut behind her and examines her parking job.

"Hey," I answer, containing my surprise.

"You leaving?" she says without looking at me. Then she opens the door again and rummages inside.

"Um . . ."

Am I?

The happy tunes quicken and grow more confused as I

157

realize my subconscious soundtrack would rather stay here with Eva than get laid.

"Nope, I just heard a car so I came to check it out. Good thing it wasn't some asshole or I would have had to kick his ass for finding our place."

She laughs. " 'Our place,' huh?"

The way she says it makes me feel like a giant tool.

She pulls a blanket out of her car and slams the door shut again. She walks past me into the clearing. When I don't move to follow her, she yells back, "Are you coming or what?"

I follow, throwing away any chance of Lindsey Jacobs for the night and probably forever.

Eva walks down by the dock and spreads the blanket out on the grassy bank next to it. We sit down together on it and face the darkening evening. I lie down with my arms behind my head and she sits and watches the lights across the lake.

"I'm in a good mood," she says matter-of-factly.

"Is that so?"

"Yes, it is."

"Why?"

"I don't know why."

"Oh."

She turns to look at me. "What about you?"

"What *about* me?"

"Oh, c'mon, John, can't you just be genuinely happy?"

"Who said I was unhappy? And what reason do I have to be genuinely happy?"

"You look unhappy."

"I'm not."

"Is that what you look like when you're happy?"

How would I know? "I'm not happy," I tell her.

"But not unhappy."

I nod. "Right."

"That's boring. At least unhappiness is interesting. Apathy is just boring."

"I'm sorry I'm boring you," I say drily. "There's no pleasing you."

"Be happy."

"Fuck you."

"I bet that would make you happy," she says, laughing. "Sorry . . . couldn't help myself."

I prop myself up on my arms and give her a look.

"Fuck you!" I say.

She just laughs again and then I can't help myself, either.

"So. John. I guess we're going to be hanging out now, is that it?"

"That's it."

I smile and lie back down on the blanket, feeling the night against my face.

"All right, but before we start having profound conversations and farting around each other, I need to know one thing: Are you a Republican?" she asks mock seriously.

"Umm . . . what's the right answer?" From the ground, I talk half to her back and half to her turned face.

"The honest one."

"No?"

"Is that the honest one?"

"Is that the right one?"

"Yes."

"Then yes."

She shakes her head. "You're funny."

"I try."

"How was school today?" she says after a moment.

"What the fuck kind of question is that? You sound like my fucking dad. You know how it was; you were there!"

"Your day is different than mine."

"It was shit."

"Why?"

"It's always shit."

"My, my, aren't *we* the resentful teenager?"

She looks down at me with a teasing smile.

"I'm not resentful. School really was shit today."

"Yeah, but why?"

"Because nothing good happened."

"When do good things ever happen at school?"

"Exactly. It's always shit," I repeat.

"There are a couple holes in your belief system."

"Fuck you. How's that for a belief system?"

"Not bad."

A breeze passes and ruffles our hair and shirts. She turns her face toward the sky and breathes a deep, satisfied sigh.

"Yeah," she says.

"Yeah?"

"Yeah."

"Yeah what?"

She smiles again at me.

"Yeah everything."

"You never make any sense."

"Wow, the two of us can finally agree."

She lies down next to me and I can feel the heat from her

160

skin. Her hand comes dangerously close to mine and the restless feelings I had before creep slowly back into my body, particularly into my right hand.

"Alarsky," I say aloud, quite suddenly, to resist touching her. Shit.

"What?" she says, turning her head to face me.

"Nothing."

"Bullshit. You just said Alarsky."

"Why the hell would I say Alarsky?"

"I don't know; that's a good question. Why?"

"I don't know, because I didn't say it."

She rolls her eyes, annoyed, and turns the other way.

"I guess things with him aren't too good?"

"You just asked me yesterday," she says to the darkness on the other side of her. "How much could have happened between yesterday and today?"

"Should I stop asking?"

"Yes . . . no."

"Which one?"

She says nothing and doesn't turn back toward me.

"Sorry, I didn't mean to —"

"Don't apologize, John."

"Okay."

After several moments, I say, "Do you wanna get out of here?"

"No. This is where I want to be."

I stare into the now black night above us and see one or two stars wink at me.

"Yeah," I say, glad I've got no comeback. The two of us can finally agree.

CHAPTER 16

At noon the next day, Jake shows up at my house.

"Dude, what happened last night?" he asks as we get in his car.

"What do you mean?"

"Where were you? Why didn't you come over?"

"I told you I wasn't in the mood."

"'Cause Sam was there?"

"God, no. Why should I care about her?"

Don't answer that.

He doesn't.

"What did you do then?"

I shrug. "Not much."

"Who were you with?"

I shrug. "Nobody."

He looks like he doesn't believe me, but knows not to push it.

Half an hour later, we walk out of Subway and eat next to Jake's car in the parking lot. I sit on the curb and bite into my sandwich.

"I bet I know what you did last night," Jake says suddenly.

"What?"

"You called someone, didn't you?"

I snort. "I told you I wasn't with anybody."

"That's code for 'I was banging Lindsey Jacobs.'"

"Sometimes you pull some amazing shit out of your ass, man."

"It's a good place to pull shit from," he says. "So were you?"

"Was I what?"

"Were you banging her?"

"Jacobs? . . . Naaaah."

"What the fuck? Why the hell not?!"

"Dude, I dunno." I shrug.

"So you were going to?"

"Maybe."

"Yes?"

"I said maybe."

"Yes, you were going to fuck Lindsey."

"I didn't say that."

"What happened? Why didn't you?"

I shrug again. "I dunno."

"Dude."

"Dude."

"Dude."

"What?"

"*Why not?*"

Because I'd rather lie on a blanket with a girl I barely know at the fucking lake and not even touch her?

God, what's happening to me?

"I . . . fell asleep."

163

Not a total lie.

"You . . . WHAT? Lindsey Jacobs was waiting, butt naked, alone in her house, for *you* to show up, and YOU FELL ASLEEP? I can't believe I'm friends with you!"

Me, neither.

"It's hard to believe someone could be *that* lame," Jake says, shaking his head and taking another bite of his sandwich. "Goddamn," he mutters through a mouthful of salami.

"Yeah. Thanks."

"Did she call you when you didn't show up?"

"Nope. She hasn't called me."

"That's it, Caesar. You lost your chance."

"Bullshit. It's her loss, not mine."

"Are you shitting me? You think after you ditched her for a fucking *nap* that she's going to call you again?"

I shrug. "It's possible."

He shakes his head. "I don't get it. How can girls *go* for shit like that?"

"I dunno, either."

He opens his mouth as if he has something else to say, but closes it again, for whatever reason.

And for several moments, nothing. Nothing at all.

I feel like I should say something, should put his mind at ease, tell him what happened, say something, anything. Say anything.

But nothing comes out. Nothing at all.

The conversation still hanging unsettled in the air, we both crumple up the wax paper from our sandwiches and get in Jake's car and drive off into the silent afternoon.

*   *   *

Late that night, I find myself uneasy and awake. I thump out
of bed, stumbling over clothes and equipment and all the other
things that fill my days, toward the door. I am almost at the end
of the hall when Kelly's door creaks open.

"What are you doing?" she asks sleepily. She stands there in
her oversize sweats, eyes only half-open.

"Going for a drive. Go back to sleep."

"You're gonna drive *now*? It's, like, two."

"I can't sleep."

"Me, neither."

"Bullshit. I heard you snoring."

"I don't snore."

"Go back to sleep."

"Can I come?"

"No."

I walk downstairs and she follows.

"Please?"

"No. I'm not going anywhere; I'm just going for a drive. You
have to go to school tomorrow."

"So do you."

"Yeah, but you're a kid, and I don't have to do anything in
school."

"Fuck you, you're a kid, too."

"Go back to sleep."

"I wanna come with you."

"No."

I open the garage door quietly and she follows.

"C'mon, pleeeeease? Pleeeeeeease? Please? Please? Please?
Please? Ple —"

"A big hell no."

As I get into the driver's seat and start the car, she opens the passenger side and gets in.

"Kelly, I said no. Get out of my car and go back to sleep."

"What if I sleep in the car?"

"Why would you do that when you could just sleep in your *bed*, which is ten times better?"

"I dunno."

"Kelly."

"John."

"Oh God, FINE!"

She grins, satisfied.

The girl can fucking get whatever she wants.

Maybe we are alike after all.

I pull out onto the black street and weave through pavement until we find our way out of the development.

"Is this, like, brother-sister bonding?" Kelly asks.

"No, this is, like, I couldn't sleep, and you wouldn't leave me alone."

She shrugs and tries to turn on the radio, but I turn it off before she can find a station.

"This isn't radio time," I tell her.

"Why not?"

"Because this is silent time. Because you're in my car and I said so."

"What's wrong with the radio?"

"No."

"Fine."

I drive for a while in silence, and out of the corner of my eye, I see Kelly leaning against the window, staring out at the night, lids drooping. I cruise the lonely stretch of highway, long fields now black in the night racing against my car along the side of the road. I only see two or three other cars the entire time we're on Route 17. But they pass as quickly as they come, tiny little dots disappearing into the silent night behind my rearview mirror.

I feel this discontent growing inside of me. Anxiety and apprehension, a jittery feeling that makes me want to drive, drive, drive . . . fly into the night. I could go anywhere. But where's that?

Kelly slumps against the window, eyes closed, arm propped up for a comfortable position. She breathes audibly, a sleeping habit since she was little, and her chest rises and falls in rhythm with her breathing. She's such a small person. Small eyes, small mouth, small face. I remember when she was so small I had to hold her hand to keep her from getting lost in the crowd. She had such a small hand.

Kelly might have a lot of places to go. If I asked her, she'd probably say she wanted to go to California or Paris or, I dunno, Mars. Where would I go? Where will I go? . . . Where am I going? As long as the road stretches on, my car will ride on. But where does the road lead to? When does it end?

Maybe I should just turn around and drive on home. My interest in taking a drive to relieve my anxiety is useless.

I pull to the right and into the opposite lane and back the way we came. Kelly sits up yawning and frowning.

"Are we going home?" she asks drowsily.

"Yeah."

She leans her head back against the window but doesn't close her eyes again.

"You drive a lot." A statement, not a question.

"Yeah."

"How come?"

"Sometimes I can't sleep."

"I'm gonna drive soon."

"Three years isn't soon."

"It's soon enough."

Then, after a moment, she says, "You're gonna be eighteen soon. You're leaving soon. Gonna be a man."

"What's so different between eighteen and seventeen? Buying porn?"

"Eighteen is when you leave."

"I won't leave forever. I won't be gone."

"Yeah, you will. Maybe not forever, but you'll definitely be gone."

I shrug.

"It's not a big deal."

She says nothing for a while, and then she says, softly, "But you're leaving."

After a few minutes of silence, I say, "I won't be going far, Kelly. Rutgers isn't far. It's less than an hour away. So I won't be gone. And besides," I add, "maybe I'll end up at Ravens. So I won't be moving away at all."

"You'll get in somewhere better than Ravens. You won't be living in the house anymore. Not that you're usually here anyway."

I shrug. "So it won't be that big of a deal when I leave."

"Great."

"What?"

"Nothing."

"What?"

I know she wants to say it but she needs prodding. But how much can she ask from me? I can't be home to hang out with her all the time anymore. It's not my responsibility to watch her or fight over the remote with her or bring home food for her. It's not. I know she misses Mom, but what am I supposed to do about it? I sure as hell can't replace Mom or fill Kelly's emptiness or do girly things with her. It's hard, but I can't help it. I'm not Mom.

I can't take care of Kelly; I need that energy for me. I need me for me.

But of course I don't say any of this. "Fine," I say instead. "Be that way."

"Fine."

"*Fine.*"

"FINE."

Silence.

She tries to turn on the radio again and I don't move to stop her. I'm too tired. I guess I'm ready to go to sleep now.

Ten minutes later, we pull up into the driveway and I park in the garage. We enter the house without a word and tiptoe quietly upstairs so we won't wake up Peggy or Dad. We slip into our respective rooms and that's that for the night.

I fall into bed and kick off my shoes into the far and dark reaches of my room. My eyes won't open for anybody.

But through the wall, I still hear Kelly call out "g'night" before I fall into a deep sleep.

CHAPTER 17

The next week slumps past without event. I wake up, go to school and get hassled, go to practice and get hassled, go to work and get hassled.

On Friday, my guidance counselor tries to hunt me down for a let's-discuss-your-promising-future appointment, but I manage to evade her college-bound grasp until last period. After practice, I jump home to shower and get ready for Danielle's birthday party.

Heat streams through my hair and down my face, falling down my chest in rivers. I pull out of the shower and wrap a towel around my waist and walk into my room.

In twenty minutes, I find myself fresh, clothed, and standing on the doorstep of Eva's house.

Knock.

Knock.

Pause.

Knock knock.

The door swings open and she stands in front of me, hair wet and eyebrows raised.

"Hey."

"Hi."

I can hear the surprise in her voice.

"What are you doing here?" she asks.

She doesn't move to invite me in.

"Sorry. I should have called you. Are you busy? I'm going to a party."

She waits for me to say something else, so I go on.

"Would you like to come with me?"

"Well, I was planning to —"

"Oh man, I'm sorry. I should have called to see if you had other plans."

That's the second time I've apologized in the past minute. This is a record for me.

"Whose party is it?"

"Danielle Tyler? It's her birthday."

"Where is it?"

"At her house."

"She won't care if I come?"

"It's open house. You're not busy?"

She shrugs. "I was just gonna stay in and get fat."

"What?"

"Watch movies, veg, eat a lot. Nice and relaxing Friday."

"Yeah, that sounds awesome," I say drily. "Don't let me tear you away from the riveting evening you've planned."

"Fine, fine. I'll go. Should I change?"

I look at her blankly. As if I ever notice what girls

wear to these things. Clothes usually end up . . . in other places.

"Right. Forget it. Let's go."

The drive is silent until Eva says, "So. Why are we going to this party?"

I shrug. "Danielle's a friend of mine and I have nothing better to do."

"Okay, let me rephrase. Why am *I* going to this party?"

"Because Danielle's a friend of mine and you have nothing better to do. Unless you count vegging as something better."

"Maybe I do. What made you think I didn't have other plans and that I'd go to this thing with you?"

"Well, you *were* free and I *did* get you to go. So why speculate?"

"It's the principle."

"What principle? There's no principle. We'll have a good time."

She laughs. "I've had a bad influence on you."

Influence?

"What do you mean?"

"Nothing," she says, chuckling to herself like she has some stupid secret.

"Alarsky might be there," I say after a moment.

"Good for him."

"You still in a fight?"

"Shut up, John," she says, almost tiredly.

"Sorry. Are you ever going to tell me what's going on between you two?"

"Maybe."

"Is it that bad?"

"Maybe."

"Are you just going to keep saying maybe?"

She cracks a smile. "Maybe."

"Good."

For a moment, I feel like I've helped. For a moment, I feel like maybe I didn't do something wrong. Maybe I protected her from hurting. Maybe she's mine to protect. Maybe I can protect her.

I can protect her.

We arrive at Danielle's house and I park in the street, where the cars are already overflowing.

"Oh shit," Eva says as we approach Danielle's front door. "I don't have anything to give her."

"No worries," I say, shrugging. "She won't notice."

"John, that's really rude."

"No, seriously. She'll be so smashed, she won't even know."

She stops and doesn't move any closer to the door.

"I have to get her something."

"It's too late; we're already here."

"What did you get her?"

"Umm . . ."

"John!"

"No, c'mon, I'm not that much of a jerk." I think for a moment. "A bunch of us gave Jenna some money and she bought something for her. Hey, listen, don't worry about it. I'll tell her you're my date and the present is from both of us."

"Yeah, like that's believable. You never bring dates."

"How do you know?"

"Well, do you?"

"Well, no, but . . . well, yes, if you count . . ." My voice trails off.

She looks at me expectantly and turns around to walk back down the hill toward my car.

I think I'm the one who needs protecting from all the shit this girl gives me.

"C'mon, it's believable!"

"That we're dating?" She practically snorts.

"Maybe?"

Does it sound *that* stupid?

"Oh God," she says, rolling her eyes. "Fine."

We enter the house where the music is raging and the air is thick with smoke. From the looks of it, the party is just starting to shape up, people bumping and jostling and taking up all possible standing room. Before we even get through the first room, Eva finds an excuse to leave me.

"I'll be right back," she says, slipping into the crowd of people.

I lose sight of her black hair and then she is gone. I manage to find my way to the bar and somehow Jake manages to find his way to me.

"Caesar." He claps a hand on my shoulder. From the pink in his face, he has clearly been here for a while and has spent most of his time at the bar.

I shrug his hand off and ask the kid behind the bar for a Corona.

"Jake."

"What's up? Who's on your list?"

"No list."

"What?" he yells over the din of Sean Paul's voice filling the room.

"No list!" I shout back.

"NO LIST?" he repeats in another shout. "Why not?"

I shrug as I'm handed an open bottle.

"Why not?" he repeats again.

"I dunno," I say, plugging the neck and turning the bottle upside down. "Not tonight."

"Why not?"

"Hey," I say loudly in his face, taking the side of his head with one hand. "Shut. Up."

I take a slow sip of beer to make it last, and then I leave him.

I drift from room to room, letting people find me and greet me and hug me, but waiting to find and greet and hug someone myself. Several prospects present themselves, but I calmly set them aside. Stacy finds me and proposes we finish what we started a couple weeks ago, while others propose new starts.

These parties will never change.

I walk out onto the back deck and into the darkening evening, where the pounding music does not reach. Several whispers of bodies hide in the shadows, eyes closed, lips locked, hands ever moving. My eyes pass over them as I lean against the railing to watch the sky grow black. Winking white dots appear one by one and try to outshine the waxing silver sliver smiling down on the night.

I drain the rest of my Corona and set it on the railing and turn to go back inside. Voices float through the black, and I hear words I quickly regret hearing.

"Eva," the voice whispers to its companion. "Eva, c'mon. Let's go inside. Upstairs."

Hurried. Hushed.

"No, c'mon," comes the insistent reply. "This is enough. Let's not complicate things."

Rushed kisses and shifting bodies.

I stand rigid against the railing, turned from the voices, listening. Hating that I'm listening. I tear myself from the railing and move swiftly toward the door before I hear any more, just as the two shadows stand up and I bump directly into Eva.

I expect her to look flustered, guilty, embarrassed — anything but pleased like she does.

"Hey."

"Hey," I mumble.

"Caesar," Brad says, slapping my hand in greeting. By the look on his face, however, it seems the last thing he wants to do is stand here and exchange pleasantries with me while he could be upstairs getting it on with Eva.

Understandably.

"Alarsky. Hey. I . . . gotta go," I say quickly, disappearing into the house.

She doesn't follow.

I drift into the basement and find the smoke down there even thicker, the music even louder. I watch as five kids stuff themselves in a closet with a huge-ass bong while a sixth bangs desperately on the door to try and get in. A guy I recognize from my bio class tries to scale the cold cement wall in order to open the window and let some of the smoke out.

"Caesar!" a voice rings out from somewhere behind the smoke.

I see Dan waving at me from the corner, blunt in hand.

"Hey, man," I say, nodding to him as I walk over.

I sit down next to him and he introduces me to the girl he's with.

"Caesar, I'd like you to meet Jenna," he says as he passes the blunt to her. "Jenna, this is my boy Caesar."

She takes a hit and giggles, stares wide-eyed at me and giggles again. Jesus, I'd recognize that awed look anywhere. It's Kelly's friend Jenna.

"We've met," I say to both of them. "Dan, what the hell are you doing hanging out with her? She's jailbait."

"What are you talking about?" Dan says laughingly as she takes another hit. "She's a sophomore."

"She's in eighth grade."

Dan laughs again and shakes his head, my words not sinking in.

"How much did you give her?" I say to him, taking the blunt and finishing it just to get it away from Jenna.

"This is our third," she says, giggling like an idiot.

Dan has a grin of idiocy to match hers.

"Thirteen, man. *Thirteen!*" I say, trying to make him hear me.

But instead he reaches into his pocket to roll another and I give up. He offers me the first hit, but I shake my head no as I stand up and walk away from the both of them.

"Heyyy," a silky voice greets me from behind.

After I turn around, Sam dances up close to me and kisses me on the cheek.

"Sam."

I don't know what else to say. Her miniskirt shows off her killer ass, and her hair pulled up leaves so much room for my lips on her neck. A sparkle in her light eyes tells me she's not at her most sober of moments, and all I can think about is taking advantage of the girl who snubbed me.

"What are you drinking?" I shout to her over the music as she runs her hand up my bare arm.

"Rum and something," she answers, eyes closed now, a smile on her lips.

"Do you want something new?" I ask, backing toward the stairs.

"Rum and something," she repeats in a murmur, not letting me leave.

I pull gently away from her. "I'll be right back," I say, starting up the stairs. "I'm getting you another drink."

As I step into the crowded hallway in front of the basement door, I try my hardest to push out images of Brad and Eva whispering in the dark with images of me and Sam making out in a bed. But as I turn the corner, suddenly the only image that manages to grab my attention is that of Jake and Kelly sitting together in a corner of the room, right by the drinks.

Holy shit.

CHAPTER 18

"What the FUCK are you doing?" I roar at Jake as I approach the corner.

"John!" Kelly exclaims with a smile when she sees me at her side.

"I'm gonna tear your lungs out!" I spit at Jake. "What the hell are you doing with my little sister?"

"Whoaaaaa," Jake says, standing up and putting up his arms in defense. "Whoa whoa whoa whoaaaaaa. I'm not doing anything with her. Kelly here and I were just having ourselves a little chat."

"Kelly, what the hell are you doing here?" I demand.

"Here? I don't know," she says, still smiling. "But wanna hear a joke?" She chokes with uncontrollable laughter. "So there's two guys sitting in a bar —"

"Fuck you, Jake," I say in a deadly voice, pointing an accusing finger in his direction. "How much did she fucking have?"

"I . . . uhh . . . I don't know," he says. "But, dude, really, listen." He gestures with his hands. "The joke. It's really. Fuckin'. FUNNY."

I shove him in the shoulder. Hard.

"What the hell's the matter with you?!" Kelly says.

"Hey, hey, hey, hey," Jake says, the same stupid smile on his face as on hers. "Liiiighten up, Caesar! Just tryin' to have a good time here."

"With my thirteen-year-old sister?! What the fuck, Jake!" And then, to the guy making the drinks, "She's thirteen! Thirteen! What are you, fucking brain-dead?! What's wrong with everyone at this damn party!"

I can't stop shouting and I want to hit everything and everyone in sight. I can feel my fury flood quickly from my brain to my fists. If Jake were anybody else, I would hit him without hesitation.

"How stupid are you?" I shout at him over the music. "Kelly, what the hell are you doing here?"

"Joooooooohnnnnnn," she says in a high-pitched voice. "What's wrong? Just let me have a good time." She smiles.

"No. More. Drinking," I say to her slowly and loudly, hoping she will understand a little. "We're going home. Now."

"Awwwww, c'monnnnn. One more," she says through a giggle.

Before I can stop her, she downs her drink in one gulp and motions for another.

"NO," I growl at the guy mixing the drinks. "Did you hear me? She's thirteen. STOP SERVING HER."

The guy shrugs. "Hey, man, whatever. This girl can have all she wants, as long as this guy keeps ordering 'em," he says, gesturing to Jake.

I turn to Jake again. "Fuck. You. Jake." I move to lead Kelly out of the room. "C'mon, Kelly, we're going home. This party blows anyway."

"Nuh-uhhhh," she whines. "This party is cool. So . . . cool . . ." She closes her eyes and leans back on her stool and almost falls off.

Jake moves to catch her, but the sight of him touching her just makes me want to kill him again.

"Listen to me," I say close to her ear. "If you want to be fucking cool, I'll take you to a better party. This one sucks. So let's go home."

"You will?" she says with a slur.

Fucking hell no!

"Yeah."

She tries to stand up and stumbles against the stool. She fumbles for something to grip and steady herself with, but she just stumbles again.

"Whoaaa," she mumbles, her smile fading. "I'm so . . ." She puts her hand to her head and moans quietly. "My . . ."

"Gimme a glass of water," I say to the guy with all the drinks.

I lean Kelly against me and give her the glass.

"Drink."

I look around as she drinks it slowly. Eva is nowhere in sight. Probably upstairs screwing that idiot Alarsky. So fuck her if she needs a ride home and I'm not here to bail her out.

"If you see Eva," I say to Jake, "tell her I went home, so she should find another ride."

"Eva?" Jake shouts over the music, not without an edge in his drunken voice. "Why would she get a ride with you? You don't even like her."

Kelly slumps against my side, eyes still closed, and fumbles to put the glass down on a nonexistent table. I take it from her, put it down, and turn to Jake.

"Now's not the time, okay?"

I put my arm around Kelly to steady her and lead her to the doorway of the room.

"It's never the time with you," Jake says into his drink.

I wheel around. "Don't you think you've done enough tonight?" I shout into his face. "Do you really want to fight with me now?"

"Oh no, that would be horrible!" he says mockingly. "The almighty Caesar! All bow before the fucking king. Nobody ever wants to challenge *him*. All hail Caesar," he spits, bitter and red-faced. "He always gets what he wants."

"Jake," I say low and cold. "Not. Now."

He points an accusing finger very near my face and stumbles a little. Slurring, he says, "Well, fuck you, man. Fuck you. Why her? Why Eva? You can have anyone you want; why did you have to pick her? We both know why: because you can't have her." He pauses to slowly take another swig. "Fuck you, John Miller. Fuck that."

"John," Kelly says faintly from my side.

And then she doubles over, lurches, and there's puke all over Danielle's white carpet.

Fuck.

"I hope she breaks you," Jake says forcefully. He looks me right in the eye when he says it.

My best friend is yelling insults at me, my little sister is wasted, the girl I came with is fucking someone else, and there's goddamn speckles of puke on my shoes.

I think it's time to go home.

Kelly spits the last of it out onto the floor, and I help her to her feet.

With one arm around her and the other hand to hold her arm, I lead Kelly to the front of the house. As we approach the front door, Eva and Brad appear from out of nowhere.

"John," Eva says when she sees me.

Brad gestures to Kelly. "Is that . . . ?"

"Your sister?" Eva says.

I grit my teeth. "Yeah."

"Honey, are you okay?" Eva speaks to Kelly's closed eyes. She tucks Kelly's dirty-blond hair behind one ear.

Okay. Great. I pull my sister past her toward the door.

"John, wait, are you leaving?" Eva says to my back.

"Yeah. So you can go home with Alarsky if you want."

"What? No, I'm going with you."

"I have to take Kelly home. I can't drop you off. Stay here."

"John. I'm going with you."

"I don't have time to argue."

Eva kisses a lonely-looking Brad and follows me and Kelly out the door.

When we finally find my car, Kelly climbs into the backseat and collapses onto her back. Eva climbs in after her and helps her to lie down so that her head is in Eva's lap. I jump in the driver's side and speed off into the night toward home.

"So . . . fast," Kelly manages in a feeble whisper.

"If you're going to hurl again, it's going to be in the comfort of our own home. Not in the comfort of my fucking car."

"Way to be a supportive brother," Eva says sarcastically.

"You have no idea what it's like to be a supportive brother," I snap.

"Or what it's like to have one."

"Faaaast," Kelly groans to Eva.

"We're almost home," Eva says to her. "Almost home."

"I drank too fast" comes a soft mumble.

"How many drinks did you have?" Eva asks gently.

"Four. Five. Six."

"Jake," I growl low to myself.

After a moment, Eva says, "She's asleep."

"Thank God."

"What happened?" she asks. "Did you know she was going to be there?"

"Hell no! You think I would have let her go?"

"How could you stop her?"

"Yell at her."

"Are you okay? Are you mad?"

Are you kidding?

"I'm seething."

"Sorry your night was ruined."

That's not the only thing that ruined it.

"Whatever."

We pull up into my garage and I notice that the third car space is filled by a car I don't usually see at this time of night:

My dad's.

"Fuck."

"What?" Eva says, helping Kelly out of the backseat.

"My dad's home."

"Fuck."

"What are we going to do?"

Kelly murmurs in her sleep and nods into Eva's arm.

We sit for a moment, hoping for a stroke or two of genius.

"Umm . . . okay, listen. I'll distract your dad. Pretend to be one of those girls all broken up over you or something. And I'll say I'm looking for you. And then . . . you slip through from the garage and take Kelly upstairs."

"He'll say I'm not home and send you away. And you'll have nowhere to go."

"So then you walk out like you've been home the whole time."

"He'll know."

"Do you have any better ideas?"

"No." I consider it for a moment. "Fine."

I take Kelly into my arms as Eva walks to the front of the house. When I hear my dad get to the front door, I open the garage door quietly and slip inside. Making sure I can still hear my dad at the front door, I carry Kelly up the back set of stairs and lay her on the cold tile of the bathroom floor. I walk to the edge of the hallway to listen for Eva's voice.

"Well," she says, sounding like she's about to cry, "do you know what time he'll be home?"

"I'm sorry, I have no idea."

I can hear the discomfort in my dad's voice.

"Can you . . . can you tell him to call Monica?" she asks tearfully. "It's really important, Mr. Miller. Please."

"Of course. I'll let him know."

"He said he'd be home," she goes on. "He said he'd be waiting for me."

"Dad!" I call from the top of the stairs. "Is someone here?"

"John? What are you doing home? I didn't hear you come in," he calls back. "I'm sorry — Monica, was it? He must have just come home."

"Caesar!" Eva cries in a strange voice. "Thank God you're here!"

I walk downstairs and into the foyer where my dad is standing with the front door open.

"Hey. Mon . . . ica."

Eva follows me upstairs as my dad walks back into the living room to the illuminated TV.

"That was quite a performance," I joke quietly.

She laughs. "You were listening? God, you must hang out with some really fucked-up girls for your dad to have bought that."

"You have no idea."

We walk into the bathroom where Kelly is still passed out on the floor.

"Get her some water," Eva says to me. "And some toast. I'll stay with her."

I return five minutes later from the kitchen with a glass of water and some nuts.

"It's the best I could do," I say to Eva, who is now sitting on the floor with Kelly slumped against her.

"Hey, Kelly, hey," Eva says softly to my sister as she shakes her gently. "Wake up."

Kelly groans a little and slips slowly back into consciousness. Eva leans the glass to her lips and tips it into her mouth.

"Blurry," escapes from Kelly's lips, and the next thing I know, she's got her face in the toilet, and the sights and sounds of nausea are coming from somewhere in the back of her throat.

Eva doesn't seem even a little disgusted.

"Does this happen every time she drinks?"

"How should I know? I didn't even know she drank. Not like this."

Kelly takes a breather but starts up again in no time.

"Did you eat anything before you went to the party?" Eva asks Kelly.

Halfway in the toilet, she shakes her head no.

"Eeesh," Eva says.

I sit down next to her and we lean against the glass doors of the shower.

"I can't tell you how glad I am that we're spending all this quality time together," she says with a smirk.

"Ditto. Although why can't we go bowling like normal people?"

"'Cause that would be half the puke and twice the fun. And what sense does that make?"

"You okay?" I say to Kelly when at last her grip on the sides of the bowl relaxes.

She nods, eyes drooping.

"Can you stand up?"

She nods, but I get up to let her lean on me just in case. I lead her to the sink.

"Rinse out your mouth and I'll help you get in bed."

She does and I do.

I lead her into her dark room across the hall and pull back the covers. Eva follows and helps her take off her shoes. Then we leave her, making sure she's sleeping on her side. I close the door, and Eva and I stand in the hallway.

"Still mad?" she says.

"Maybe."

She looks me right in the eyes. "Now what?"

I match her look. "I don't know."

"Do you know what time it is?"

"No. Do you care?"

"No."

I pause for a moment.

"I think I'm still mad."

I walk into my room and she follows. I flip on the light, gesture to the chair, and stretch out on my bed. She sits down and stares at the blank walls and empty spaces in between, and silence falls in the air. She spins absently in the swiveling armchair and I lie still and waiting.

"It'll be all right," she says into the silence.

"What will?"

"Things. With Kelly. Other things. All things."

"Maybe."

"Everyone needs someone to tell them that things will be all right. I'll be that someone for you."

I don't know what to say to that, except, "You're already someone."

This time, I'm the one who surprises her.

"All right," she says.

And for the first time tonight, I believe it will be.

CHAPTER 19

Saturday morning is hellish. I jerk awake and out of bed, my head a flood of names and faces, but only one really registers. I stumble into Kelly's room.

Still asleep.

I stand over her sleeping form, waiting for her to wake up. If I were her, I'd stay asleep. The hangover will be enough, but coupled with my wrath, it could be the worst morning of her life.

I leave her room and return ten minutes later with a glass of water and proper breakfast. I set both on her nightstand and sit down in the gray armchair next to her desk to wait. My eyes close slowly and Kelly's room droops out of sight.

I fall out of sleep again when I hear Kelly begin to stir.

"Kelly," I whisper.

She rolls over and groans loudly.

"Kelly, wake up."

She lies still for a moment, eyes closed, then stuffs her head under the pillow and moans louder into it.

"Suck it up."

"UUUGGGGGGHHHHHH" is the muffled answer.

"C'mon."

"*MMMMPPPPHHHHHHH.*"

"Come ON."

I pull the pillow off her head. She doesn't move.

"Kelly, wake up. You need to eat something."

I nudge her lump of a body.

Still nothing.

Nudge harder.

"UUUUUUUNNNNHHHH."

Harder.

Harder.

Harder.

She pulls herself up slowly and then collapses again onto her face.

God, she's impossible.

Finally, after some more forceful prodding on my part, she does manage to pull herself awake and slump against the top of her bed in a sort of daze. Her eyebrows furrowed in pain, she tries to grasp for sleep to release her from the hurt. She makes a sound of ache and I hand her the water.

"Fucking. Hell," she says to herself, taking a gulp.

"Yeah."

She squints against the morning light.

"Can you . . . ?"

"Yeah."

I pull down the blinds and sit on the edge of her bed. I gesture to the plate of eggs and toast on her nightstand, and she reaches for it gratefully.

"Damn. Thanks."

"Yeah."

She grits her teeth, and her face contorts in pain as she chews slowly. I grab Tylenol for her from downstairs and she swallows two after her last bite of toast. She sighs against the top of her bed and I sit back down in her chair and wheel it to the side of the bed.

"Feel any better?" I ask gently.

"Yeah, a little. Thanks so much."

"Mm-hm. Yeah. *Fuck you.*"

"What?"

"Now that you're good and comfortable, I get to yell. What the FUCK were you doing at Danielle's house?"

"John, aw, c'mon, please, not now. Please," she begs through the pounding in her head.

"Yes, now. Fucking now. What the hell is wrong with you, Kelly? How did you even get to the party?"

She closes her eyes in frustration, trying to piece the memories together.

"Jenna asked me if I wanted to go."

"Well, what the hell was she doing there?"

"She lives there!"

Jenna Tyler. Danielle's little sister.

FUCK. I should have known.

"I can't believe you thought you could go."

"Why couldn't I?" she says with indignation.

"Because something could happen."

"What could happen?"

"SOMETHING DID HAPPEN!" I yell into her face. "ARE YOU STUPID?"

"What happened? I had a good time? Yeah, that's fucking terrible."

"DO YOU NOT SEE WHAT I SEE?" I motion to her lying in bed.

She says nothing, but takes another gulp of water.

"You think you're so cool, huh," I say to her. "Kids are always so obsessed with being cool. Don't be stupid. You're not cool."

"What's wrong with wanting to have fun?"

"Nothing, until you're stupid about it."

"Thanks, Perfect Brother Who Never Makes Mistakes."

"Oh, fuck you."

"Yeah, fuck you, too."

"I saved your ass."

"Saved me from WHAT? From having a good time?"

She struggles against the pounding.

"Having fun puking up a storm in somebody else's house? Having fun being barely able to walk? WHOO-HOO, IT'S A BLAST!" And I'm on a roll. "You think you would have gotten home last night if it hadn't been for me? You think Jenna would have helped you? You think she was sober enough to give a shit about you? You think she was gonna take a break from being 'cool' to fucking care? I saved your ass."

"Bullshit."

"Who else was gonna help you?!"

"What about JAKE? He was helping me! Jake — yeah, that's right, that's what I said. Jake, your best friend! Jake!" she starts to scream madly.

"What the fuck are you talking about? You're so naïve. Jake wasn't helping you; he was fucking getting the drinks for you!"

"What the fuck are YOU talking about? He only got me one!"

"How is that helping you?"

"He said I could only have one. And then we were just talk-ing! JUST TALKING! He told me not to drink too much or too quickly and . . . and he was HELPING!"

"You said you had six drinks!"

"Well . . ." She hesitates. "I did. But it wasn't his fault! He didn't know I'd already been drinking!"

"Kelly. What the FUCK did you do?"

"God, John, just . . ." She winces again from the pounding. "Just leave me alone."

"No. I'm not leaving you alone."

"What do you want?!" she shouts.

"I don't know!" I shout back.

"God, what's your problem?" She sighs after a while, more to herself than to me.

I answer anyway.

"You. You're my problem. Where do you get off drinking all of a sudden? Are all your friends doing it? Is it the thing to do?"

"Where do you get off giving me a peer-pressure bullshit lecture? Where would you be if you didn't give into your own image and all that bullshit?" she says fiercely.

"You have no idea what you're talking about. I don't do any-thing that I don't want to do."

"What makes you think that I didn't want to do it?" she fires back.

"Why *would* you?"

"Because it's FUN! Is that so wrong?"

"Why is it fun?" I ask accusingly.

"I don't know — why don't you tell me? You're the one who gets drunk so much."

193

"I don't get drunk that much," I inform her.

"You're always drinking," she counters.

"Always drinking and always getting drunk are two different things. Don't act like you know what you're talking about."

"Then teach me."

"What?"

"Teach me about that stuff! About drinking, about drugs: Tell me how to do things right. You're my older brother!"

"Tell you how to do things right? Don't drink. Don't do drugs. You'll be fine."

"Ugh. Fine. Whatever. Don't tell me. But someone else is going to tell me all about drinking, and what if they're wrong? What if they tell me the wrong shit and then I get fucked?"

"Then that's your problem. Don't ask. Don't believe them. And then you won't have a problem."

"You're not helping."

"I'm not trying to help; I'm trying to yell."

"Why can't you accept the fact that I'm growing up?"

"You're thirteen. That's hardly growing up."

"I'll be in high school next year," she argues.

"Congratulations."

"Things change!"

"Yeah, they fucking do. So what? You think that you're going to high school, so you should throw yourself into drinking and drugs and sex?"

"Isn't that what *you* did?"

"We're going in circles."

She sighs.

"Can't you just wait till you're a little older?" I ask. It's almost like I'm pleading.

"I will never be old enough to you. I will always be younger, and that's too young."

"Why are you so obsessed with growing up? Can't you just be a kid?"

"Being a kid sucks."

"Enjoy it."

"Oh, get over yourself. You're only four years older than me."

"A lot happens in four years."

"Yeah, perfectly nice people turn into *you*," she says with disgust.

"I'd be insulted, except that I was never a perfectly nice person."

"Fuck you."

"Likewise."

"So what do you want?"

"For you to stop."

"Funny, that's what I want, too."

"You want me to, what, stop caring? Stop looking out for you? Stop saving your ass?"

"Stop giving me a hard time."

"Stop drinking, and I will."

"*You* stop drinking, and *I* will."

"No. That's not how this works."

"Don't you get it, John? You drink, so I drink. You screw up, so I do, too!"

WHAM.

I stare at her while she holds her head and downs the rest of the water.

Finally I shake my head and say, "Dammit, Kelly, I should have just left you there last night. Teach you a lesson."

195

"Good, then LEAVE ME ALONE!" she screams all of a sudden. "Just. Leave. Me. Alone!"

"You know what? Fine. I will leave you. Good luck explaining your hangover to Dad."

I stalk out of her room and back into mine, punching the door closed.

From the floor, Eva wakes with a start and sees me standing, fists clenched and angry.

"What's wrong?" she asks sleepily.

"Forget it," I grumble.

"You talked to her?"

"Yeah."

"Didn't go well?"

"Yeah."

"It'll be all right."

I don't answer. I sit down next to her on the sheets I had spread out for her on the floor. She stretches her back and winces.

I repress my fury.

"Damn, I'm so sore."

"You're the one who insisted on the floor."

"I wasn't about to kick you out of your own bed."

I shrug.

"What time is it," she mumbles to herself as she glances at my alarm clock.

10:13.

"What are you doing today?" she asks as she brushes her hands through her mussed hair.

I shrug. "Nothing except work tonight. You?"

"Same."

I try to keep the conversation simple. But Eva cuts right through the bullshit. She takes a long, hard look at me and asks, "You okay? Still mad?"

I stare stonily to the side. I should have known nothing can ever be simple with her.

"Just forget it," I say. "Let's talk about something else."

"Okay."

"What happened with Brad?" I ask slyly.

"I didn't tell you last night and I'm not going to tell you this morning, either."

"I didn't ask you last night."

"Yeah, you did. As you were falling asleep."

"That doesn't count. I can't be held accountable for the things I say when I'm that tired."

"Great. I'm still not telling you."

"Fuck you."

"That's what you said last night, too."

"Good. At least I'm consistent."

She laughs.

"Wanna go to the gazebo?" I ask.

"Now?"

"Yeah. Unless you want me to drive you home."

"No, let's go."

"Cool."

"I gotta get home before we go to work, though. I have to shower," she says.

"Fair enough. I can't hang out with you when you smell anyway. Really, it's unbearable."

"Dude, I know."

"You should have that checked out."

"The doctors say it's a lost cause. I'm destined to walk the earth a smelly disgrace. Forever."

"Damn. That's a bit harsh."

"God sucks."

"Mmm."

Beat.

"You're Christian, right?" she asks.

"Yeah, more or less. Why?"

"So you believe in God."

Wait, what the hell? Couldn't we talk some more about how you smell? Do we really have to talk about God before noon? How the hell did we get *here*? I swear, with this girl you need a map.

But some part of me must want to follow her, since I say, "Yeah. Do you?"

"Not really."

"Why not?"

She shrugs. "I don't like thinking that I'm not in control of my life. And I don't like giving God credit for things I did or blaming God for problems that are my fault. Plus, look at how much warfare He causes. Not worth it. People are so stupid about religion."

"It's just because they believe it so strongly."

"Do you?"

"Not really."

"Why not?"

I shrug. "I dunno. It's not important to me."

"Why not?"

198

"I dunno."

"But you believe in Him. Her. It."

This whole conversation is going much further than I thought it would. "Yeah," I say.

"You don't sound sure."

"I'm not."

"Okay. That's fair."

"Religion . . . it's not really something I think about."

"We don't have to talk about it if you don't want."

"No, it's not really that I mind; it's just that I don't know how I feel exactly. I never think about it."

"Ever?"

"Not really. I mean, right after my mom died, my dad started going to church a lot more. And it seemed like everyone was always talking about God this and God that. But after a while, things became normal again. I don't really think about it. Him."

"Because it's not important to you."

"Right."

Right? Is it? I really never paid attention to the fact that I never paid attention.

"But is it not important to you because you never think or talk about it? Or do you not think or talk about it because it's not important to you?"

"I don't know. I guess it could be important to me. If I was raised religious or if all my friends were really religious."

I wonder again why she cares so much. Why she cares about what I care about. Why I suddenly want to care about everything. Just so she cares.

I add, "Neither of my parents cared or care very much about it, I don't think."

"I see."

"What about your parents?"

"They're both Buddhist."

This doesn't surprise me much. "Are you Buddhist, too?" I ask.

"I believe in some of it. It's more of a philosophy than an actual religion."

"I don't really know what that means."

"Me, neither. It's just what they tell me."

Beat.

"Wait . . . are your parents white?"

It sounds stupid as soon as I say it. But she laughs anyway.

"My dad is. He's French. My mom's Vietnamese."

"Cool. I'm white and boring."

She laughs.

"Generic," I continue. "The usual Irish-British-Western European mix."

She nods.

"So tell me," she begins, "doesn't religion ever come up with your friends?"

I try to picture it, but I can't. "For fuck's sake," I tell Eva, "we don't exactly sit around and ponder the meaning of life; we just don't talk about shit like that."

"Jake's your best friend, right?"

I'm not sure at the moment.

But I say, "Yeah, why?"

"What religion is he?"

"Christian."

"What sect?"

"I don't know."

"Does he go to church?"

"Yeah."

"Is he religious?"

"I don't know. No."

"Why does he go to church?"

"What the hell is this? Jesus. I dunno, because his parents make him?"

"Do you think you know your friends well?" she continues.

"Why?"

She looks thoughtful for a moment.

"What do you talk about with your friends?"

"What?"

"When you sit around, what do you do? What do you talk about?"

"We just . . ." I shrug. "We don't. We just . . . are."

"But you hang out."

"Right."

"What do you do?" she asks again.

I'm not sure I would have had her stay over last night if I knew this was going to be the morning after.

"We . . . we drive," I answer. "We eat. We drink. I don't know!"

"Why do you do the things you do?"

"Why do you ask so many questions?" I counter.

"I'm just . . ." She shrugs. "Just wondering. So Jake's your best friend?"

"Right."

"Who's your best girl friend?"

201

"My best girl friend? Umm . . ."

The faces of all my girl friends flash through my head and I try hard to think of the one I'm closest with.

"Well, how would you define that? Like . . . the girl I talk to the most? The girl I sleep with the most? The girl I hang out with the most? The girl I've known the longest?"

"It should be your standard, not mine. It's your best friend."

I think about it, then shrug. "I don't have one."

"Well, who do you like the most out of all your girl friends?"

"I dunno. I like them all the same, I guess."

"There's not one you like having conversations with?"

"Conversations?"

"Yeah."

"Umm . . ."

Who's the last girl I had a conversation with? Eva? Before that? Her again. Before that? Sam? That conversation didn't go too well, considering I was just trying to get her naked. Maybe I don't have conversations with girls.

"You don't have conversations with girls?"

"Of course I do."

"Well, then, who do you like talking to the most?"

"You."

I said it.

She smiles. "Besides me."

"Besides you?"

Who is there besides you?

"I don't know."

Pick a name. Any name.

"I don't . . ." I trail off.

She gives me an expectant look.

202

"I don't . . ." I shrug, grasping for my words. ". . . like to talk."

For a moment, she looks deep in thought, not saying anything.

Then, "Let's go."

"What?"

"Go. Let's go. The gazebo."

"Oh."

"You still want to?"

"Yeah . . . but . . ."

She just stares at me.

"Don't worry," she reassures me. "Don't worry that you've told me all your deepest, darkest secrets. We can still pretend you're shallow."

She smiles and I stare.

"So." She looks at me expectantly. "You ready, pretty boy?"

With you, I'll never be sure.

But I say, "Yeah. Let's get outta here."

CHAPTER 20

"Here we are again," she says as we pull into the bushes near the gazebo.

"What is it about this goddamn place?" I mutter. "Can't fucking stay away."

She laughs. "I know what you mean."

We both get out of the car and walk into the clearing and toward the water's edge.

"Let's just never leave," I say. "Let's just stay here forever and never go back. We won't have to deal with any bullshit the world gives us. Then it'll be all right."

She smiles sadly and doesn't answer for a moment.

"But what will we do for food?" she finally asks.

I sigh and sit down on the dock.

"Don't lie to yourself," she says, sitting next to me. "If you're upset, let's talk about it."

"Talk about it?"

"Yeah," she says with a small laugh. "I know you're a robot devoid of human emotion, but it wouldn't kill you to try."

"It might," I say.

"It won't."

I shrug. "What do you want me to say?"

"What do you want to say?"

I shrug again. "I dunno."

She stares down at our reflection on the surface of the lake and moves her toe in small circles on the water. The wind washes in and out through the grass and across our tired faces. The pale gray sky stirs and I stare out at the other side of the lake.

We don't say a word.

As we sit there in the late morning gray, I suddenly feel very aware of Eva sitting next to me. Her female heat radiates from her skin, and I swear I can smell a faint scent of I-don't-know-what from her hair. My body calls to me and I want to touch her, want to feel the warmth of her skin against mine, her against me.

But my body won't move. I can't tell if it's my brain or my balls stopping me, but at this point there's hardly a difference. In any event, my hand only drifts slightly in Eva's direction and doesn't leave its place at my side.

What's wrong with me?

I don't understand why I want to touch her so badly or why I can't, and as the minutes pass, the feeling only gets worse. I urge myself to say something or do something quick. Anything.

But what?

"Hey," I say to the air.

"What?"

"I don't know."

There's a pause, and then she laughs. It's not a ha-ha laugh. It's an Eva laugh. It laughs at everyone, at the absurdity of *everything*. Out of the corner of my eye, I watch her toe stop moving around in the water. She pulls her legs to her chest and wraps both arms around her knees. Every single movement makes me feel that familiar ache. And yet every part of my body (well, *almost* every part) tells me to stay put.

"What are you laughing at?" I say. "What?"

"We're being stupid."

Stupid?

We?

"We're being stupid," she says again. "We're being heavy and serious and . . . and we're being stupid."

We?

"What do you mean?"

She shrugs and looks away to her right.

"Wanna go swimming?" she says suddenly, shooting me a wink and a smile.

"Are you kidding? The water's, like, fifty fucking degrees."

"So?"

"So . . . c'mon, what are you, suicidal?"

"Fine. No swimming. But let's *do* something."

"Like what?"

"Like, God, I don't know. Something stupid."

"I thought we were already being stupid."

"Okay, yeah, but we might as well *do* something stupid if we're going to *be* stupid."

"Should we get drunk?"

She looks at me and shakes her head.

"C'mon, John. You can do better than that. This isn't a stupid let's-go-puke-off-a-bridge bonding experience. If we're going to be stupid, we're going to do it right."

Beat.

"So . . . you wanna go puke off a bridge?" I ask.

"Yeah. Let's go."

We leave the lake and start walking along Route 6.

"You know we have no drinks, right?" I ask her as we walk.

"What?" she says. "What the fuck is the point of puking off a bridge onto lots of unsuspecting little cars if you're not at least a little dizzy when you do it?"

"Oh, I, uh, we can turn . . ." I gesture behind us when I look at her face and realize she's kidding.

She smiles at me and points as the bridge comes into view.

"That it?"

"Yeah."

"That's not a fucking bridge."

"What are you talking about? Of course it is."

"A *bridge* is made up of precariously crisscrossing metal and stretches across water. *That* is a dinky piece of shit made of cement that overlooks more highway. I don't know what the fuck *that* is, but it's not a bridge."

I stare at her. "You talk a lot of shit. C'mon."

I lead her up the hill to the middle of the overpass and we lean against the side that looks over the north end of Route 84.

"This view sucks," Eva says after a moment.

We watch as the flashes of dark colors pass under us on their way out of town. They whiz by in short bursts of sound.

"You first."

She gestures to the side of the bridge.

"What?"

"Well?"

"How do you expect me to throw up? I didn't even eat break-fast," I say.

"Hmm. That could be a problem."

"Aren't there other ways of being stupid?" I venture. It actually takes courage for me to do it.

"Yes."

"Can't we do them instead?"

"No."

"Why not?"

"Because I said so, all right?"

"You're impossible."

"So are you."

"Me? What?"

"You are!"

"At least I'm not a temperamental, bossy, self-righteous snob."

"At least I'm not an arrogant, apathetic, A-crowd ASSHOLE!"

"Was that really necessary?"

"I was on a roll."

"You make me laugh."

"Likewise."

"Should we proceed to the upchuck, then?"

"Maybe breakfast first."

"But we just got here. Now we're going to turn around?"

"Not yet."

"Good."

"We could *spit* on the cars instead. I always wanted to do that. Living in New York, I never really got the chance."

"So this is your moment to compensate for your deprived childhood?"

"Something like that. Plus, what else are we going to do?"

"Good point."

We stand side by side, leaning forward against the wall, still staring down at the cars as they pass us by. Neither of us makes a move to puke, eat, spit, do any of the things we say we will. We just stand and we watch.

Somehow things seem better that way.

After twenty more minutes of silent car watching, we decide to head back to the lake to get my car and go for some breakfast.

As we're walking back, Eva says, "John."

"Hm?"

"Did you have a fight with Kelly?"

"Maybe."

"Are you sure you don't want to talk about it?"

"What's your obsession with talking all the time? No, I do not want to talk about it. No, I do not want to talk. No. No. No talking."

"Are you sure?"

"No."

"Should we —"

"Talk about it?"

She doesn't answer.

I sigh and relent.

"Yes, we got into a fight. Yes, I'm still a little upset. Yes, I am confused. Yes. Yes, I want to talk about it."

She waits for me to say something else.

"She won't listen to me. I don't want her drinking. She's just a kid."

"If you could go back to when you were in middle school and take back all the drinking and shit, would you?"

209

"I dunno. Probably not."

"If you maintain that what you did was okay and you don't regret it, then how can you expect her to have a strong opinion against it?"

"I don't regret anything."

"Bullshit."

"I don't."

"That's just what people say when they don't want to feel sorry for themselves. It's not what they mean. Everybody has regrets."

There's something, I dunno, *personal* about the way she says it.

"Why?" I ask her.

"Because people are stupid. They make mistakes. And they know that."

"Doesn't mean they have to regret them."

We walk the rest of the way in silence, feet scuffing gently across the late-morning pavement in steady rhythm. We get back to my car and drive to the diner, checking first to make sure Molly's not on shift.

"Does your dad care that I spent the night?" Eva asks while we are waiting for our food.

"He doesn't know."

"Would he care?"

"I dunno. Maybe."

"Has he ever caught you with a girl?"

"My dad? No. I don't bring girls to my house."

"Why not?"

"I don't know. It's weird. I just don't. I don't generally have people over."

"Even Jake?"

I shrug. "We don't hang out at my house a lot. We mostly hang at his house."

"Why?"

"I said I don't know."

"Weird."

"Yeah. I've never had girls over so I don't really know how my dad would react."

"How can you . . . if you never have girls . . . ?"

"Parties. Their houses."

"You don't take them to the gazebo? Sweep them off their feet, whisper sweet nothings in their ear, and then fuck their brains out?"

I try to imagine it, but I can't. It just feels wrong. Like having sex in my sister's room or with a teacher watching.

"No," I tell her. "Parties. Their houses. I wouldn't want to go to the gazebo the day after if I knew I'd fucked a girl there the night before."

"Why not?"

"I don't know."

"Because it means something to you?"

"The sex? Hell no."

"The gazebo."

"Oh. Maybe."

Maybe it does mean something to me, but does she have to make me sound like such a pussy?

"Besides," I say, "I don't usually have to sweep girls off their feet."

"Why?"

"Because most of them just want to fuck."

"I find that hard to believe."

"Maybe. Maybe not. It depends on the girl. You'd be surprised how many girls have inner sluts."

"Girls are stupid."

"Sometimes I do have to charm them a little, though. Lie a little."

Why the fuck am I telling *her* my methods?

"Guys are stupid, too."

"Yeah," I say.

"Don't lie to me, okay?"

I can't make any promises.

"I'll try not to."

"You're supposed to say 'okay.'"

"I know."

The waitress (much older than Molly, thank God) brings out two plates of food and slides them on the table. With a smile and a wink at me, she walks away.

I have to stop coming here.

"Did she just wink at you?"

"Yeah."

She laughs. "You're unbelievable."

"I know."

I stick a fork in my eggs and swirl it around on the plate as she spears a bite of her omelet. Our forks scratch against our plates in a sad sort of way.

"It's not my fault, you know."

"What's not?" she asks.

"The fact that I'm wanted."

"It's your fault if you want it, too."

"Can you blame me?"

"Maybe."

"Well, what am I supposed to do?"

"Whatever you want."

"That's what I'm doing."

"Fine, then."

"Fine."

"Do you enjoy yourself? Is it good for you?"

"What, sex?"

"Yeah."

"It's fine."

"Fine? You go through all that trouble for 'fine'?"

"What trouble?"

When have I ever had trouble?

"Seems like there could be trouble."

"Sex isn't troublesome."

"Are you sure?"

"Trust me. I'm an expert."

"You're a bastard."

"I know."

"So then why do you do it?"

I shrug.

"Because I like it. Why *don't* you do it?"

"Who said I don't do it?"

"Do you?"

"Do I do it?"

"Yeah."

"Sometimes."

"Oh. Alarsky."

"I didn't say that."

"You thought it."

"Shut up."

"Okay."

I swallow the last of my eggs and reach for the glass of orange juice.

"Don't say it," she says.

"What?"

"Don't ask."

"Ask what?" I say innocently.

"About him."

"Who?"

"Screw you."

"Alarsky?"

"Screw. You."

"You need to come up with more original comebacks."

"Just get the check."

As I wave down our winking waitress, I can't help but think that despite all the shit from last night, it was worth it just to buy Eva breakfast.

CHAPTER 21

Days slip by and get lost in thick blue sweatshirts and flying orange leaves. I watch the morning unfold as I drive to school in the pale November gray. I pass stretches of dirty white highway and blurs of orange and red and brown. My foot presses steady and smooth on the gas as I fly down the road, a black memory and nothing more.

I turn into school and pull up into an empty spot in the student parking lot. Gathering my books behind me, I slam the door shut and pocket my keys.

And walk.

Into the school, through the lobby, up the stairs, to the locker. I don't speak to anyone all morning, though I can't say I'm disappointed. I haven't spoken to Jake since Danielle's. We find ways to avoid each other, which I make easier by avoiding my friends altogether. I've spent the past two weeks working as much as possible and hanging out with Eva when time permits. I've passed up several opportunities to speak to anyone who might want to raise their voice.

So I just keep on walking.

Away.

I once had a friend who told me Wednesdays are the best day of the week because after Wednesday passes, the school week is already half over. I ponder this as I stare at the clock through history class and count down the minutes until this Wednesday has passed.

"Caesar" comes the familiar sound of agitated administration.

I turn my head and slide only an inch from my slumped position.

Crap.

"Ms. Tenen."

My guidance counselor stands in the doorway of my history class, arms folded, an expectant I've-been-looking-all-over-for-you expression in her eyes.

"I'm sorry to interrupt, Mr. Johnson. Do you mind if I borrow Mr. Miller here for a moment?" she says to my teacher.

Double crap.

"Not at all," my teacher replies with a wry grin.

Asshole.

I pull out of my chair, my body trying desperately to stay glued to the seat I have made myself comfortable in, and walk out of the classroom. I follow Tenen to her office and sit down in the big chair across from her desk, designed to fool students into comfortable submission.

"Caesar," she says in her sweet but stern let-me-guide-you voice.

"Susan," I return with the same patronizing tone.

She grits her teeth in slight and subtle irritation. Then, recovering, she says matter-of-factly, "We had an appointment scheduled two weeks ago."

"What appointment?"

"I scheduled it for . . ." She checks her computer. "The twenty-third. What happened?"

I shrug innocently. "I have no idea. I don't remember any appointment."

"Caesar."

"Susan."

"Ms. Tenen," she corrects me.

"Ms. Tenen," I repeat for her benefit.

She tries again.

"First, how do you like your schedule?"

"I could drop a couple classes."

"Which ones?"

"The first four."

"Caesar, you have to go to class."

"Why's that?" I ask her with mock seriousness.

"Because otherwise you won't graduate."

"Don't I already have enough credits to graduate?"

"You still need to take English."

I shrug. "So I'll switch periods. Can I just drop the first four so I can come in at, like, noon?"

"You're not dropping your morning classes," she says flatly.

"Well, then my teachers can't punish me for falling asleep in class. I'm taking their classes against my will."

"Everybody goes to school against their will!"

"As my guidance counselor, should you really be telling me

that? You wouldn't want me losing faith in the public education system."

God, this is fun.

"Caesar."

"Susan." I raise my eyebrows in challenge.

"*Ms. Tenen.*"

I wink at her.

She heaves an exasperated sigh.

"We need to talk about SATs."

"What about them?"

"You only took them once."

"So?"

"Don't you want to try again to improve your scores?"

"Lemme guess, I'm supposed to say yes."

"That would be nice."

"You said I did fine."

"You did do fine."

"So why do I need to take them again?"

"So you can do better than fine."

"What's the point?"

"To see what you can achieve."

"You mean to get into a better college?"

"That would be nice, too."

I shrug again. "Whatever."

"Well, what *are* your college plans? Applications are due in the winter and you still haven't told me."

Another shrug, just to piss her off. "Dunno."

"Time is running out, sweetie. Your future isn't your future anymore. It's your present."

How many times has she used that one on her students?

"Good, so I plan to live in the present. No use in worrying about the future if it's already here. Can I go?" I start to stand up, but she stops me.

"Caesar, are you even planning to go to college?"

"Can you get me out of it?"

"Caesar . . ." she says warningly.

I sit back down with a sigh and stare at her sullenly. The knocking pendulums on her desk click quietly against each other in steady rhythm.

Click.

Click.

Click.

We stare at each other across her cluttered mahogany desk, my expression defiant and hers determined. Neither without a hint of exasperation.

"What's wrong, Caesar?" she asks with her understanding counselor tone.

"Nothing."

"You can talk to me."

That's okay. Really.

"I'm fine."

Really.

"Everything okay at home?"

I drop the facetious act and snap, "That's none of your business."

"I apologize."

"I'm missing history," I say curtly.

I get up out of my seat and throw her a last look before walking out the door.

"Later, Susie," I call back.

*   *   *

It's around midnight when Eva and I end our delivery shifts and pack things up at Papa John's.

"Okay," she says, tossing her bag into the passenger side of the car. "See ya."

See me? How 'bout now?

"Hey, you wanna do something?" I call to her from outside my car.

"Uhhh . . . no, y'know, I'm not really in the mood."

I walk around my car and stand in front of her open door. "Why not?"

She shrugs. "I dunno. I'm tired."

"C'mon, you can afford to waste some time with me. We can go back to the bridge."

She doesn't seem to hear me. Her body faces me, and her eyes hover near mine, but she seems to only talk through me. "Forget it, John. I just wanna go home and sleep."

It's reasonable, but something about the way she says it doesn't seem right. I can't help but feel like she's not telling me everything. Her empty excuses seem all too familiar.

"You wanna crash at my place?"

"No," she says, as if it's obvious. "I want to go *home* and sleep. What's wrong? You wanna talk or something?"

"No, I just . . ."

Don't want you to go.

She looks at me. "I'll catch you later, John. Call me tomorrow if you want."

" 'Bye."

She pulls the door closed, starts up, and rips out of the parking lot in a matter of seconds. I watch her go and stare after the tail-lights as they disappear into the night. I get in my own car and head home, a knot of disappointment tying and untying nervously in my stomach. It's just Eva. Just Eva.

Eva.

At school, I walk the halls like a zombie, ignoring calls and waves without so much as a nod. Things are starting to feel more and more strangled every day. After lunch, I walk slowly through the halls to pre-calc, and amid the jostling and shoving, someone bumps my elbow in passing. I turn and there's Jake, as startled as I am.

"Hey," he says, trying to keep it casual.

"Hey," I return with the same cool voice, nodding.

He falls into step with me and we say nothing for a moment as we walk to pre-calc together.

"What's goin' on?" he asks when I don't speak first.

"Not much," I answer with a shrug. "You?"

He shrugs in reply.

"Haven't seen you around much," he says carefully.

"Haven't been around much," I explain without explaining.

He nods, staring off to the side as we walk, trying to think of something to say to break the tension.

Then he laughs. "Yo, you missed it. It was awesome; at Dan's this weekend he told us how he got stoned with Danielle's little sister — it was fucking hilari . . . ous . . ." He trails off when he realizes what he has said.

I don't answer.

We walk.

Our strides fall naturally together, and with this subconscious act, things are patched without being patched. Jake and I don't talk about what happened. We don't talk at all. We start to hang out again, here and there when I don't have work, there and here when we don't have practice.

Life goes on, just like that.

But nobody talks.

And nobody cares.

Days slip by into a sort of numb routine, school and practice and work and parties. People don't talk and nobody cares and nothing changes. I still have to drive Kelly around, I still drink too much Corona for my own good, I still don't know what to do with myself. Tenen starts to call my house asking for my dad, but I let the machine deal with her, since no one else wants to.

I see Eva less and less, and when I do see her, it never seems to be enough. I don't know why she starts to avoid me, but I do know I can't stand for it.

"Where have you been recently?" I ask her one night in the parking lot after we help close up. "I feel like we haven't hung out in a while."

"What are you talking about? I see you every day."

"We haven't gone to the gazebo in forever."

"It's almost winter. It's too fucking cold to go to the gazebo."

"We could do something else," I offer.

"Sure, but not tonight, okay?" she says distractedly as she opens her car door.

"Why, what are you doing tonight?" I ask casually.

"I'm busy."

"Try to be more vague," I say jokingly, though even I can feel the edge in my voice.

"Okay," she says, not playing along. "See ya later."

She closes her car door and I watch her drive out of the parking lot and down the road.

Seems I'm doing that a lot these days.

CHAPTER 22

Monday night I lie restless in my bed, studying the details of my white ceiling. The neon in my alarm clock laughs itself red, as the quiet colon grows louder with every blink.

Blink. Blink. Blink. Blink.

Every second, every blink, is another shove, another poke, another jab in my unsettled stomach.

Blink. Blink. Blink.

1:16 already and not a single blink from my own eyes.

I dig in the darkness until my hand comes in contact with the familiar feel of a stiff sweatshirt. I pull it over my head, slide my window open, and duck out into the cool of the night.

I sit down on the rooftop and curl my arms around my legs to protect them from the bitter night frost. I pull my hood over my head and rock back and forth against the cold. I let the night burn me in every place that it can, feel the cold against my skin and the pricking, stabbing sensation that makes me numb. I feel the night snap against me and fall to the ground in icy pieces.

A slow freeze.

It hasn't been very long since school started in September. Only a couple months, and already the wind is changing and I need a haircut. All the things that are supposed to be good suck. All the things that are supposed to suck do. Things are different but the same and I am the same.

But different.

I want to understand it but I don't. I want to know her but I can't. I want to make things right with the people around me, I want to fall asleep with a sense of contentment and wake up with a sense of anticipation, I want I want I want but I won't . . .

Do.

Anything.

I reach back inside my room to pull out my flannel comforter. I wrap the warmth around me.

I just don't know what to do with myself. These sporadic nights of introspection aren't enough, I need something more than that. Something more solid, something more secure. Something that's not me, that's not a constant battle between brains and balls, something, someone, that has more to offer me than just me.

Because I'm not enough.

The next day has that feel of a discontent Tuesday waiting to be made right. After work, I find Eva and tell her to get in my car.

She talks to me without talking to me.

"Not today, John. I have some stuff to do."

This time, the rejection is clear. And it's not okay.

" 'Some stuff'? Eva, you have 'some stuff to do' every goddamn day. What's with you lately?"

225

She looks surprised, not by what I said but that I actually said it. "I'm just busy today. Why are you getting upset?"

"I'm not upset," I say automatically, wanting it to be true. "Can you just, can we just . . . can you just get in my car?"

She stares at me. "But I'm *busy*," she repeats.

"Is it more important than talking to me?" I say boldly.

"Well . . ."

She hesitates as a look of guilt crosses her features. We stand facing each other in the dark parking lot of Papa John's Pizza, Eva disoriented and me despairing.

"I think I might need you," I blurt out in desperation.

Before it sinks in, I can feel the weight of the words I've been waiting to say all this time.

Oh God. What have I done?

"You . . . what? What are you talking about?" Eva says, seeming to finally realize that I'm there.

The way she says it makes me want to grab the words right out of the air and stuff them back in my mouth, where they belong.

"I don't know."

My heart pounds in my ears and I can't look at her.

"John . . ."

"Yeah."

"C'mere."

She moves toward me and takes my hand, putting two fingers over the inside of my wrist. She leans into me, her face right up to mine, only a breath away. In spite of myself I feel my pulse quicken at an abnormal rate, and right away she knows. I pull away and back against my car hastily as she stares at me, shocked.

"What are you doing?" My voice jumps an octave.

"What are *you* doing?" she exclaims.

"What the fuck" is the only way I can answer, completely caught off guard.

"What's going on with us, John?" she asks.

"What do you mean?" I say, just a hint of hysteria in my voice.

"You know what I mean. What's going on with us?" she repeats.

"What's the right answer?" I try to joke.

"That there is no us."

The answer I don't want to hear.

"But that's not right. There *is* an us. There's you. There's me. That's us."

I fight her with my desperation, try to make her feel what I feel, hope she sees what I see. *I'll fight for you*, I want to say.

"No," she says, shaking her head. "No."

"Why not?"

"Because, no!"

Her voice jumps a little higher.

"No, just not with you, not us. Please, just . . . no," she says pleadingly.

I must not look too happy, because then she says, "No, no, I didn't mean — no, look, John. It just can't be like that, okay? I can't, it can't . . . and we can't . . . so just . . . please."

"Please what?" I say coldly, trying to act as if I never blurted anything at all.

Deny. Run. Maybe we can forget.

"Please don't," she says.

"Don't what?"

"Don't do this. But don't be upset. And don't . . . don't walk away."

"I don't want this."

"Don't be upset," she repeats, cutting me harder than the first time.

"I'm not upset. I'm fine."

"You're fine?"

"I'm *fine*. I don't know what you're talking about."

Blame. Run. Deny.

The words come out before I can stop myself.

"I don't know what you're going on about. You're acting crazy. I just wanted to talk, and you're acting all weird."

She rolls her eyes at me. "Don't pull this shit with me, John," she says seriously. "We both know I didn't bring this on."

"Bring *what* on?" I shout, as if I don't know. "You're totally impossible! You never say *anything* that I can pin down. Everything has some deep hidden meaning that I'm supposed to figure out! I have no idea what you're talking about, so don't blame this on me."

"You're the one who was freaking out because I HAVE OTHER PLANS! You 'need' me? What the fuck is that? Bullshit to evoke my sympathy?"

Not bullshit.

"I'm sorry that I tried to say something NICE to you!" I am almost yelling now. "I promise I won't do it again."

"JOHN!"

"WHAT!"

"WHAT IS GOING ON WITH US?"

"I DON'T KNOW!"

228

"WHAT DO YOU WANT?"

"I DON'T KNOW!"

Why did this have to happen? Why did we have to evaluate where we are and think about all that heavy shit? Why couldn't I keep my mouth shut for five minutes?

Eva sighs. "Hold on," she says.

She pulls out her phone and makes a call.

"Hey . . . Listen, I'm so sorry, but . . . yeah . . . mm-hm." She laughs at something, nodding. "Yeah . . . I know." She rolls her eyes, a smile teasing her lips. "Yeah . . . no, it's not that," she says with another laugh, probably directed at me. "Okay . . . okay . . . thanks for — okay. I'll call you tonight . . . 'bye."

She flips the phone shut and tosses it into her car before locking the door. She walks to my car, past me, and slides into the passenger seat and sits waiting expectantly. I don't know what else to do, so I get in and drive us to the gazebo.

When we get there, neither of us moves to get out of the car. We sit in the bushes in the pitch black of night with the heater on, neither of us moving or speaking.

"I never thought I'd talk to you like that," she says finally, breaking the silence. "Never thought I'd have to."

I hate the way she treats me like a child, some inexperienced moron she has to teach.

"What do you mean?"

"You know, defining our relationship or whatever. Not you. I never thought you."

I hate the way she singles me out, makes it perfectly clear I'm not at the same level as her and her friends.

"What is that supposed to mean? I am normal. I do have relationships with people."

229

"Obviously," she says, unfazed. "I just meant that you don't like being — I don't know. I was obviously wrong."

"Being what? Being sensitive? Being human? Being a good friend? What, Eva? Just fucking say it!"

"Being heavy."

"Oh."

Beat.

I love the way she catches me off guard, makes comments I don't expect, smiles when I expect a scowl.

Fuck.

"I feel like we're missing something here," Eva says.

"You're the one who canceled your plans to come with me."

"Well, it seemed important. But if you don't care . . ." She looks at the clock on the dashboard. ". . . I can still make it to meet Brad."

Brad.

"Are you two together or what?" I ask without thinking.

"What, having to evaluate our friendship isn't enough? Now you're asking me to define mine and Brad's?"

"That's not what I —"

"No, for your information, we are not together. Happy?"

Yes.

"Why should I be?"

"Because you're a heartless bastard who doesn't want other people to ever be happy."

"Yeah, but besides that?"

She doesn't say anything for a minute.

"I think he's in love with me," she says finally.

My heart plunges.

"Are you in love with him?" I ask.

"I don't know. Maybe?"

Maybe?! The answer is no! Alarsky is a boring son of a bitch who can't play defense for his life! What the hell do you see in *him*?

"Yes or no?"

"We both know it's not as easy as yes or no."

Do we?

"Yeah. But if you love him, why aren't you together?"

"I didn't say I love him. And . . . it's complicated."

"You always say that. 'It's complicated, it's complicated.' What is so complicated?"

"I just, we just, I . . . I don't know."

"You *do* know. Tell me."

She doesn't speak for a moment.

"We were dating for some time."

Ow.

"And I think I did love him."

OW.

"But then he slept with my best friend."

OUCH!

"And then he moved away."

"Damn."

"Yeah."

"I don't see what's so complicated about it. It's very simple: He's a complete asshole."

"He was drunk."

"A drunk asshole is still an asshole."

"You would know."

"Shut up."

"But then I moved here, too. And he wanted to pick up right

where we left off, and I didn't know how to respond to that. I had told him it would never be like it was again."

Yeah, that worked out REAL well, judging by Jackson's party.

"And then. . . . " She shrugs. "I don't know. I told you, it's complicated."

"He hurt you bad."

She nods.

"Then why . . . ?"

She shakes her head.

I say nothing, only stare straight ahead into the darkness on the other side of the windshield.

"I don't know what to say."

"Don't say anything."

In my head the scene plays out: We sit by the water of the lake and don't speak. All I do is take her in my arms, and we sit together in comfortable silence, and it's beautiful. But despite my fantasies, I feel the distress in the air. I want to fill the silence with the touch of her hand or her face or her lips —

No, don't think about that.

I watch her out of the corner of my eye, staring out the front window, her head rolled slightly to her right in weariness. She feels me looking at her.

"What?" She doesn't turn. Just keeps staring out the windshield.

"What?" I say defensively.

"Nothing."

"Should we get out of the car?"

She shrugs.

As I open the door and step out, I feel the tension rush out of the car and into the night. The stars lie sprawled and uncaring in the black sky and the pale shine of the moon is the only light in the dark bushes. The cool air cuts against my face and moves across my eyes.

I shove my hands in the pockets of my jeans and lean against the side of my car, facing the unknown of the forest around us. Eva opens her door and rounds the car from behind and slides up onto the edge of the trunk. She rests her feet on the bumper and leans back on her hands, watching the dark with me.

We are right out of a magazine: beautiful girl with the good hair sitting on the trunk of the beautiful car, tall and beautiful guy with the good jeans leaning against the side of the beautiful car, both silent and brooding and beautiful in the beautiful night.

Except that I'm freezing my ass off out here.

I don't know what to do.

Have I been rejected? I can't even tell. Such a simple thing, to be turned down by another person, but of course Eva has to go and complicate it with her complicated ways. I wasn't even aware I had put myself in a position to *be* rejected, but leave it to Eva to confuse me on this front as well.

I don't understand anything these days.

"It's cold," she says.

"Yeah."

"Does it snow a lot here?"

"Yeah."

"It never snowed in Arizona."

"Arizona?"

"I lived there for a couple years. Never snowed."

"The snow here is nice."

"It snows in New York."

233

"It's not as nice as here."

She doesn't say anything.

"What's it like there?" I ask.

"Where, New York?"

"Arizona."

"It never gets cold."

Our conversation is choppy, long pauses stretching between replies. We don't face each other, don't talk to each other, just respond to the air without emotion. We talk about nothing, fill the quiet spaces of the night with our words of nothing.

But it's more like the quiet spaces fill our conversation, become the spaces between our short, staccato sentences.

"It's cold," she says again.

"Yeah."

I shift my weight, and the mulch and twigs and needles crunch softly in the dirt beneath my feet.

I furrow my eyebrows. "Why does everything have to be complicated?"

"It doesn't. They don't. We make it that way."

"Is that true?"

"Sometimes."

"But I don't like this. I don't like feeling heavy."

"Then don't."

"I don't know."

"That's okay. It'll be all right."

"I can't believe after what you told me about Brad that you're comforting me. Shouldn't it be the other way around?"

"Maybe," she says, and I hear the quiet smile in her voice.

"Okay. It'll be all right, Eva."

She laughs a half laugh.

"Thanks."

For a second we're us again.

I step to the back of the car and slide up next to her on the edge of the trunk. She wiggles closer to me for warmth and hugs her crossed arms closer to her body. I lean my arms on my legs, and we sit side by side, not looking at each other, just staring out at the darkness surrounding us and the car. The moon has moved higher in the sky and hangs over us now, shining a half shine down with its dim light.

It's warmer now.

The yelling seems worth it.

"What are you thinking about?" she asks after a moment.

"Nothing. What are you thinking about?"

She laughs. "Nothing? How can you be thinking about nothing?"

"What are you thinking about?"

She laughs again. "Everything."

"How can you be thinking about everything?"

She smiles and shakes her head.

We don't look at each other.

"Do you feel different than before?"

"Before when?" I ask.

"I dunno. Before before. Before today. Before yesterday. Do you feel different?"

I shrug.

"I dunno. Sure. Do you?"

"Yes. And no. And yes."

"Are you still cold?" I ask after a moment.

"Yes. No."

"Me, too."

It feels good, it feels right. It feels like us.

"We should go swimming," she says.

"Are you suicidal?"

"Not at the moment, no."

"No swimming then."

"Fair enough."

Then she says, "I'm sorry if I haven't been around recently."

"What have you been up to?"

I feel her look at the ground.

"I've just been busy. With. Things."

"With Alarsky?"

"Sometimes."

I wait for her to explain more, but she doesn't.

"This was stupid," she says after a minute. "We shouldn't be stupid. Let's not think about it."

"But you're the one who —"

"Sometimes I'm wrong."

"No way."

"Let's not fight again."

"Okay."

"Though maybe we should."

"Are you arguing with yourself?"

"Yes. No. Maybe? I don't want to talk about what we should talk about," she says.

"Neither do I."

"Though maybe we should."

"Maybe."

"Things might change."

"I don't want that."

"Maybe we don't have a choice."

I stare into the forest.

"Maybe."

"Damn," she says.

"Damn," I agree.

"You need me?"

She said it.

"You said we wouldn't —"

Talk about it.

"I know, but . . . maybe we should."

No, we shouldn't. We should just go on being whatever we are instead of trying to be whatever we think we should be. We should just go back to the way things were before I opened my mouth, before I said how I felt, before I ruined it all. We should laugh and banter and *be*.

But of course I don't say any of this. Instead I say, "Forget it, okay?"

I feel her turn toward me, lean one leg up on the trunk, try to get me to look at her. I stare at the black of the trees.

"John . . ."

I feel the warmth of my mood slip from my head out through my fingers and feet.

"What?" I say coolly

I don't turn.

"Did you mean it?"

"I don't know what you're talking about."

"Would you please take a little responsibility for what you said?"

"No. This isn't me. This isn't what I do. You are not what I do. You know what I do? Girls in short skirts. I do girls. That's what I do. I don't do this," I say without an ounce of emotion in my voice.

"We just . . . we can't."

"I said forget it."

"John, can we please talk about it?"

"Talk about what? Talk about how you hang around me all the time and then the second I mention anything about our relationship you fucking run? Shouldn't it be the other way around?"

I feel the heat rushing back to my head. *Go on.*

"Talk about what? Talk about you and Brad? Talk about you throwing that in my face? Talk about the tension between us that you — *yes, you*, don't give me that look — help create? Talk about what? What, Eva, what would you like to talk about?"

"I never gave you any inclination that there was something between us!"

"Okay, right. Sure."

And the shit starts anew. I feel fury return to replace reason, feel the Know and the Want knock heads.

"I don't want to hurt you —" she starts to say, touching my arm.

I pull away and slide down from the back of my car to face her.

"Don't give me any of that emotional bullshit. You've been messing with me for three months and I'm sick of it."

"*Messing* with you?! What the fuck are you talking about, John? Is it so hard for you to imagine I'm not attracted to you? Is it so hard for you to imagine rejection? Why can't you accept this as it is, John? Look, I'm sorry if you've been getting the wrong idea, but —"

As she yells I see rap CDs and Jake's bedroom carpet and Sam's hair, arms, eyes. I see rejection. I see failure. I see spinning out of control.

I fight back.

"But you're just too good for me? But I'm just fun to fuck with? I'm your little pet jock plaything who's fun to prod with your stupid life-evaluating questions and your stupid, STUPID brown eyes? Is *that* it?"

I start yelling to the woods and pacing around angrily with my back to her.

"Don't yell at *me!*" she shouts back. "You're the one who shows up all the time just *begging* for someone to talk to you about your stupid, STUPID, obviously deep-rooted issues!"

"*I* have deep-rooted issues?! LOOK WHO'S TALKING! I'm not the one fucking the guy who fucked my best friend!"

"Fuck you!"

The forest shakes with our anger.

"All you ever do is poke into my life," I say, "but when I mention one thing about Alarsky you flip; you act like *I* need to be fixed, but then *you* act just as broken. You say one thing and then do another. How the hell am I supposed to believe in you, Eva? How am I supposed to know what to do when you're just as fucked up as I am?"

Run? Don't run. Stay. Fight. Yell.

"You think I *poke* into your life? Listen to yourself! You're practically begging for someone to talk to, what the hell am I supposed to do, walk away?"

"Yes, you're right, I come up to you every day and spill my guts to you. That's exactly how it is."

"Well, obviously you don't *ask*! You're '*Caesar*' — you're too fucking macho to ever ask for help."

I see nothing but verbal blows, think of nothing but how to beat them back. Progress and peace have crumbled, and I'm left with nothing but a sword laced with insults.

"I don't fucking need your help."

"No, but you fucking need *me*!"

"Fuck you!"

"You said it, not me!"

"No, I said it, and then I said *forget it*! But you don't fucking forget anything!"

"How am I supposed to 'forget it'? How am I supposed to ignore what you said?"

"Because I said so!" I yell.

"What do you want from me, John?!"

"Nothing anymore! Forget it! Forget everything! Just forget it all!"

"Is that really what you want?" she shoots feverishly. "You want to forget everything?"

"You're not worth remembering," I spit back furiously.

And then there is nothing. She doesn't speak, doesn't shoot again, doesn't even look at me. Somewhere inside of me a tiny speck of remorse tugs at my heart, but my brain smacks it down in a second. In the past three months, I have undergone the most emotional stress since my mother died. And I can fucking thank this girl for that.

She deserves what she gets.

I am urged to drive off and leave her deserted at the lake, but if she dies, she won't suffer enough. The drive back to Papa John's is spent in smothering, smoldering, *screaming* silence and as soon I get to the parking lot, she opens the door and slams it shut behind her. Still smoking with fury, I squeal away from her and out of the parking lot as quickly as I can.

It's her turn to watch me drive away.

CHAPTER 23

I speed home in absolute rage. I replay the conversation over and over again in my head, the way it could have gone, the way it should have gone, and finally the way it went. With each replay, I grow more surprised, more confused . . . *angrier*.

How could she say all those things to me? That I'm desperate for her help? That I'm desperate for *her*?

I grip the steering wheel tighter and my right hand turns an ugly shade of pale. My house comes into view and I pass it, not wanting to submit to its steadiness.

I'm not fucking desperate for anything. Or anyone. I don't *get* desperate, period.

All she's ever done is be a condescending smart-ass. What the hell do I need her for? No wonder the past two months have been hell for me, what with Chris and Sam and Kelly and Jake and everyone. Eva is the source of all my shit; none of this happened before she got here.

Bitch.

I've been messed with. Since when did I become the mess-ee? My whole life I've been the mess-er.

I've never felt so worked in my life. And now what? Do I want to cut her off, do I want to forget about her like I said? Do I want to forget everything? Is that what I want?

What do I want?

What does *she* want?

Wait, who cares? Who cares, who cares, who cares about her? Who cares what she wants?

I care.

I care?

I *care?*

Oh God. Look what she's done to me.

Decide, decide, decide what you want. Decide what the answers are, who's right and who's wrong, decide what you should do. Decide . . .

To forget it all.

That's what Caesar does, and that's what I'll do. Push it out, forget it all, make it a memory, one that's not worth keeping. Get on with my regularly scheduled program, drink, eat, smoke something. Hit, fuck, hurt someone.

It's just so much easier that way.

Once more around the block.

The next morning on my way to school, I make a conscious effort to replace Eva in my mind.

Okay, every time you start to think about Eva or what happened, think about . . . Jenna Farrell's rack instead. Much, much, much more appealing image. This is step one in my plan to forget what happened. Hopefully, one step will be all I need, but I am willing to take drastic measures if necessary:

Actually hooking up with Jenna.

Look, it's working already. Am I good or what?

Or what.

I pull up into the school parking lot and grab my books and walk toward the school. A dark blue Honda passes me as I cross the parking lot, and she flashes into my mind.

I think quickly of Jenna.

Right. Jenna. Right. See, it's working.

I walk into the school.

I end up having to spend most of the day thinking about Jenna, and when I see her after last period, I am almost glad. Which is a strange feeling, considering in all the time I've known her, I've never once been glad to see Jenna.

"Hey," she says as she approaches me at my locker.

"Hey."

"What's up?"

She leans on the locker next to mine.

"Not much, you?"

"Nothing."

"How're things?"

"Not bad. We haven't hung out in a while."

I hadn't noticed.

"Yeah, I know. You want to do something this weekend?"

She straightens a little with surprise.

"Yeah, that'd be good. What do you want to do?"

I shrug. "You figure it out. Call me."

"Okay."

She smiles slowly in an attempt to look sexy but I can feel the giddiness right beneath the surface, weekend plans clicking into place, new underwear being bought. I feel like a good person for doing her this favor.

"'Kay. 'Bye," I say, giving her a small wave and slamming my locker closed before heading down the hallway to the gym.

"'Bye!" she calls to my retreating back.

Score.

I change in the locker room and stride out into the gym, where some guys are already jogging around a little to warm up.

Practice is filled with a different kind of scoring. The season is just starting to heat up and games will start soon. Arms pump, wrists flick, the sweat pours. The ball speeds up as we seem to fly in slo-mo, and hands chase and race to tap the ball in or out of the net.

Score another for us.

Right as I'm dribbling toward the net and about to shoot, there she is again in my head.

No! Jenna's tits!

I miss the shot, a little bit because of Eva's face and a little bit because of Jenna's tits and mostly because I'm a total moron.

"What's the matter with you?" Marsh mutters as he streaks past to get the rebound.

My first instinct is to hit him, but these days I'm not too keen on listening to my instincts. After all the trouble they got me into with Eva . . .

NO! TITS!

Dammit.

After practice I drive home and, for lack of anything better to do, I try my hand at a little pre-calc. Takes me about twenty minutes before I realize I have no idea what I'm doing and that the solution is to not do it at all. I pack that away and sit at my desk staring out the window.

This is not how this is supposed to happen.

I want to go to the gazebo but there's always the chance that she'll be there, and as much as Jenna's boobs save me when I'm alone, I don't know how well I would do face-to-face with Eva. So . . . no gazebo for me. What else can I do?

I kill time with TV and a little Instant Messenger and then around 6:00 or 7:00, my dad knocks on my door.

"John? You home?"

"Come in," I say.

"Hey, do you guys want to get Chinese takeout tonight?"

SHIT. I was so busy avoiding Eva that I totally forgot about avoiding my family.

"Uhhh . . ."

"Don't try to get out of dinner. You haven't eaten at home in weeks. What do you want?"

What do I want?

Kelly stops in my doorway for a moment.

"Mexican," she says before she walks into her room.

"You want Mexican?" my dad asks me.

"I don't care," I say, not taking my eyes off the TV screen.

"Well, you're the one who has to go get it," he says. "So you better want it at least a little."

"What?" I turn my head to him. "Why do I have to pick it up?"

"Because, *John*, I'm tired. I had a long day at work."

"Well, I had a long day at school."

"Well, that's too bad because now you have to go pick up dinner." Without letting me answer, my dad retreats down the hall, calling back, "Get me a chicken quesadilla."

Sigh. I roll my eyes and shut off the TV and grab my jacket and keys off the floor. In the hallway, I knock on Kelly's door, shouting, "I'm getting dinner. What do you want?"

"Are we getting Mexican?" asks the voice on the other side of the door.

"Yeah. What do you want?"

"Two burritos" is the reply.

"Fine."

"And can you get me a beer?"

WHAT?

I start to speak (yell, really), and her door swings open.

"Jeez, I'm kidding," she says when she sees my face. "I'm coming with you."

Ha. Ha. Ha.

Kelly and I haven't really been around each other very much since Danielle's party. It hasn't been the silent treatment, but there's been a tiny bit of tension in the air whenever we're around each other. This is the first time Kelly has voluntarily gotten in my car in a while, and I feel at a loss as to what to do.

I drive.

"What's been going on with you?" Kelly asks the silence.

"Hm?"

"What have you been doing?"

I shrug. "Same ol'. You?"

She shrugs in imitation. "*Same ol'*."

247

"How's . . ." I don't know what to ask about. ". . . school?"

"Fine." Then, bluntly, "Are you still mad?"

"What?"

"About Jenna's sister's party."

"I'm not mad. I'm . . ." I hesitate, searching for the right word.

"Mad."

"No. Maybe."

She looks out the window.

"Did I throw up a lot?"

"Yeah."

"In your car?"

"No. You would have known if you puked in my car because you'd still have bruises from when I kicked your ass."

"You're mad because I drank," she says frankly.

"I'm mad because you shouldn't have been there in the first place."

"Why not?"

"Because you're too young. And clearly not ready."

"I'm not too young. It was fun."

"Of course you thought it was fun. You're in middle school; anything high school is fun. Sweatpants with our school logo on the butt are a fucking blast to you."

"What's wrong with that? Of course I want to be older. Everybody is always trying to act older. What's wrong with that?"

"It's stupid."

"Why is it stupid?"

"It just is. Act your own age."

"Like you?" she accuses. "Kids in high school try to act older, too."

"We *are* older."

"You're not being fair."

"I don't care."

"Are you still mad?"

I'm just not up for this conversation. "Today's really not the day, Kelly," I say.

"Why? What happened?"

"Nothing."

"Something happened. What happened?"

"I got in a fight with my friend."

"Who? Jake? Eva?"

"Jenna," I lie.

"Jenna? The slutty one?"

"That's being a bit vague, but yes, she is one of the girls I know who tends to be . . ." I search for a better word and fail. "Slutty."

"You had a fight with her? About what?"

"Forget it."

"You already started. Now you have to finish."

For a moment, I don't answer. I slow the car as I hear the warning of the train gates start to close somewhere in the distance.

Stuck in the silence and the traffic, I have no choice but to speak.

"I didn't have a fight with Jenna. It was with Eva."

"You guys had a fight? It's about time."

That, I did not expect. I pull up the parking brake, turn off the engine, and look at my baby sister.

"What?"

Kelly shrugs. "It couldn't go on all happy and loving forever."

She looks right back at me, with this why-is-my-brother-so-clueless attitude in her eyebrows.

"What are you talking about? Where do you get this shit?"

I try to play it off, but she's got my attention.

"I just . . ." She shrugs again. "You seemed too . . . happy."

"I seemed *happy*?"

"Not happy, but like . . . I dunno. Different."

Different?

"How?"

She doesn't look at me when she talks, just plays with the locks on the door.

Click. Unlock.

Click. Lock.

Click. Unlock.

Click. Lock.

"Why wouldn't it last long?" I ask. "Because I'm incapable of keeping relationships with people who aren't like me?"

Did I just say that out loud?

"No," she says, laughing. "Because it was too good to be true."

"How do *you* know that? What are you doing, spying on us? You've only ever seen her, what, like, twice?"

"No, I've been around."

Click. Unlock.

"What does that mean?"

"Anyway, I'm just trying to say that I'm glad you two are fighting."

What the fuck? This is further confirmation that the asshole gene is prominent in my family.

"You're *glad*? Thanks a lot."

"No, I mean, it's bad, but . . . everybody fights. You couldn't have gone very much longer without fighting. It's healthy."

"Where are you getting this stuff?"

250

"What? It's true!"

"You're telling me I should be happy that I'm on bad terms with Eva? I'm ecstatic."

"Not *happy* per se . . ."

Click. Lock.

Did my little sister just use the phrase "per se" while giving me relationship advice? What the hell is going on?

"I just . . . it's healthy," she says again.

Click. She leaves it on unlock.

"Great. I'm healthy. My misery is *healthy*."

"Misery? You? It's worse than I thought."

"Who are you?" I say with a half laugh. "Where do you come from? You have opinions and theories about my friendships with other people?"

"Just her. She's different, John."

Well. I definitely can't disagree with that.

That, it seems, is the whole problem.

CHAPTER 24

Later that night, as the world comes down, I sprawl out on the roof, my arms open and my face to the sky as the heavens pummel me with wave after wave of rain. I want to fight back, to meet fate with fist and fury. I want to kick the clouds.

For once in my life, I have something worth fighting for. But I know I can't.

I won't win.

The next morning on the way to school, it occurs to me that I don't really feel like going; I feel like driving.

So I do. Past the school, past the diner, past the gym. To the gazebo.

Well, Caesar. You have just proven yourself to be thoroughly predictable.

The grass squeaks against the rubber of my sneakers as I fly into the gazebo, dodging sheet upon sheet of the continuous rain. I don't have any overwhelming urge to throw myself headfirst into the lake and inhale. So I still must be at least a little sane.

I think it's necessary that I sit down with a look of misery and let the rain fall on me. I don't know what else I can do.

So I sit.

I wait.

It rains. Hard.

And it's hard. God, it's so hard.

I feel it. I feel the warmth in my skin wash away with the rain, feel my jeans get heavier as the drops gets steadier, feel the world take a giant piss on my head. I feel the cold. I feel the numbness.

So much that I can't feel.

Once the world has hurt you enough, you reach a quota for pain and you stop feeling it. And then you can scream at the sky because there's nothing left for it to throw at you.

Or so you suppose.

A crack of thunder and the sky splits. A great flash and the hair on the back of my neck curls against my skin.

BOOM.

A tree across the lake is fried in the time it takes for me to let out a single breath. Holy shit. The trunk is split all the way down to its roots and chips of bark are everywhere. Everything surrounding the tree remains intact, unscathed. It's a beautiful, horrible thing to see such destruction in such a short time.

I become aware again of my sopping state and the pain comes back. Something has got to change. I can't just drive off every time something bad happens.

John, what have you gotten yourself into? You knew from the beginning girls wouldn't be worth it. And you still had to go and mess with perfection. You just had to talk to her. You never talked to any of them but you had to talk to *her.*

And now you're just talking to yourself.

It's all right, though, right? I got this far without her and I'm quite capable of getting on without her. I don't need this and I don't need her. I *do* need food. And a clean shirt.

I squeak against the old wood of the gazebo as I pass up its stairs and out the other side to the clearing where my car is parked. I pop open the trunk and pull out a shirt and towel I've stowed away. I lay the towel on the driver's seat and sit down to kick my shoes off into the car and peel off my drenched socks. The wind knocks my car harshly from all sides and I feel it down my spine as I pull off the shirt clinging to my frame. I wait for the car to warm up before turning the heat on full blast.

If this is it, if senior year means sitting soaked and shivering in your car with the heat on, if this is all it's going to be, then I don't know what I'm doing here.

I need comfort sex. I've never had to be comforted before, but I imagine it's got to feel pretty good to have such a reliable backup plan. I could call so many girls . . . they'd even skip class to come and meet me. Then again, in the past half hour I've resolved to get over this about twelve times. And each time it still resulted in me in the middle of the woods in nothing but boxers. Which is all right when you're with a girl, but pretty pathetic if you're alone.

My phone buzzes against the passenger seat where I stashed it.

Bzzzzzzzzzzzzzzzzzzzzz. Bzzzzzzzzzzzzzzzzzzzzz.

A text. Jenna.

where r u

I sigh and toss the phone aside, not bothering to answer.

What difference does it make? I'm out of her reach now. I'd go back to school, but what's there for me? I'd go home, but what's there for me?

I know what I need to do. I need to move.

I pull my dry shirt over my head and pull back out onto the road in the pouring rain. There's not much to do on a day like this, especially if all your friends are at school, where you're supposed to be. I could probably text Jenna back and she'd meet me somewhere, but that girl talks too much. I need someone who can't keep her mouth shut but for . . . other reasons. I browse through my mental database of girls or friends or whatever you want to call them. There's always Sophie, but I think that girl has contracted so many STDs that she can't even keep track of them herself. That's just gross.

Stacy? Too recent.

Lindsey? Probably still mad.

Sam? Sam. She seemed a little desperate last time we met; I wouldn't be surprised if she's come to her senses about hooking up with me. Sam? There's always Sam.

My windshield wipers go into overdrive as I blaze past the blurry fields of Brown Farms on my way to God knows where. Corn-husk colors blend right into the gray of the sky and against the dull of the forests behind the pasture. And I am gone in a second, nothing more than a streak of black against dull gray.

Outside, the gas stations and strip malls slide in and out of focus with the *streeeaaaaaak streeeaaaaaak* of the windshield wipers. I pass the McDonald's, the Ford dealership, the bank. I pass in and out of downtown Laurence in a near flash, and soon I'm all alone on 95.

I should get a haircut. I've been thinking about that for a while and I just haven't gotten around to it yet. I need to get this mess out of my eyes, out of my way; a haircut could be just what I need. I could make decisions, I could make resolutions and promises that I'll get over it, that I'll never think on it again. I could do that, but that requires conviction. And that requires energy. And that requires more than just sex.

I need to do a lot of things. I need to get over myself. I need to make this go away. I need to turn around and get something to eat. I need I need I need and I will . . .

Do.

Something.

Make.

Something. Of myself.

I take exit 18 and drive until I find the nearest Taco Bell. I'll be perfectly honest, there is absolutely nothing in the world better than a Taco Bell chalupa in the middle of a Tuesday afternoon. Besides, I'm desperate.

Sitting in Taco Bell I scroll through my mental black book. Who can I call? Maybe I could give Lindsey another shot. She's anxious enough to forgive and forget pretty quickly about me blowing her off.

I flip open my phone and punch Lindsey a text.

meet me @ ur house @ 2

Within fifteen minutes, I receive her reply:

ok

And suddenly things are feeling up.

"Caesar, what are you doing?"

I open my eyes to Lindsey standing outside my car, tapping on the window. Startled and still groggy, it takes me a few moments to realize I have fallen asleep since I parked outside her house around 1:30. I step out of the car and kiss Lindsey's warm and wet cheek. The biting air cuts cold through our heated glances, and I feel the familiar tugs and pulls in all the right places of my body, all the familiar feelings you feel when you know you're just about to get laid.

It's good to know that at least some parts of me are still functioning properly.

Lindsey watches me with hunger and doesn't hesitate before moving toward me.

"Don't you want to go in —" I start, before she cuts me off with a squeeze.

"Haven't you ever wanted to do it *in the rain?*" she whispers in my ear, taking her time to make sure I feel every syllable of her words in my spine.

I let her lead me to the back of her house, hands reaching, tongues searching the whole way. The rain does add something sensual to it, something that doesn't disappoint me in the least. As the two of us lie naked and warm on her surprisingly comfortable patio, the world slips away into a blur behind the curtain of rain falling cold and pricking on our skin.

When the heat is gone, Lindsey and I retreat inside and

upstairs to her room, where we duck quickly under the covers. She nestles into the crook of my left arm and places a warm hand on my bare chest, saying nothing before closing her eyes. I must admit I miss the simple feel of a girl's hand, the feeling of smooth legs under my touch.

Imagine all the great things I've been missing these past few months I've wasted with . . .

Don't think of Eva.

I'm afraid to get out of here and leave behind the warmth of Lindsey's sheets because I know once I'm alone, the questions will start again.

I pull Lindsey closer to me, catching a whiff of her shampoo as she murmurs against my side.

I fall asleep.

I wake an hour later, Lindsey still snuggled against me. The day is slowly wasting away and I can feel the questions start to creep back into my mind. Eventually I'll need the answers.

But not before I give Lindsey another go. Maybe Lindsey is the answer to all my problems; maybe all I need is this, here: her hair against my cheek, her hand against my stomach, our legs entwined. Maybe this is the solution.

How can one girl be the answer to the problems caused by another? Are girls simply interchangeable? Do we spend our whole lives bouncing from girl to girl to girl, exchanging one with another until all our relationships just become one gigantic rebound?

I hope not.

Lindsey stirs and sighs into my arm as she opens her eyes slowly.

"Hey," she says sleepily.

I fight the urge to ask, "Hey, so what kind of movies are you into?" Even in my head I can hear how idiotic that sounds.

"Hey," I say instead.

"Did you get any sleep?"

"Sure," I mumble vaguely, my thoughts preoccupied by the chestnut tendrils brushing the side of her bare neck.

I wonder if she *could* replace Eva. I wonder if she has the capacity to be just as good.

I wonder . . .

But my thoughts are interrupted by Lindsey's lips. On my lips. On my jaw. On my neck. On my chest. On my . . .

What's the point?

CHAPTER 25

I start hanging out with Lindsey on a regular basis. Every day we cut our last two classes and meet at her house after school to fuck like rabbits. These sex sessions are great; Lindsey is great and the sex never gets old. But it's actually during those postcoital moments that I feel like there's something worth sticking around for. We cuddle for an hour or two before one of us has practice or a meeting, and on occasion we exchange bits of conversation, bits of information, bits of ourselves.

It's nice to be with her, to keep warm on these winter days. It's nice to stare up at someone else's walls and still feel the familiar unsettling feeling I do when I stare at my own. I just wish that poster of a half-naked David Beckham wasn't there.

And Lindsey herself is not too bad. In terms of relationships and school and her family, we have a lot of things in common. I've even managed to shove out other . . . distractions that have been plaguing me recently. Well . . . it's more of a nudge than a shove. All right, more of a tap. But it's progress.

*   *   *

The Friday of the third week in December, Jake calls me up while I'm at Lindsey's.

"Yo," I answer.

"Caesar!" he says jovially. "Where you been, son?"

"Around," I say. "What's goin' on?"

"Who's on your list tonight?"

I laugh shortly. "No list, man. No list."

"C'mon," he says. "How can there be no list? Where are you?"

"Nowhere, man."

"Aw, shit, you've already done it, haven't you?" he says laughingly. "I don't get it!"

"Caesar? Who is it?" Lindsey asks sleepily, moving a hand up my stomach as she pulls herself up against a pillow.

"Sorry, did I wake you up?"

"Caesar! What the fuck? JACOBS?" Jake yells into the phone with disbelief.

I swear under my breath.

"YOU'RE FUCKING LINDSEY JACOBS?!" he screams.

From my side, Lindsey giggles.

"She can hear you, dude," I tell him.

"Hell" is all he can say.

"Right. Well. Talk to you later, then."

I flip the phone shut and toss it on top of my shirt on the floor.

"It's supposed to snow tonight," Lindsey says against my chest. "Let's go outside later and do it in the snow."

I laugh. "You're crazy. We'll get pneumonia."

"I know, but it'll be worth it."

For a split second I have the urge to invite her to go to the gazebo with me. But I know she would want to have sex, and that's really not the point. Yet part of me wants to know how she would react, what she would say, where she would walk.

Would she sit where Eva sat? Could it ever be like it was with Eva? Eva, who I've completely avoided. Eva, who's completely avoided me.

Jet-black hair flashes through my mind and Lindsey stirs against my skin.

"I've gotta go," I say.

"Hmm?"

Her eyes flutter open and I meet her ocean blue gaze.

I pull my arm out from behind her and kiss her quickly before I stoop to grab my shirt and wallet.

"Where are you going?"

"I can't stay."

She slips out from under the sheet and wraps her legs around me from behind. I feel every inch of her beautiful body pressed against my back, inviting.

Oh Lord. Give me strength.

It takes all my willpower to pull her legs off me and to put my shirt back on. I can't look her in the face or I'll never go back.

"Hey, I'm really sorry."

I kiss her again and then I'm out the door.

The lake is frozen when I get to the gazebo. It's been over a month since I've been here, but the well-worn tracks from my car are as deep as ever. Bundled up in my sweatshirt and jacket, I crunch across the dirt and grass to the gazebo. I lean against the archway facing out toward the lake. Everything is still and lifeless; the lake is a sheet of ice, the trees silent and naked in the dark. It's that kind of mind-numbing cold that only comes in winter, when the chill gets into your shirt and hangs out by your heart, and your shiver comes from somewhere deep within.

I think about Lindsey. Things with her could potentially be good. I shouldn't fuck it up. But I will. I know I will. I can't fight who I am, I can't change the way I am with girls. And I certainly can't change the way girls are with me.

I walk away from the gazebo, take the creaking steps one at a time, out across the clearing and toward the water.

It's a massive mirror. The lake has been transformed, one solid ice block that won't move for the next few months. My reflection remains the same. The turbulence of storms, the flexibility of spring, have ended. The stagnation of winter has settled in.

It starts to snow.

I walk slowly out to the dock and stand at its edge, watching the gray of the sky and its falling swirls. White patches collect where the ice is dry, the snow falling a little bit faster every second.

"I hope you're not planning on going for a swim."

A million things race through my mind in less than a second, but one thought rings out clearer and louder than all the others:

Eva.

I turn and don't say anything. There she is, standing halfway between me and the gazebo, one hand on her hip and the other by her side. As soon as I see her face, all the progress I've made with Lindsey is shattered.

"John."

"Eva."

She doesn't say anything more. She walks out onto the dock, but doesn't look me in the face, sitting down on the side and letting her legs swing over, her feet resting lightly on the surface of the lake. The snow falls swiftly on our hair and shoulders.

Silence fills the air between us, and I try to hide the discomfort I can feel written all over my face. The tension is heavy, but neither of us wants to be the one to break it. A thousand things run through my mind that I could say, that I probably *should* say, but nothing comes out.

Am I not good enough for you? Is anyone good enough for you? Why did I tell you I needed you? Why don't you need me? How can you need Alarsky? Will anyone *ever need me?*

Is it too late to go back?

Millions of thoughts come tumbling into my outbox of words, but nothing leaves my mouth.

"Don't talk for a sec, okay?" Eva says suddenly.

"Okay."

"Just listen for a little bit."

I prepare myself for some speech, some dissertation on what went wrong in our relationship. I expect diagrams.

But she says nothing. She wants me to listen to nothing.

I try to concentrate on the whirling white, on the simple silence, but after several minutes, my mind starts to wander.

Why *shouldn't* I bring Lindsey here? What's so special about "our place" that's worth remembering? Have you brought Alarsky here? Did you have sex here? Why does it matter? Did you guys go swimming together?

Do you love him?

I want her to say something.

"How do you feel right now?" she asks, breaking the silence.

"What?"

Six words and already she's got me off guard.

"How do you feel right now?" she repeats, turning her head toward me.

"I . . . I feel all right?"

"You feel all right or you *want* to feel all right? Or you *think* you feel all right?"

"I . . . what? All of the above?"

This girl drives me crazy.

I sit down next to her off the side of the dock, but neither of us looks at each other now. We talk to the night.

"Wh . . . uh, how do *you* feel?" I attempt.

"Fine."

Right. This is going . . . great.

"I'm just asking, because I want to know where you are right now. In terms of this. In terms of getting over this."

"Is there something to get over?"

We both know damn well that there is.

"That depends."

"On?"

"Us. You."

"And what about you?"

"What *about* me?"

"Dammit, Eva."

"Sorry. What would you like me to say?"

"I would like things laid out for me in clear-cut terms so I can figure out how the fuck to react!"

"You know it's not that black and white."

Of course I fucking know that. That's what makes it shitty.

265

"Things just . . . change," she says with difficulty.

"This quickly?"

"Sure. Relationships change. People change. Shit happens."

"And you don't want to do anything about it?"

"Maybe things just stopped being fun. Stopped being interesting."

Like a fucking slap across the face. Heat rushes to my head and my heart drops and I can't look at her. I can't believe what I'm hearing.

For a moment, I say nothing, just feel the weight of her words hang heavy between the swirling flakes.

For a moment, nothing.

And then:

"What the fuck?" I ask the air. "What the fuck does that *mean*? How can someone just stop being interesting? How the fuck do you turn someone on and off like that, Eva?"

"Well, why don't you tell me? You seem to be an expert at it."

"That's different; those girls mean nothing to me. Are you telling me you hung around for three months because it meant nothing to you?"

I can't stand to look her in the face, but out of the corner of my eye I see that she won't look at me, either. Her long black hair falls over her profile, a dark curtain for her to hide behind.

"What if that's what I'm trying to say? What would you do?" she asks without much emotion.

"Fuck you, Eva," I say, and hear the pain in my voice.

"Maybe I just stopped caring."

"Why?"

"Hell, I don't know."

"Because of Alarsky?"

"Because of a lot of things. I'm sorry, John, what do you want me to do?"

"What the hell is the matter with you?!"

"If only I knew," she says to the air.

Finally, I turn my body to face hers, resting one leg on the dock where the snow has made it white. My other leg hangs cold and frozen over the edge, nearly touching the surface of the frozen lake.

I stare straight at her.

"Oh no, don't turn this into a I'm-so-fucked-up-that-you-can't-blame-me deal. This isn't out of your hands."

She doesn't look at me, just stares at her hands as she plays with the frayed edges of her jacket.

So I go on. "You made a choice. You *chose* to stop caring. You *chose* to let things get complicated."

At this, she finally seems to have a reaction. Flicking her eyes from the snow over the lake to my face, she quickly pushes her body to face mine.

"*Me?* Don't pin this on me! Things got heavy and dramatic and it stopped being worth it. It stopped being worth hanging around you to have so much baggage. And for God's sake, we weren't even having sex!"

"So ultimately you chose between hanging out with me and hanging out with your other less emotionally attached guy friends?" I say sarcastically. "Please. You have more baggage than anyone I've ever met. Listen to yourself! We're not fucking, so it's not worth sticking around for? You're pulling a goddamn Caesar."

"No, what I'm saying is, having emotional *shit* with you isn't even reasonable! Because there's no sex involved!"

267

"Because there's no sex, then it doesn't make sense to have problems?"

Maybe the *problem* is that there is no sex, my balls suggest.

"Do *you* have any problems with girls you don't have sex with?" she asks.

"I don't *know* any girls I don't have sex with!" I shoot back, exasperated.

"I'm just saying . . ."

"This makes no sense?"

"Right."

"Well, I could have told you that."

She fingers the bottom of her jacket again and speaks with her eyes lowered.

"It's just not working. We just stopped working. We disagree on too many levels. We don't understand each other."

"I thought that was the point."

"The point is," she says without looking at me, "it got shitty. And now it's too late to go back."

"You're not even going to fight for it? You're not even going to try?"

She talks to the dock now.

"Try for *what*? What do you think we had, John? What do you think we *could* have? Where did you think it was going?" she says.

"You're supposed to be the relationship expert, not me. Why don't you tell me where it was going? I'm not the one who has intense relationships left and right; I'm the screwup! *You're* supposed to fix *me*! Isn't that the way these things are supposed to play out? C'mon, you've seen the movies. FIX ME, EVA! FIX ME!"

Her hands fly to grab the sides of her face as she turns away from me angrily.

"FUCK YOU, JOHN!"

A beat.

A beat.

An eternity of beats.

After many moments, Eva goes on more calmly, still talking to the darkness. "All right." She takes a deep breath. "Let's . . okay, let's try again. If you had things your way, how would it be?"

I don't answer right away, so she follows with, "Would we have sex?"

My first instinct is to say yes. But for once I'm sure that wouldn't solve anything. It would just bring us into a whole new world of complicated bullshit.

I lean against a spike jutting out of the dock and consider the question. Consider Eva.

"If I had things my way . . . everything would go back to the way it was," I say. "We would hang out all the time. We would have fun together. We would go places together. You would continue being my first . . . I don't know what. And I would hope that somewhere down the line, you would feel like I was your first something, too. Anything. And you wouldn't make me feel like shit. At least not without asking."

"That's what you want?" she says, finally giving up on talking to her jacket and focusing back on talking to the snow. She pulls both knees into her chest and tucks her bare hands into the sleeves of her jacket.

"I think so."

"And do you think we can have that?"

I pull a pair of wool gloves from my pocket and toss them in her direction.

"Maybe? I don't know, maybe it's too late. What do you think?"

She stares at the gloves, then at me, then back at the gloves. She doesn't reach for them, as if to tell me her defiance of me extends to her hands as well.

"I don't know, either. I don't think we can," she says.

I stare back.

"I figured you would say that."

Then I ask, "Well, if you had things your way, how would this go?"

She shoves her hands into her pockets and takes another deep breath.

"We would come here. And be us, together. And then when we weren't here, we would be us, apart. And we'd care but we wouldn't worry. And it would be detached but by no means emotionless. I guess that's what I would want. No bullshit, no drama. Just us."

"And why the hell can't that happen?"

"Because life is full of bullshit. And so are you, sometimes."

"And you."

"Yeah."

But even with the bullshittiness, can't it be worth it? Can't I be good enough to not care about all the crap? Why does it have to change?

"I don't understand . . . how can it be over?" I say, almost desperately. "You're . . . you're The Girl. You're supposed to make me listen to the right kind of music and teach me about art and tell me things that are going to change my life. How can you give up on me?"

"John, I'm *not* The Girl. I'm *not* perfect . . . and, to be honest, some of the CDs I own are kind of embarrassing. And you're *not* The Jock. You're *not* stupid —"

" — and, to tell you the truth, beer pong *isn't* all that fun."

She doesn't laugh. She doesn't even move.

"I don't want to be The Girl," she says quietly to herself. "I don't want you to look back on your life and think I was the one who changed everything."

"Well, it's a little late for that."

She doesn't know how to answer; I wouldn't know how to, either.

I feel like I've just cut my chest open and handed Eva my heart. And she's just sitting there, tossing it from one hand to the other, staring at it, trying to figure out what to do with it.

"You really think we don't have fun together anymore?" I ask the silence.

She doesn't answer again. Every tenth of a second that she remains silent kills me a little bit more.

Finally she says, "I can't pretend we don't have fun together. We . . . we do. It's just . . . the bullshit isn't worth it. The weirdness. The unspoken tensions. This is what it comes down to: You think this is worth exploring, but I've been down this path. I don't want to know how it turns out. I don't . . ."

"Think it's worth it."

Think I'm worth it.

Again, she takes her time to respond.

"I don't know."

"You do know. You just don't want to hurt me. Say it. You and Alarsky. Not you and me. You don't want to tell me like that, but face it: You've made your choice. If you're so big on honesty, why don't you just say it? Why don't you just tell me? What's my problem, Eva? And tell me, for fuck's sake, what *yours* is!"

"I can't."

I don't answer, only fume in her direction.

She picks up my gloves and stares at them as she talks.

"I can't tell you what Brad's got that you don't. I don't know. I don't know, I don't fucking know! I don't know anything. I don't know what I want or what my problem is. And I sure as hell don't know what *your* problem is. I wish I could be sure and tell you it's this and this and this but I *can't*. I'm just as confused as you are."

"Except you *are* sure of one thing, right? You're sure that we can't be friends anymore?"

"I never said that," she says quietly, defensively.

"Well, *something*'s not working!"

"Well, I don't fucking know what it is!" she says, raising her voice again. "I don't know what to do, either. Don't you see? I can't save you any more than you can save yourself. That's your problem, John. You think you can rely on me to make you happy, but you can't. I can't help you the way you want to be helped! I'm sorry."

She lays my gloves in her lap.

"You're wrong!" I tell her, realizing it for the first time. "What about connection? What about everything you've told me about: about people, about relationships, about finding yourself in someone else? How can you tell me you can't rely

272

on other people to be happy? How can you say that when you're obviously happy with Alarsky? You're lying! You're fucking lying to me! You aren't telling me you don't need anyone; you're telling me you don't need *me*."

She doesn't look at me. She doesn't even turn in the direction of my voice. She just stares out at the frozen lake, at its illusion of solidity and permanence. She doesn't move.

Because it's true. Because we both know it's true.

And there's nothing that hurts more.

"I don't know what I want," she says.

"Join the fucking club."

Neither of us says anything for several moments. Eva shivers into the darkening night, her black jacket and hair catching the sky's crumbling pieces.

"So what have we decided?" she asks.

"What do you mean?"

"Do we have closure? Is this over?"

She starts to get up.

"Are you leaving?" I ask in a slight panic.

"Well, yeah, why not? I don't see any point in sticking around."

For once in my life, I'm fucking *trying*, I'm the one sticking around . . . and this is how it turns out?

"Fine," I say disgustedly. "Whatever. Fuck you."

She relents and sits back down, facing me this time. "No, c'mon, don't let this end with a 'fuck you.'"

"Screw you?"

"Fuck *you*, John."

I shrug. "Stop trying to run, Eva. I'm not. So you sure as hell shouldn't be."

"Well, what do you want me to say?"

"Does it matter?"

Silence again. Tense and thick. The freeze is starting to work its way up my arm to my shoulder. My hands are already too stiff to move fluidly. I'm pretty sure this is a bad sign.

Winter's white blanket has fallen on all the land around the lake and around our bodies on the dock. Night has come and my face burns.

She says, "I want to make things right. I do want things to go back. But you understand they can't?"

She finally looks at me.

"Yeah."

She goes on. "I don't want you to think I don't value you. Or our time together. That's not how this is. We just aren't on the same page. I can't handle more than one out-of-balance relationship at a time. My emotional energies are all tapped out. I only have room for so many fucked-up relationships in my life."

"So there you go, you just said it. Ultimately you don't have 'room,' and it comes down to me and Alarsky. You chose."

She doesn't answer for a full minute. When she finally does, her tone is quiet and pained.

"I love him."

I can't believe it.

"God, Eva, how can you even say that? What do you see in him?!"

"What do you want me to say? We connect on this whole other level!"

"Bullshit!"

As much as it would suck if Alarsky was some sensitive

274

indie-artist jackass, I think it's worse that he's not. It's worse that he's an average student and that he's on the team. It's worse that he hangs out at parties like Jackson's and that he's exactly like me. But he's the one who got The Girl.

"What, you're pissed off? You're not even hurt?" Eva challenges.

"Fuck you, Eva. You're in no position to tell me how to deal with my emotions."

"What's that supposed to mean?"

"Haven't you noticed? You're not exactly an expert on being sane."

"Well, of course I knew that! You're telling me it took you all this time to realize I have my own issues?"

"Oh, go fuck yourself."

"I never told you to believe in me, John. I never said, 'Trust me. I know all the answers.'"

"You sure as hell made it seem like you did!"

"What you chose to believe is not my fault!"

"Fuck you! Just look at the way you talk to me!"

"What do you mean, the way I talk to you? Explain."

"See, right there! That! Your fucking interrogations, your constant challenges. Your need to always make me explain myself! Your 'hows' and 'whys' and 'what do you means.' You're always badgering me, trying to soak everything out of me. For someone who asks so many questions, you sure as hell don't have many answers!"

"Okay, yes. Maybe. Yes, obviously I played a part in this image you've created of me. I'm not perfect."

"Well, I think *that's* become overwhelmingly clear."

Fight. Push back. Don't let her bring you down.

"Thank you. I try," she tries to say drily, but I hear a little bit of hurt in her voice.

Push on.

"Maybe you're turning out to be less than I thought you were."

"I'm impressed that you said that," she says. But I hear her barriers. "Maybe you're turning out to be more than I thought *you* were."

"See, a normal person would be hurt by what I just said," I say, banging on her emotional wall. "But not only are you not hurt, you're impressed? What the fuck, Eva?" I spit.

"I *am* hurt. But I'm impressed by your honesty. And your ability to let go."

Oh, don't do me any favors.

"Seriously," I say bitterly, shaking my head, "what the fuck is wrong with you?"

She shrugs but won't look at me. "It never seemed to bother you before."

"That was then."

"What, now you hate me?"

I turn away.

"Should I?" I ask the darkness.

Nobody responds.

But in that silence I hear Eva's heart crack, the invisible tears break at the brim and fall down her cheeks. I've won.

But it means absolutely nothing.

Finally, I speak.

"You have no idea how much I wish I could," I say truthfully.

"I want to hate you so badly. I want to hurt you like you hurt me." I pause. "I want you to break. But I can't fight anymore. I forfeit. You win."

"This is hardly a game," she says, her voice recovered.

"No, but it is a battle."

"Who are we battling? Each other?"

I turn and look her in the eye.

"Ourselves."

The cold burns against my face in response, and I shove my hands deeper into my pockets.

"John, I'm sorry if I hurt you."

"You did. But I think it's going to be all right."

She smiles, a real smile. "Well, I could have told you that."

"You did."

The silence snaps in the night. The wind tosses our words and carries them across the frozen lake until we don't feel them anymore.

Finally I say, "So I guess it's not over. But it's not not. We've decided . . . what, exactly?"

"To wait, I guess."

"For?"

"I don't know. We'll stop when we're ready. We'll know."

"As usual, you're completely full of shit."

She smiles at me from the other side of the falling white curtain.

"Yeah. But you know you love it."

Yeah.

I'd give anything not to.

Without saying anything, I move toward her and take her by

the shoulders and pull her against me. I hold her tight against me, feeling her respond slowly but with strength. Pressing her face into my jacket, she wraps one arm around me and keeps the other between our two bodies, resting it right where our hearts meet.

This kills.

In reality, the embrace probably doesn't last longer than thirty seconds, but it feels as if it lasts for all of three months. Everything that wasn't said, all the understood feelings that were never fully understood, flows into our arms and through each other.

This really, really kills.

We break apart, not daring to look at each other for a moment. And then she pulls me gently toward her, eyes closed, face tilted, leaning me down, kissing me softly on the forehead. I watch as she walks down the dock, across the grass, past the gazebo, and disappears into the brushes.

Her shoes leave a trail of footprints from where I'm standing to where she's going.

CHAPTER 26

It's almost the new year. New Year's Eve is the time when all the rich wastes gather from the far corners of suburbia at Stacy Kinder's to get smashed and run into things. Granted, this is almost every weekend for us, but there's kind of an unwritten rule that New Year's is supposed to be more fun than usual.

"So. New Year's. Stacy's?"

Jake greets me on Monday with a hearty hand slap.

"Yeah, sure." I shrug.

"Although now that you're with Lindsey . . . I guess you've got no agenda with anybody else?"

I shrug again.

"Whatever," I say. "We'll do Kinder's."

"We'll do Kinder?" he jokes. "Fine, but I call shotgun."

Jake leans against the locker next to mine as I shuffle around in the sea of papers for my bio book.

"So, what's been goin' on? What'd you do this weekend?"

I shrug again.

"Yes, thank you, you've really painted a picture for me," he says.

Another shrug, but this time to get rid of the image of Eva's back as she walked away on Friday.

"It was fine. Hung out. Y'know."

"No, I don't know. Especially since you weren't with us. Since you were with . . . ?"

"People?"

"Jacobs?"

"Why do you assume —"

"Jacobs?"

"I —"

"Jacobs?"

"Fine."

Let him believe his own fictions.

"Why aren't you celebrating?"

"Celebrating what?"

"This is a record for you."

"What?"

"This is the longest you have continuously fucked one girl. I'm surprised you don't have your anniversary branded on your forehead."

"Great, Jake." It's depressing that he keeps track.

"Sorry. It's just all anyone can talk about."

"Fuck everyone."

"You seem to have done that already."

I don't answer for a moment, and Jake looks a little regretful for being Jake.

"You okay?" he says then.

"Huh?" I can only imagine what he must see in my face.

"Did something happen?"

I grunt a no and he doesn't pursue the matter further, but I know he knows something is up.

"Nothing happened," I reassure him. "I'm fine."

It's his turn to shrug.

"Whatever."

"Whatever."

"So. Stacy's?"

"I said fine."

"New Year's Eve as seniors! We better make it count."

"I'm sure Kinder won't disappoint."

"True, that."

I can't believe it's almost the new year.

Later that day, I sit in English and stare at the back of Francesca's head while Mrs. Donahue scribbles notes on the board for midterms. Seriously, who gives a shit about midterms at this point? What difference will they make this late in the game? In the last stretch before the end of senior year, who really gives a shit about anything?

As if on cue, Tenen appears in the doorway.

"John. My office. Now."

She starts to walk away but turns back, then says to Mrs. Donahue as an afterthought, "Oh, sorry, Karen. I hope you don't mind."

Mrs. Donahue waves her off absentmindedly, still scribbling away.

I drag myself out of my seat and follow Tenen. I plop down into her worn brown chair and settle so I have the optimal view of the tiny pendulums, clicking away into the silence.

Click.

Click.

Click.

"This wild-goose chase is getting old, John. I'm tired of trying to hunt you down, especially when you don't even bother to show up to class half the time."

"I'm here now. What do you want to talk about?"

"Well, it's too late for you to take the SATs again, obviously. But generally, college. Applications are due in just a few weeks. Have you even started yours?"

"What do you take me for?"

An idiot, which might be what I am.

"How far along are you?"

"Far enough," I say vaguely.

"Well, since I've been doing this for twenty years and you've been doing it for about four months, I'll be the judge of that. What have you done?"

"Oh, you know, this and that. I've got one or two done."

She takes out a pad of paper.

"Okay, tell me your exact list."

"I . . . how about later?"

"Later? John, it's December twentieth! How much time do you think you have?"

"Look," I say finally, tired of this game, "let's just accept it. Don't dick around with me; we both know I can't really get in anywhere. There's no real point. You were right the first time — I haven't started. And I'm not going to start. I'm going to Ravens with the rest of the 'slackers,' so let's spare ourselves."

I start to get up, wanting so badly to knock over those stupid clicking balls.

"John," Tenen says worriedly, "sit down."

I don't move from where I'm standing in front of her desk.

"What's going on?" she asks with concern.

"Nothing. Why do you always ask that? I'm fine."

"You seem upset."

I look at her sitting there behind her desk, in her mahogany world where everything is just a number, a grade, a percentile, a probability. She doesn't understand, but I don't hate her for it. She wants to but we both know she can't. I wish I had more energy to wish, to want, but I just can't. I can't care about what she's saying; I can't want what she wants me to want.

"I'm fine. I've really got to go."

I turn and walk out her door, not stopping even when I hear her call after me.

I don't go back to class. I stop at my locker for my jacket, and then I leave. I don't sign out. I walk right out the front doors and through the student parking lot to my car. The day is bitter and dry and my now very long hair blows in my eyes.

I really think it's time for that haircut.

By the time I get home, it's around two o'clock. I walk up to my room and unlatch the screen from my window. I grab my comforter and step out onto the roof and settle in the afternoon cold to wait.

For what, exactly? What, who am I waiting for? Closure? Resolution? I know I want to go to the gazebo and I want her to be there. But I can't. And that's sort of the point.

Have I fucked it up with Lindsey? I haven't called her since last week, haven't made any attempt to talk to her. It could have been good, but I couldn't go through with it. Is it too late?

283

Could anyone forgive such blatantly rampant assholeness? Do I even want her to?

Standing unarmed on the roof, I lay myself open to the sky. The gray hits me in all the wrong places, knocks me down one gust at a time. My head feels naked.

I feel the same restless urge that would normally make me want to drive, but I know that at the end of the day all I'd be doing was driving in circles until I had to come home. So I think I'll just stay. I think I'll just wait.

"What the hell are you doing?"

I turn to see Kelly standing next to the open window, one hand on her hip and the other by her side.

"What the hell are you doing?" she repeats.

"Sitting."

"Why?"

"I dunno."

She eyes the window for a moment and then climbs over the sill and sits next to me. Silently I hand her some of my comforter and she huddles beneath it.

"Aren't you supposed to be at school?" she asks.

"Yes, Mom."

Beat.

"Why aren't you?"

"I didn't want to be there."

She stares at her feet. "What's up?"

I shrug.

"You . . . okay?"

"Why does everyone keep asking me that? I'm perfectly fine. I'm breathing normally, my liver is still intact, and I can see out of both eyes. I'm perfectly fine."

284

"Relax, I was only asking."

Shrug.

"Sorry, things are just . . . weird right now."

"How?"

Shrug.

"John? Oh, c'mon. How?"

I don't look at her.

"I don't know."

It's the truth, isn't it? I really *don't* know. I really don't know anymore about anything than I did before, do I? I mean, fuck. I'm just as confused as ever.

"You do know. You just don't want to say it."

She faces me, her eyes as frank as her questions.

"I don't know."

"Well?" She pokes my side through the fabric of the comforter. "What does it have to do with? A girl?"

"No . . . maybe. No."

"Who?"

"I don't know. It's . . . it's not a girl. It's me."

"What's wrong with you?"

"I don't know."

Silence for a moment.

And then, "Talk to me."

More silence.

And then, "Well, what do you want to know?"

"What did you do?" Kelly asks.

I turn my head to stare at my little sister, her face set against the gray of the sky. She stares back at me with her light eyes that match Dad's, and for the first time — whether it's actually there or not — I see a little bit of me in her. Something about her gaze seems familiar; the look in her eyes is the same thing I see in the mirror every morning.

For the first time I see Kelly in my hallways, by my locker, in my car, at the diner.

And it's not easy.

"I don't know exactly. Things just went wrong."

My mouth bursts to say her name.

"With Eva?" Kelly says before I can.

"Eva. Everything."

"What happened?"

"Things just . . . didn't work out," I say vaguely. Then, after a moment of thought, "I just wasn't what she needed. Things weren't mutual. Things got fucked up. It was bad."

I shrug.

"Go on," Kelly urges.

I shrug again.

"I don't know what else to say."

She rolls her eyes and shifts her weight against the roof tiles.

"Please. There must be more."

"I . . . what do you want me to say?"

She rolls her eyes again.

"Jesus, how did it happen? Did you try to kiss her? Did you have sex? Is there another guy? Another *girl*? Did you have a fight? Is it over over? Are you just being John? C'mon, what *happened*? There must be some part of you that knows how to tell a fucking story!"

Kelly, the relationship expert. Go figure. I guess all those late-night gossip sessions amounted to something.

"There's another guy," I say finally. "Hence no kissing, no sex. Hence the end."

"She picked another guy over you? This chick's got balls."

"Fortunately, she doesn't . . . that would make things a hell of a lot more complicated. But, yeah, my thoughts exactly. She said they 'connect on a whole other level' or some bullshit like that."

"What's he like? Is he, like, fucking amazing blow-your-mind-away awesome?"

"No — that's the thing. He *sucks*."

"What?"

"He just . . . he sucks! He's lame. He makes lame jokes and he sucks at basketball and he's not as good-looking as me."

She shoots me a look.

"He's not," I say matter-of-factly. "But he loves her. And she loves him. And it's all a little too much for me," I say sullenly.

And then the heat rushes back to my head.

"But honestly? He's a boring piece of shit!" I spit.

"It's all relative. Maybe she thinks you're a more boring piece of shit."

"Great."

She smirks at my uneasiness before shrugging and saying seriously, "Look, you know it's not supposed to be easy."

"What?"

"Relationships. Falling in love."

"What would you know?"

She shrugs. "You'd be surprised."

I am.

Then she says, "Well, do you think it's true?"

"What?"

"Do you think you're boring?"

"No, I don't."

"So what are you going to do about it?"

287

"What do you mean? What the hell can I do about it?"

"Prove her wrong."

"How?"

"Well, how do you usually woo girls?"

Cool stares. Smooth smiles. White lies.

"I dunno. It wouldn't work on her."

"Why not?"

"She's just not that type of girl."

"I'm sure you can think of something. You're Caesar."

"Not today. Maybe not anymore."

As we speak, I watch the sky. I can feel the heat from her body between the folds of flannel, but I can't look her in the eye. I don't want to see what she sees in her coward of a brother. I don't want her to see me defeated.

But we both know she knows.

She shrugs into the silent afternoon and says, "So it's over then?"

"I'm not sure. I don't think I want it to be. I guess it just stopped working for her. She stopped wanting to be in the same places I was. I guess you're right — I bored her. But she . . ." I pause. "She never bored me," I say softly.

Kelly doesn't say anything, only wiggles closer to me under the blanket. We don't speak for that moment, just sit in the settling afternoon cold.

"The worst part is that . . . she's always talking about talking, y'know?"

"What?"

"Like . . . she's one of those people who's always talking about their feelings and their thoughts and all that crap and I'm not . . . I'm not like that. But she talked to me anyway. And after

288

a while, I talked back. I talked and I talked and eventually I said things I never thought I would. Or could."

"So isn't that good?"

"Well, that's the fucked-up part. I finally said what I really wanted to say. And what happened? I got burned." I shake my head. "Why bother at all?"

"Maybe it's supposed to be worth it," Kelly says earnestly.

"Maybe it's not."

"Only one way to find out."

"I was afraid you'd say that."

"Jesus, I've never seen you like this before. Pull yourself together!" With a puny punch, she knocks me in the shoulder.

"That's because I've never felt this way before. But I just don't know what to do!" I say pathetically.

"All you can do is wait. Wait for it to pick up again. Or wait until you're over it. You'll bounce back."

"I hope so."

"You'll find someone else in no time. There *are* other girls out there," she says pointedly, almost condescendingly.

Other girls? Lindsey's face flashes into my mind.

"Well, yeah," I say. "Of course there are. And for a long time, I thought that's all there was. But they're all so bland! That's the problem, isn't it? I don't want other girls. I don't need other girls. I wanted *her*."

Kelly laughs.

"It's not them. It's you," she says.

"How's it me? You're saying I'm bland?"

"No, I'm saying give someone else a chance. You might be surprised."

"What?"

"Here's a suggestion: Try to not be a complete asshole."

"*What?*"

"It's not her. It's you."

"So what are you saying, that Eva's not really that great?"

"I'm not saying she's not great. I'm saying someone else could be just as great. You think she's the only one when maybe she's really just the *first* one. You think she's The Girl, but she's really just *a* girl. And so many girls would be willing to be Your Girl. If you would just see them. If you would just give them a chance."

I marvel at my sister. "How come I never knew you knew all this?"

She shrugs.

"You never gave me the chance."

Maybe it's true. Maybe she's right. Maybe I've been missing out all this time on all these girls. But I gave one girl a chance, and look what happened. Do I really want to risk it again?

"Let's say you're right," I tell Kelly. "Let's say I do take an interest in one of these girls. Let's say she doesn't return the feelings. Let's say I get burned again. What do I do?"

Kelly shrugs.

"Get over it."

When I don't respond, she says, "Look, just because you're going to start being a real person doesn't mean you have to turn into a little crying wuss. Be yourself; do what John would do."

"I still have to figure out just what that is."

"Join the fucking club."

After a moment, I say, "Maybe I was wrong about you, Kelly."

"Wrong about what?" she says cautiously.

"I dunno . . . maybe you are ready."

"For what?"

"School. Things. Guys. Shit." I shake my head. "I dunno."

"Drinking. Sex. Shit."

"Yeah, something like that."

"And, what, now you think I'm ready?"

"At least for the drama part," I say.

"What is so scary about me growing up?"

I don't answer for a moment, let the bitter gray chill wash over our hair and faces first. I see her slipping from my fingers, the last few years falling as quickly as sand.

"Look," I say in a last feeble attempt to protect her, "don't get hurt, okay? I don't want to come home from college and have to kick some freshman punk's ass."

"You're afraid I'm going to get attacked?"

"No, no. I just . . . I don't want anything to happen to you. And, y'know, something *could* . . ."

Images of Kelly at keggers and tailgating parties and pregames fill my head as pimple-faced freshmen weaklings mock me with their roofies in the background. With effort I push them out.

"I know you want me to say I can handle myself," Kelly says. "And I'd like to think so, too, but . . . I can only promise to be careful, all right? I'll do the best I can."

"One more thing."

"Yeah?"

"Don't get involved with guys like me."

She looks me in the eye, taking me seriously. "Right. Okay."

"Promise me you'll be smarter than I was."

Now she smiles. "Trust me, that won't be a problem."

291

"Good."

She tries to hide a grin, but I see, and then I know. I know what I see. I see me. I see the past and the future meet at this moment, and I know.

I know we're ready.

PUSH

YOU ARE HERE.

www.thisispush.com

Meet the authors.

Read the books.

Tell us what you want to see.

Submit your own words.

Read the words of others.

this is PUSH.

☐	0-439-09013-X	**Kerosene** by Chris Wooding	$6.99
☐	0-439-32459-9	**Cut** by Patricia McCormick	$6.99
☐	0-439-29771-0	**You Remind Me of You** by Eireann Corrigan	$6.99
☐	0-439-27989-5	**Pure Sunshine** by Brian James	$6.99
☐	0-439-49035-9	**Tomorrow, Maybe** by Brian James	$6.99
☐	0-439-24187-1	**Fighting Ruben Wolfe** by Markus Zusak	$6.99
☐	0-439-41424-5	**Nowhere Fast** by Kevin Waltman	$6.99
☐	0-439-50752-9	**Martyn Pig** by Kevin Brooks	$6.99
☐	0-439-37618-1	**You Are Here, This Is Now: The Best Young Writers and Artists in America**	$16.95
☐	0-439-67365-8	**Perfect World** by Brian James	$7.99
☐	0-439-69188-5	**Never Mind the Goldbergs** by Matthue Roth	$16.95
☐	0-439-57743-8	**Kissing the Rain** by Kevin Brooks	$6.99
☐	0-439-48992-X	**Splintering** by Eireann Corrigan	$6.99
☐	0-439-54655-9	**Lucky** by Eddie de Oliveira	$6.99
☐	0-439-12195-9	**I Will Survive** by Kristen Kemp	$6.99
☐	0-439-38950-X	**Getting the Girl** by Markus Zusak	$6.99
☐	0-439-62298-0	**The Dating Diaries** by Kristen Kemp	$6.99
☐	0-439-53063-6	**Lucas** by Kevin Brooks	$7.99
☐	0-439-51011-2	**Born Confused** by Tanuja Desai Hidier	$7.99
☐	0-439-73646-2	**Where We Are, What We See** by Various Artists	$7.99
☐	0-439-73648-X	**Heavy Metal and You** by Christopher Krovatin	$16.95
☐	0-439-67362-3	**Johnny Hazzard** by Eddie de Oliveira	$8.99

Available wherever you buy books, or use this order form.

Scholastic Inc., P.O. Box 7502, Jefferson City, MO 65102

Please send me the books I have checked above. I am enclosing $_____ (please add $2.00 to cover shipping and handling). Send check or money order — no cash or C.O.D.s please.

Name_____ Birth date_____

Address_____

City_____ State/Zip_____

Please allow four to six weeks for delivery. Offer good in U.S.A. only. Sorry, mail orders are not available to residents of Canada. Prices subject to change.

www.this is **PUSH** .com

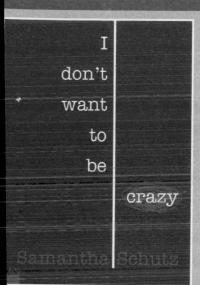

PUSH

Just like life.

BE A PUSH AUTHOR.

Enter the PUSH Novel Contest for a chance to get your novel published. You don't have to have written the whole thing — just sample chapters and an outline. **For full details, check out the WritePUSH area on www.thisispush.com**

PURE SUNSHINE BRIAN JAMES

you remind me of you
a poetry memoir
by eireann corrigan

KEROSENE
chris wooding

cut
Patricia McCormick

FILLPUSHNC